MURDER AND MARGARITAS

A BLOCK ISLAND MYSTERY

JUDY TIERNEY

Murder and Margaritas: A Block Island Mystery

Produced and printed by Stillwater River Publications.

Visit our website at **www.StillwaterPress.com** for more information.

First Stillwater River Publications Edition

ISBN: 978-1-968548-80-3

Library of Congress Control Number: 2026914628

Publisher's Cataloging-in-Publication
Provided by Cassidy Cataloguing Services, Inc.

Names: Tierney, Judy, author.
Title: Murder and margaritas : a Block Island mystery / Judy Tierney.
Description: First Stillwater River Publications edition. | West Warwick, RI, USA : Stillwater River Publications, [2026]
Identifiers: LCCN: 2026914628 | ISBN: 9781968548803 (paperback)
Subjects: LCSH: Reporters and reporting—Rhode Island—Block Island (Island) | Nurses—Rhode Island—Block Island (Island) | Murder—Investigation—Rhode Island—Block Island (Island) | Interpersonal relations. | Summer—Rhode Island—Block Island (Island) | Block Island (R.I. : Island) | LCGFT: Detective and mystery fiction.
Classification: LCC: PS3620.I382 M87 2026 | DDC: 813/.6—dc23

1 2 3 4 5 6 7 8 9 10

Written by Judy Tierney.
Cover and interior design by Elisha Gillette.
Published by Stillwater River Publications, West Warwick, RI, USA.

Dedication

Of course to Ron, and also to my former mentor, Donna Diers, RN,MSN, avid nursing scholar and researcher, and mystery genre fan, who introduced me to nursing and to novels by Dick Francis.

I no longer practice nursing but I still read mysteries. The character Addie Morton, R.N. with her cap collection is for you, Donna.

FOREWORD

Readers who are familiar with my previous novel, *The Washashore Murders,* might wonder why *Murders and Margaritas* is set on Block Island, Rhode Island, instead of the fictional community of Nor'easter Island. The characters have not packed up all their belongings and moved, en masse, to a new place. Nor'easter Island was a thinly disguised Block Island, where I lived in the same cedar-shingled cottage as character Dita Redmond for a number of years. I decided I owed it to my former home to make it the true setting for *Murder and Margaritas.* The characters, businesses, and sites, however, are all still fictional, as are the murders. The only real murders I ever heard of on Block Island occurred years before I arrived.

Judy

PROLOGUE, 2 A.M.

It's 2 a.m., and the man is impatient. Shrouded in a black hoodie, he drums his fingers against the dashboard of the cargo van. He's watching for the lights to go out in the only pub on Block Island that stayed open this winter. When they dim and he sees the bartender, Harry Ring, lock up and leave, he shifts a foot and mutters, "One down."

He waits again until he sees the police vehicle that's been idling outside the pub motor up and drive off. The man in the van knows it won't be back. Joe is the only officer on duty this shift, and it's time for his 'lunch break,' which he always takes at the station where his mistress awaits his arrival. Satisfied that no one is about and knowing that in the off-season on this thinly populated island, once the bar closes, odds are that no one else will be afoot, the man steps out of the van. He hurries to its rear doors and opens them wide. There are no rear seats. The body is laid out on the floor, feet pointing toward the back doors. It's not been in rigor mortis long. He grabs the ankles and yanks it part way out, then heaves it over his shoulders. The woman's body sticks out across his back, but he's confident there's no one to notice. Besides, it's a new moon and cloudy. There's no light. Even if someone happens by, he will not be seen.

The woman is light, skinny actually, a pack of bones. Her shoes are loose, and one drops off. He lets it be. That he is carrying a dead person doesn't bother him. He's done it before.

He had hoped to move quickly across the expanse of grasses and reeds that led to the estuary, but the recent rains and high tides, as well as a brief warm-up, had left the ground somewhat muddy, though not full muck. He slips and slows down to keep his balance, swearing because his boots will be dirtier than he had expected. Then he remembers no one will follow him into that morass for months. The holes where he sank in will fill by then. The woman will lie undiscovered, at least until spring. He drops her off his shoulder, removes his gloves, and shoves them into his pockets. Then he retraces his steps as quickly as the ground allows.

When he gets back to the van, he opens the back doors wider and leans in. He pulls his boots off one at a time and places them in a large plastic garbage bag. Then he grabs the extra pair of athletic shoes he always stores in the cargo space. When he has them on, he jumps into the front seat, starts the engine, and heads to the airport, where he parks in the small lot. He shifts his seat back and sleeps until the diner inside the old hangar opens.

Going inside, he orders a cup of coffee and chats with Laurie, the owner, until it's time for the first flight to the mainland. When he sees the captain climb into the plane, he pays up and strides across the tarmac, plastic bag in hand, and boards the 6-seater, two-engine aircraft.

PART ONE

EARLY SPRING

ONE

Addie Morton pushed a shock of red curls from her forehead and positioned her nursing cap over them. She fastened it in place with two old-fashioned bobby pins. This particular vintage cap resembled an upside-down paper cupcake holder with a black stripe. It was one of her favorites among the 20 different ones she'd collected. Pinning a cap on was the first thing she did every day when she arrived at work at Block Island's only medical clinic.

She'd been glad, as a newly graduated nurse, that no one in the profession wore a cap anymore. They seemed to her like relics from the early twentieth century and foolish-looking in an age of technological health care. She never could have foreseen that she would be one of the last few nurses, maybe even the last nurse, to wear one. She'd taken to wearing it because she felt it cast a professional aura, even if a few red curls escaped and added a slight look of insouciance. On days when she dealt with running-at-the-mouth, drunk and disorderly tourists, the cap helped her channel what she called her inner "Big Nurse." But mostly, the cap helped her set her own boundary between her personal self and her role as a nurse for the island patients who knew her as a friend or acquaintance, or as a recently single parent of a school-age child. With her redhead's pale skin, blushes and flushes crept swiftly over her face when she least desired them. The cap helped maintain an official distance.

When it was secured, she stepped away from her tiny office into the waiting room and plumped the upholstered chairs, the ones with the worn white, pink, and green floral-patterned pillows, and straightened the magazines on the side tables. She reflected on the fact that every medical waiting room she'd ever seen or worked in started the day with these neat stacks, as though this small act of housekeeping let patients know their care was in good hands.

Satisfied that the waiting room furnishings were all in order, she went to the front desk behind the waiting room window. The clerk was not yet in, so she checked the day's roster that was lying open on it. This morning, the clinic's first patient would be the infant of her best friend, Dita Redmond. If ever Addie needed garb to make her look official, it was with her best friend. Dita was coming with her two-month-old infant, Janie. Addie thought about the high hopes Dita spoke of for Janie: future cancer researcher, senator, Olympic star. But then, doesn't every mother start out with highfalutin dreams? She had them for her own boy, Danny, too. Why, people even concocted special scenarios for their dogs these days, describing them as the smartest dog ever, genius level, or the gentlest of all the animals they knew; so there was nothing wrong with daydreaming about your kid.

Abbie was humming to herself as she prepared the clinic for the day. When she was working, she was almost happy because she didn't think about the downward spiral of her personal life. Also, she hoped her life was about to get back on track again this very day when she had a couples-therapy session scheduled with her estranged husband, Mel.

It was spring on Block Island, her favorite time of year, when the tourist shops prepared to open, including her mother Rachel's "The Lorelei" gift shop. Cardboard boxes with merchandise piled up on doorsteps in town. Summer-cottage owners trickled over from the mainland to check their houses after the long winter, and restaurants would soon be opening on weekends. Spring was a time of hope on Block Island.

She was pulling Janie Redmond's chart, along with the others scheduled to see the doctor that morning, when a commotion at the double doors of the emergency entrance drew her away from the front desk to the patient exam area. She stopped humming. She heard Dr. Bennett's voice outside speaking to the ambulance crew. Then she heard him almost race inside.

"Addie," he called. "We need the camera. There's a body on Ocean Avenue in the wetland by the clam flats. We need to go."

She reached up to remove the bobby pins holding her cap, setting it down carefully on the desk; she wouldn't need it out by the estuary. She hurried to help Dr. Bennett. He'd already yanked open a supply cabinet and removed the boxes holding the gear they would need: gowns, caps, gloves, and booties. She counted the items he handed her and stacked them on a small desk where the doctor wrote his notes.

"I'll get the camera and call Dita to push her appointment back two hours," she said. "Dr. Bennett, are you sure it's a body? Not a live person?"

"Chief Gomez called me and said the guy who called it in thought it looked as though the body had been out there for quite a while—definitely not breathing and quite discolored," he replied, picking up the stack of supplies.

Addie handed him a plastic bin. He threw them in and headed to the back door where the staff parking lot was located.

"I think I have enough. Let's go in my car." He tossed the bin into his trunk. "The ambulance will follow. I'll call the medical examiner. Do you have the tablet so we can Zoom with him?"

"I'll run back in and get it," she said. She ran, but not fast, knowing there was not the pressure to rush that they would have had if the person was alive. Besides, she did not run for a hobby like her friend Dita. She moved fast only as necessary.

When she returned to the car, Dr. Bennett was talking on his phone with the ME. She heard the latter say he wasn't able to get to the island that day. Fog had descended on his closest airport, so there were no flights. He was much too busy to spend hours getting to the ferry dock and then taking another hour to get to the island. In these situations, Dr. Bennett was already cleared to act as medical examiner. He would send photos of the victim and the surrounding ground to the official ME.

Addie was not happy about accompanying Dr. Bennett as a photographer. She wished he'd have one of the EMTs take the pictures and let her stay at the clinic. Since her brother Joel's body had washed ashore, she was panic-stricken by the thought of even being near anyone who'd passed away. She braced herself for the task ahead. It was time to get over her brother's untimely death. She needed to remain professional. Dr. Bennett's voice telling her they would have to wade through the slop in the estuary pulled her out of her thoughts. The frozen wetland melted and puddled in spring, then liquefied into muck. The doctor had brought plastic booties to protect the site surrounding the body from their footsteps as well as protect their own shoes.

"I grabbed a couple extra pairs of those shoe covers. We'll need to change them when we get close so as not to track extraneous swamp material onto the site," the Doc said.

As Ocean Avenue was only a couple of miles from the medical center, they arrived at the scene in under ten minutes. The EMTs pulled up behind them at the curb, and they all gathered at the edge of the swamp. The serene beauty of the spot was not lost upon them: the curve of the shoreline, the reeds shining in the early morning sun, the calm shallows. Addie leaned on the car to slip on her booties, then the gown, the hat just big enough to cover her curls, and the gloves. She followed Dr. Bennett into the wetland, her feet squishing in the muck and making a sharp 'pock' sound when she pulled them out. Each time, she repressed a complaint. Slowly, they made their way to the body. Addie stopped when she could see the corpse, which appeared to be a woman with a mane of white hair. She snapped pictures of the entire scene, the body, and the area around it.

"I think we should change our booties here," Dr. Bennett said.

"There's a narrow band of beach sand a little further up," Addie said. "Let's go around her and change there."

He agreed, and they continued to the beach where they leaned on each other to reboot. A snowy egret, returned from its winter home, was fishing the shallows. It lifted its head for a second to see them. Then they trekked on, and Addie took clumps of the grassy area near the corpse, the hard sand next to it on the other side, the patch of grass under its feet. One sneaker was missing.

Dr. Bennett beckoned Addie closer. It was a woman. She was on her back, legs akimbo, one arm overhead and one across her belly. Addie took a deep breath and snapped additional photos.

"Send them over to the mainland," the doctor said, and Addie forwarded all the pictures.

They waited while the ME on the mainland spent some time looking at them. Addie turned away from the body and chatted with the ambulance crew. Then the ME returned to the screen and told them to photograph the woman's other side. The EMTs flipped her onto her stomach. Her shirt was pasted to her back with dried blood and mud. Addie swallowed a retch. The woman had bled out. This did not appear to be an accidental death, a sudden heart attack, or a stroke. She heard Dr. Bennett's voice but not what he was saying. Then she heard him shout her name.

"Addie, are you listening? I need pictures of all this."

She pulled herself out of her drift and walked around the woman snapping photos. There seemed to her to be nothing a killer, if there was one, had left behind, but then she was not trained to search for that. Perhaps the ME would notice irregularities. She sent all the photos in one batch to the mainland. The medical examiner left the Zoom again to look at them.

"This woman has been gone a while," Addie murmured. "Has no one missed her?"

Clots of white hair surrounded the deceased woman's skull. The torn clothes on her frail, bony body were the kind that active older ladies prefer, navy cotton twill slacks and a repeating print cotton tee. Her sole remaining shoe was a sneaker brand often advertised for walking seniors.

"This really doesn't look to be recent," she reiterated, almost in disbelief.

She struggled to control her grief, to be professional.

Dr. Bennett set his jaw and appeared stoic. "She looks like she was in her sixties," he said, turning to the ambulance crew and police. "I don't recognize her. Anyone else?"

Addie saw relief on their faces, a relaxing of jaws and shoulder muscles as they shook their heads, no. They were all year-rounders. She knew every one of them as well as their medical problems: the two policemen, including George Gomez, who was the chief and had had appendicitis several years ago; the two volunteers on the ambulance crew, one of whom had a drinking problem he struggled with and the other, acid reflux; the doctor, who had a problem controlling his libido. Addie wished she didn't think of their diagnoses every time she encountered them.

If the victim was a local, at least one of those guys, if not all of them, would have known her. They would have recognized a summer cottager, the mainlanders who owned or rented homes regularly, as well. Addie noticed how relieved they were the corpse was not one of their own.

The medical examiner returned to the Zoom call and gave them permission to move the body to the medical center where they would remove her clothing and examine her further.

They discarded their protective clothing into a large, black plastic garbage bag, stowed it in the ambulance with the body, and Addie joined the Doc in his car again for the return ride. She watched the chief stumble on his way to his cruiser. He picked up what looked to be a shoe and took it with him. It looked like the one on the corpse's foot.

When they arrived at the clinic, Addie headed to an examining room and retrieved several pairs of gloves from the wall container and a pair of shears before joining the others. She handed out the gloves and passed the shears to one of the EMTs as the stretcher was wheeled in through the double doors of the emergency entrance, then they followed and entered the larger examining room.

Addie straightened up to compose herself -- she was a professional, after all -- and strode over to the table, her eyes blinking under the bright examination lights. Though she suspected the worst, when she was closer, she choked. The stench was overwhelming.

Dr. Bennett "tsk, tsked" as his head moved back and forth, tossing his abundant salt-and-pepper hair. He popped the top of a bottle of air freshener and sprayed, overlaying its chemical odor on top of the air of decay.

"Her shirt's covered with dried blood. Addie, let's remove it and take a quick look. Then we'll send her to the mainland to the coroner."

She took the shears back from the EMT she had hoped would have this particular job and sliced off the front of the torn tee shirt. As she worked, she noted in a flat voice between her teeth so she wouldn't have to fully open her mouth, "The morning boat already sailed."

Block Island was reachable only by sea or air; there was no bridge. The spring ferry schedule would not start until the following week. For now, Tuesdays and Wednesdays had but one boat in the morning and one in the late afternoon.

"Then she'll have to go into cold storage for the day," Dr. Bennett said. "I'm so sorry, Addie. I should have realized this would be difficult for you."

Addie thought, *yes, you should have*, and with a flash of intuition understood that this doctor, often involved in extramarital dalliances, was a deeply flawed, uncaring human being. His bonhomie with people was a learned and superficial convenience. How hard it was to draw competent and caring physicians to this remote island, she thought. Her subconscious kicked in all on its own to add *and caring husbands*.

She'd retreated into herself and was backing out of the room when Bennett's voice brought her back.

"Can you call the ferry office when we're done here and reserve a spot for the ambulance this evening, Addie?"

There was always a couple of places reserved on the ferry auto deck for emergency vehicles. If there were none, last minute travelers filled the spots instead. Addie expected the deceased would be transported to the mainland in the ambulance aboard the *Emma Ann,* the winter ferry vessel.

"Who is this woman," Addie whispered, almost to herself. "And how did she end up dead in the swamp?"

"None of us recognize her," Gomez said, though this had already been acknowledged. "You sure you don't, Addie? You see so many of the tourists here."

Addie shook her head. Dr. Bennett said he'd been trying to think whether she was someone who'd come in over the previous summer as he had a good head for faces.

Especially for women, Addie thought.

She stepped back to take notes as the doctor moved closer and examined the corpse top to bottom, reciting any bruises and scars including a surgical incision below her belly button indicating a possible C-section. He and one of the ambulance guys flipped her over to do the same on her posterior, and tried to pull the rest of her tee shirt off. It was torn but pieces were stuck to her. It looked to Addie like she had bled out. When they managed to remove the cloth, Addie staggered backward, and drew in a deep breath. A large portion of flesh on the woman's back ripped away with the shirt.

"Shot in the back," Dr. Bennett said, with a grimace. "I could probably dig out a bullet, but they'll do that during autopsy."

Stating the obvious, more to himself than any of the others, Chief Gomez lowered his voice and said with a touch of sarcasm, "Definitely not suicide."

Addie put down her notebook and snapped the photographs. She felt overcome with grief and fear. Here was an aging woman shot in the back, dead, on their own island, a place where until her brother Joel's murder she had felt so safe.

"Could she have been shot right there?" she asked, her voice quavering. "Surely someone would have heard it."

"If she was killed during hunting season, anyone who heard the shot would have thought it was someone chasing a deer," Chief Gomez replied.

Or Dita, Addie thought. Her friend Dita, a reporter, had stuck her neck out investigating Joel's death and had been hunted like prey. She'd almost gotten herself shot.

"But I think this lady was killed somewhere else and dumped there," Gomez continued.

Dr. Bennett agreed. Then he asked, rhetorically and just a bit too glibly, his thick white mustache bobbing, "A day-tripper perhaps, who met nefarious ends?"

Addie backed away from the table, moving toward the door. "She has no coat, not even a fleece, and no winter gloves," she said. "She looks like she was going to the store for a loaf of bread in summer."

"It must've been sometime in the fall. Too many people around in summer," the chief said. "We'll know more after the autopsy."

Addie let out a loud sigh. This was not the way life was supposed to go on Block Island.

They clustered in the hallway now; all of them had slowly moved away from the corpse and its noxious odor. Dr. Bennett closed the exam room door to keep the stench from following them.

"Who found her?" Addie asked. "Who was out there?"

She wondered why anyone would have been mucking about at this time of year.

Gomez replied, "Blaze Connors. He had a break in construction projects and thought he'd do a little clamming off the beach before all the tourists arrive."

There was a low chorus of gasps in the room; Blaze was well known to all of them. He ran a construction crew that had recently renovated one of the larger hotels. The crew was on hiatus right now until new spring projects got underway.

Addie knew him also. She wondered if he was taking his blood pressure medicine as she'd urged him to do.

"He's probably not a suspect, but we can't rule him out yet," Chief Gomez said hastily, looking straight at the ambulance volunteers. "I know you guys are friends of his, so I'm telling you right now. He's not in the clear. And, yes, he's in shock. Went over to the airport to sit with his pals at Laurie's diner."

Addie couldn't talk about it anymore. "I have to get ready for our first patient," she said, and she swallowed. "I mean, our first live patient."

"Go. We'll finish here." The doctor motioned to the EMT's to move the body onto the stretcher again and to place her bag of clothes with her. He looked over at Addie. Her face felt contorted as she struggled to cope. She could see a realization pass over his face, and she thought, *Yes, I am feeling queasy and upset because my brother Joel was murdered also before he washed up in a storm tide.*

He looked away from her and asked over his shoulder, "Dita's baby's the first, right?"

Addie murmured, "Yep."

She was already on her way to wash her hands. She hyperventilated over the sink as she scrubbed. Then she heard the stretcher rolling down the hall again and the refrigerated drawer in the utility room clacked open and shut.

"That's that," she heard Dr. Bennett say as he removed his gloves with a snap.

She dried her hands and took a deep gulp of air, grateful she'd brought a potpourri of dried lavender picked from last fall's garden for the washroom that morning. The clean floral scent that wafted up from the corner of the sink helped settle her stomach. She heard the beeping of the ambulance back-up alarm as it left the driveway, the crinkle of the paper on the examining table being removed, probably by Dr. Bennett as no other staff had yet arrived. This episode was over. She re-pinned her cap in front of the mirror and returned to the front desk just as Dita came in, on time, an unusual occurrence for her.

Dita crossed the waiting room with a sure step. Addie watched with interest as her tall, willowy friend moved with the grace of a cat gliding along the top of a familiar fence. This was the woman who used to trip on her dance partner's feet. The infant was swaddled in a cerulean blue blanket. Dita clutched her close to her bosom like a delicate treasure.

Addie smiled and thought how most mothers brought their new babies to the clinic strapped into an infant car seat, but Dita had rarely strayed a foot from Janie since the child was born. Thinking about that wiped away the brutal image of the murder victim.

"Nice to see you," Addie said, and she really meant it. "Dr. Bennett's finishing up with someone. Come around to the back. I'll get Janie ready for the exam." She leaned forward and brushed Janie's cheek with her forefinger. It was doubly refreshing to feel the infant's soft skin after undressing the desiccated corpse.

Janie gurgled.

"She likes me," Addie said.

"The Mustache got someone important to see so he had to move my appointment back?" Dita asked, using their nickname for Dr. Bennett, a middle-aged man in the midst of a mid-life crisis whose carefully groomed mustache was his most prominent facial feature. Rumor had it he'd been in affairs with several island women. But Addie, still feeling somber, was not in the mood for jokes, and she let the reference slide. Normally Dita's remark would have forced at least a snicker out of her, despite how buttoned up she tried to be when she was on the job.

"Did he forget about us?" Dita asked.

Addie realized Janie's appointment was of the utmost significance for Dita and, in her mind, it should be for everyone else also. She half-anticipated Dita stomping a foot next. Addie hesitated, trying to figure out how best to explain. Dita was a reporter for the local newspaper, "*The Island Gale*," and Addie did not know whether the information about the body should be made public as yet.

Finally she said, exaggerating her syllables, her Rhode Island dialect breaking through, "Look, Dita, something's happened, but if I tell ya, it's between us. You can't use it for the paper until we get the okay."

Addie thought Dita looked bored. She was. Almost nothing ever happened on Block Island until tourist season began, and Dita didn't believe Addie's news would be earth-shattering.

"Everyone always wants to talk off-the-record. What's new about that?" she asked with a shrug. "So tell me, did The Mustache's wife come over and catch him with Sharon? Or is he after you?"

Addie gave her an exasperated look and hissed, "No, and lower your voice."

Dita smiled, and her eyes lit up. She whispered, "Okay, just sayin'. I forgot you have your nursing cap on."

"It's not about him," Addie said, clearing her throat, and told Dita about the woman whose body lay in the refrigerated drawer.

"Who is it?" Dita asked, ticking through in her mind the elderly women she knew.

"Don't know yet," Addie replied.

"Don't know? She can't be one of us then."

On Block Island, the words *one of us* always referred to the community of year-rounders.

"No," Addie said.

"How'd she die? Any idea?"

"Shot. In the back."

Dita wheezed and held Janie closer. She herself narrowly escaped such a fate two years ago when a drug gang was running rampant on the island and Dita was investigating their crimes. The thought of new murders on the island, well, made her feel as though she was lifting off the ground with fear. Addie put her hand on Dita's back and maneuvered her into a chair. She was totally Addie Morton, RN, now.

"Slow down, breathe out, you're about to have a panic attack. It's okay. Breathe."

As she spoke, Addie reached out and took Janie into her arms. Then she waited for her friend to calm down. Once she'd settled, she passed Janie back to her and continued preparing the room for the exam. She turned away to lay paper on the baby scale.

"I guess we're more alike than I thought. My stomach turned when we were examining the Jane Doe. Now you're sick. We're both pretty squeamish, my friend," she said. "But you're okay now."

She heard a muffled groan from Dita. "Or are you?" She looked back over her shoulder.

Dita had begun to shake. Her rosy cheeks were draining, and she was gasping. "Whoops, Janie's going to fall," Addie exclaimed, dropping the paper and leaping to place her arms under the infant, securing her in her own arms once more. She felt as thoughtless as Dr. Bennett. She'd spread the news of the murder as casually as he had.

"Breathe slowly. You'll be okay," Addie told Dita as she opened a drawer with one hand, removed a paper bag, and handed it to her friend to stop the panic attack. "Breathe out into the bag and in again. I'm so sorry. I was more concerned about keeping the news quiet than with your feelings."

Dita took a few minutes, and then she dropped the bag into her lap. "I'll be all right. That was quite a shock. You can give Janie back now."

"Sit on the news until you get the story from the chief, okay?" Addie asked. "And let me have Janie for a couple more seconds so I can love her up."

She tickled Janie's cheek and smiled, and yes, she was rewarded with a tiny smile back. *Gas my eye,* she thought, recalling the doctors of prior decades who thought babies didn't flash a love smile back. Addie unwrapped the infant and handed her back to Dita.

"I promise I'll hold my story," Dita said with some exasperation. "But at least get the woman's picture to the realtors. Maybe one of them met her."

"Good idea. I'll pass it along. Now I need to get Janie's shots ready." Addie left to get the vaccines. Had she not been called upon to assist with the deceased woman, she would have prepared them earlier. Poor Janie would be immunized today for diphtheria, whooping cough, and tetanus in one shot, polio, haemophilus influenzae type B and pneumonia in another, and the rotavirus liquid would be squirted into her rosebud mouth. Addie had checked Dita's record yesterday, and found she'd been immunized for the illness initialized RSV. She would pass those antibodies to Janie in her milk, so the baby would not need yet another shot.

Addie put the premixed hypodermic needles on a tray with the oral vaccine and brought them into the examining room just as Dr. Bennett arrived there. She stepped aside to let him get close to Dita and Janie.

"Isn't she a sweet one," he said, reaching out to touch Janie's hand. He smiled. "May I?" He focused his big blues on Dita.

"Of course," she replied obediently. She held Janie out and he took her in his arms, cooing softly, focusing on her now.

"She certainly seems to be thriving," he said, placing her onto the baby scale. "Dita, I hear your mother's looking for a house here."

Dita glanced at Addie, who knew Dita would want to tell him to stay away from her, but Dita kept her mouth shut and just nodded. Evidently Janie's well-being was more important than telling the mustache to keep it in his pants. Addie was glad Dita had restrained herself and she shot her a smile. Dita gave the most minimum of shrugs in return, but Addie caught it.

The doctor called out Janie's weight and length. Addie recorded them on Janie's chart. Then Addie spoke up for Dita.

"How lucky my friend is to have her mom move over to help her. Now she has a sitter so she can help Sean at the gym. I doubt she'll have much time to socialize."

Sean was Dita's husband, and his fitness business was starting its second year. Dita wasn't planning to monopolize her mother's time. She actually hoped she would find a social life on Block Island, but she was well aware why Addie had said that, and she flashed her a smile.

After listening to Janie's heart and testing her reflexes and fontanelles, the doctor passed her back to Dita. "She looks great. No problems?"

Dita shook her head.

"Good. Come back in a month. Addie," he called out, "you can give Janie her shots. And, Dita, she can have some ibuprofen later if she's cranky." With that, he turned to the door to leave, but then skidded to a stop and glanced back. "I suppose Addie told you about the body. You'll be wanting to talk with Chief Gomez. He'll brief you on the details."

Then he was gone. He was one of those people who could seem to dissolve into space when he left a room, sometimes without announcing his departure. Dita wondered whether he was like that with his lovers—poof, and disappear.

"Guess I don't have to wait to write the story," Dita said as Addie followed the doctor out of the room to set up the vaccinations.

Addie returned in a jiffy with her tray of hypodermics. "Hold her so she doesn't move around. I'll be as quick as I can." And she was.

When Addie finished, Janie began to howl. "Oh dear. I should have asked the doc to give her her shots. She's never going to like me now."

"She won't remember. Come over to see us later," Dita said, trying to rock the now hysterical infant.

Addie handed her the blanket Janie had been wrapped in. "Rewrap her so she can't squirm out of your arms."

She helped Dita snuggle Janie up. The screams resolved into sobs. Dita again invited Addie to the house. "We can talk, and you can check on Janie."

But Addie couldn't. "I have a meeting with the therapist and Mel."

"Today? Here?" Dita was definitely interested.

"On the mainland, this afternoon," Addie said. Seeing Dita's eyebrows lift in question, she added, "We need supplies for the clinic, so Jack's letting me fly over and back for free on Block Air."

"Are you getting a taxi over there?" Dita asked.

"No," Addie responded. "Mel will meet me at the airport, and we'll go to the meeting together. Afterward, we'll pick up the pharmacy order, and he'll take me back to the airport. Don't ask anything else now. I'll call you tonight."

Dita realized she'd been dismissed. She was disappointed not to be privy to more details.

"Okay. We're so lucky to have Jack and his airline on the island," she said. She shifted Janie, gave Addie a sideways hug, and added, "I hope your meeting goes well."

By well, she meant she hoped Mel was returning to Addie.

Then she went to the waiting room window where the clerk, who'd arrived during Janie's exam, handed her the bill. Before she stopped in to see Sean at work, she'd find the chief and get a statement and a picture. Someone was bound to recognize that woman.

Addie watched Dita walk to her car. She thought about how Dita had taken it upon herself to prove Joel was murdered, and then she found who did it. Addie was grateful to Dita and admired her for pursuing her hunch even though everyone, herself included, had disagreed with her and tried to make her stop digging. If not for Dita, Joel's death would have forever been documented as a suicide or accidental.

Addie thought the woman with the white hair and one sneaker deserved a name, and her killer needed to be named as well. Dita would not be able to throw herself into an investigation with the depth she had for Joel's, given that she had Janie now and Sean had a new business. Who would fight for this Jane Doe? The ambulance volunteers might be more interested in protecting their friend, the contractor who found her. Addie wondered what brought him to that swamp this time of year. It wasn't a popular clamming spot, though she couldn't deny there were some crustaceans there. Surely he would be on the suspect list.

Should she, Addie Morton, RN, help find the killer or killers? Perhaps, but first things first. She had a feeling this couple's therapy session today with Mel would be a major turning point for them, a make-or-break session. She wanted him to come back. She wanted them to be a family again. She was hopeful it would go that way.

TWO

Janie was asleep in her crib, her breathing deep and rhythmical. Above all, she was quiet. No one but Sean and Dita, and Tuffy, their golden retriever, would ever know that Janie had just spent the previous fifteen minutes shrieking until a dose of pain medicine kicked in, alleviating the effects from her shots.

"At last," Sean whispered, slinking out of the room, fearful of making even the slightest noise that would reawaken the infant.

Dita followed him, glancing back one last time to make sure her sweet one was definitely in slumber mode. She shut the bedroom door as softly as possible, tiptoed down the stairs, and sank into the living room couch next to Sean.

"That was tough," they said in unison.

With Janie asleep, Dita realized she needed to eat. "I'm starving. Let's flip a coin for supper duty."

"Maybe we should call the Washashore," Sean suggested. "Harry might send someone with an order. Tonight's special sound good?"

"Okay, fine with me." Dita knew the pub's specials, and she liked them all. Today was Monday, so it was probably chicken parmesan with their own tomato sauce.

Sean made the call, and after a brief conversation, he turned to Dita. "Harry doesn't have anyone to bring it." Harry was the owner, and often the bartender, of the pub. "I'll pick it up if you want."

"Fine," she said.

That would be a good time for her to call Addie to catch up on how the couples' therapy session went. It was after 9 p.m., and she was pretty sure that on a school night Addie's little boy, Danny, would be in bed by now, or at least upstairs in his room. "Let me know if anyone at the Pub knew that poor woman, the one they found today."

"Sure. Must be today's topic of conversation among the drinkers," he said, grabbing his shoes, "other than if Boston's winning the hockey game, of course."

As soon as Sean left, Dita called Addie's cell phone. Her friend picked up immediately.

"Well," Dita asked, "how are you?"

"Devastated, but more for Danny than for me."

Dita's heart sank. This was not what she'd been hoping to hear.

Addie took a breath and blurted out, "Mel wants to make the separation permanent."

Dita had been expecting a report on progress toward saving the marriage. She was taken by surprise. She almost dropped the phone.

"No!" she exclaimed. "Oh, Addie, ouch!"

"Right. He finally admitted his affair. He doesn't know if he wants to marry this Marissa he's been seeing when he works on the mainland, but he knows he doesn't want to stay married to me. He didn't even say it was the island he needed to leave. I had thought he might ask me to move to the mainland with him, which you know I would do, but... he just wants out. From me."

"Double ouch," Dita said.

She heard Addie let out a sob on the other end of the phone.

"To think after all these years together he has no strong feelings for me," Addie said, sobbing harder. "Dita, I don't understand. What happened? Why? And what do we tell Danny?"

"I'm so sorry. I'm so sorry," Dita said. She wished she could hug her friend. Addie had always been so strong, even during the aftermath of her brother Joel's murder, and Mel had been a big help then. Addie's anguish made Dita feel wounded. She didn't know how to comfort her.

Addie choked back her sobs so she could speak. "You thought it was devastating when you found out Loretta had betrayed and used us. Imagine if it was Sean, how much worse."

"Yes, of course," Dita quickly agreed. "Addie, you don't think he might still change his mind?"

"It's been eight months, and he hasn't. This is permanent. He was quite clear. I hope I can afford to stay in the house. Mel's paying child support now, but who knows how long he'll continue." She paused, and then she blurted out, "I'm so relieved I had that abortion. How would I have managed alone here with another baby?"

Two years ago, Addie had had suspicions that Mel was having an affair with someone while he worked his two weeks a month off the island. Then she discovered she was pregnant. Much as she wanted another child, Addie knew the timing was wrong. After weighing the options, she and Dita flew over to the mainland, ostensibly for a professional meeting and clothing expedition, and she checked into a women's health center. No one but Dita knew. "We're here for you, Addie. You're not alone."

"I know, and I appreciate that. Actually, Mel said Sean had visited him..."

Dita broke in. "On the mainland?"

"Yeah, he went to Mel's office and tried to convince him to come back. I guess Sean thought Mel was in the throes of an infatuation he would get over."

"Well imagine that," Dita said, feeling a surge of affection for her husband. *Good for him,*she thought.

"I know you're ambivalent about your mother moving here," Addie said, "but I'm sure glad mine is close by. I couldn't get through this without her. Dita, never did I expect Mel, of all people, to act like this."

Neither had Dita. They had spent so much time together, the four of them and Danny, brunching on the weekends, hiking on the island trails, playing cards, and hanging at the Washashore Pub. Their little foursome plus Danny seemed lopsided now as a threesome; Janie was too small to count. It would be especially difficult for Sean, who'd spent so much time doing projects and enjoying a beer with Mel.

"It's going to be hard for Sean, too," Dita said. "He's losing his best friend."

Thank goodness Sean had the fitness center, and Teddy, Dita thought. Teddy and Sean rode their motorcycles together. Cruising on bikes erased the fifteen-year age gap between them. Then Teddy hit it big in the tech world and bought the Double-ender Inn. He offered to set Sean up as manager in his fitness center with the option to buy the business in two years. Sean wouldn't have as much free time now to miss Mel, not to mention he and Dita had a steady income at last. But he would miss him, as would Dita.

"I can't tell you how upset this makes me. I don't understand him either," Dita said, though marital breakups on Block Island were all too familiar a tale. A couple can't make ends meet on the island, so one leaves to work on the mainland, returning weekends or whenever they can. The island partner becomes a work widow, and the bonds between the couple fray.

Addie cleared her throat. "I'm feeling sorry for myself, but I'm also starting to feel very angry. His behavior is infuriating. He was always so even-tempered, so accommodating, willing to be the good guy at work and at home. Was he actually seething inside? Even now he seems nice to me when, really, he's stabbing me in the back. Oh, I just don't want to be with you, he explains with his meekest smile. Is he trying to disarm me into passive acceptance?"

Dita thought it was good that Addie was angrier than she was sad. Turning his despicable behavior against herself would only hurt and disable her.

"You're absolutely right," Dita said. "You should be angry. Don't let him smile and smooth-talk you into accepting low alimony and child care. He's making my blood boil. And speaking of mothers, because you were a few minutes ago," Dita continued, "I'm picking mine up at the ferry tomorrow, and we're meeting with Dahlia Brown. She's got her own real estate business now. She's taking Mom to see a few houses."

"Good. You'll see, your mom will be a big help." Addie yawned. "It's been a long day. I'm going to clean up the supper mess in the kitchen and go to bed. I'll talk to you tomorrow."

Dita heard the truck pull into the front yard. "Okay. Sean just drove in with our dinner anyway. But remember, I think something's wrong with Mel, not you."

It was Addie that Mel was married to, but Dita felt he'd left her and Sean as well. She was furious, furious that Danny would grow up with split households, if he was lucky. She was furious that the man had been part of her and Sean's lives and then sailed away when the mood hit him like flotsam in the tide. She wondered, had they ever really known him? He'd always been a calm presence, willing to help with whatever they needed. But was there a different person under that façade? Certainly, she'd been introduced to that kind of shapeshifter with Loretta, leader of the washashore gang. She was beginning to think she needed to look a little deeper at the people who surrounded her.

And in her kitchen, wiping the table and loading the dishwasher, Addie was also wondering whether she'd really ever known Mel. Unlike Dita and Sean, who met in college, she met Mel when she came to the island for the job as the clinic's nurse. She'd summered here as a child with her mother and father, but hadn't stayed through the winter before. Mel was commuting on and off the island even then as the part-time town planner. She and Mel had gravitated toward each other over that winter. He was one of the few white-collar islanders; she was one of the few washashores with a year-round full-time job. They never exactly fell head over heels, but she wondered whether anyone really did.

Until now he'd been a good father to Danny and a good husband to her, but was he just going with the flow? Acting? Addie glanced around the kitchen. They'd picked out the flooring together, and he installed it. They'd shopped for the furniture and fought over the backsplash tiling, she pushing for the blue, he the white subway tiles. He was part of this house, unlike the husbands who haunt but don't inhabit a space. His fishing rods still stood against the garage wall. He'd left them behind. His collection of science fiction books still filled the shelves of a whole bookcase. He'd told her he hadn't found a permanent place to live over there yet. When it was his weekend for Danny, he came to the island and stayed at their house, and Addie either stayed with her mother or went away to the mainland.

She dried her hands on a white linen towel with an embroidered duck, pushed the button to run the dishwasher, and went upstairs to bed, looking in on Danny first. She'd never figure out what went wrong unless Mel told her, and he didn't seem to want to do that.

THREE

Dita startled awake at 4 a.m. Janie's tiny, empty tummy had turned her into a howling banshee. Who could sleep through that? She looked over at Sean, snugly asleep next to her, not even a twitch, and the words, *Oh, right, fathers*, raced through her mind.

"Hmmph," she said. "I'm coming, Janie."

She willed herself out of bed, shuffled over to Janie's cradle and picked her up, then returned to sit in bed and feed her. They both fell asleep again until 6:30. Sean had already gone to the gym to open at 5:30 a.m. for the group of realtors who exercised together before they went to work. Dita was so exhausted she'd not heard him.

Janie stirred, cuddled next to Dita, and searched for her breast.

The rising sun sent a red glow through the slider. Sean and Dita never lowered their shades in the off-season, as there was no one out there to peer in. Dita looked out beyond the yard to the dunes, Scotch Beach, and the ocean. She watched the surf lap onto the shore while Janie lapped her milk. The waves looked as though they barely had the energy to land. This languid sea would be good for her mother's crossing. Yes, she reminded herself, her mother, Caroline, was to arrive this morning to look at houses. Caroline had decided to move to the island to be near her long-awaited grandchild.

First though, Dita needed to pick up a few groceries. She put Janie back to bed while she showered and dressed; then she dressed the infant. She fed Tuffy and let him out. By 9:15 they were in the car, headed down

Corn Neck Road past the dunes and the herd of deer running along the tops, thank goodness not across the road in front of her. Teddy's van was at the surfing lot, though he'd not find a wave today. She slowed to say hello, and they both rolled down their windows. He was just taking a look at the sea, he told her, and he'd be on his way to grab the ferry on its next trip off. He had a consultation on the mainland. Dita might have guessed he had a meeting to attend, as his usually ruffled hair was combed, and he had shaved. He couldn't resist saying good morning to Janie, so he climbed out of the van and opened Dita's back door. She noticed he had a dressy leather jacket that fit loosely over his slightly overweight body. She liked Teddy a lot. He was not only Sean's friend and financial savior, so to speak. He had become the boyfriend of her friend Rachel, Addie's mother. Teddy leaned into the car close to Janie and cooed and tickled and smiled, before letting Dita go on her way to the parking lot of Gerri's Island Pantry, the sole grocer on the island. The locals shortened the name to "the gyp," pronounced with a soft g and the i changed to y. It carried most everything at prices which made the cost of a ferry ride to the mainland for food reasonable, but it was there when you couldn't make the trip.

Once parked, Dita struggled to pull Janie's carriage out of the trunk with one hand while holding Janie with the other. Dita pulled, she pushed, she twisted to no avail.

"Let me help. I'll hold Janie for you," called Dahlia Eastman, her mother's realtor, her voice loud as a tuba in the brass section of a philharmonic orchestra. She strode toward Dita and reached out for the infant. "It's easier if you leave her in the car until you get the carriage out. Hand her to me."

Sometimes people's names befit them. Dahlias are showy like roses, hard to ignore. Dahlia Eastman was a solid but not obese woman, with wavy hair that behaved, and a photogenic face. Like the flower, she was not to be ignored. Dita was glad Janie's cry, strident as it had been this morning, did not reverberate like a brass instrument. She held the baby out and thanked Dahlia, then tugged again at the folded carriage contraption that seemed welded into the trunk, this time using both hands. She gave a good yank to free it, and when she did, almost fell over backward onto her derriere. Finally, she cranked it open and latched it.

"I'm already exhausted," she said to Dahlia. "We build rockets to go into space, but we can't invent a baby stroller, even a small one, that folds up to fit easily in a trunk and unfolds without injuring the baby's parent."

Dahlia lowered Janie into the seat and then glanced around the parking lot, though there was no one nearby to hear her. Even the seagulls were gone, out fishing in the calm waters on this stellar day.

"I wanted to talk to you, Dita, before your mother arrives. I recognized the photo of the murdered woman, and I called the chief right away."

"Really?" Dita asked. She had expected a sales pitch on a house for Caroline and had been only half-listening while thumbing through her phone. Now she gave Dahlia her full attention. She placed her phone in her pocket and rocked Janie's carriage back and forth in place. "Who is she? Should I have recognized her?"

Dahlia turned her head, scanning the parking lot to make sure no one else had appeared. Dita wasn't sure why the realtor needed to maintain secrecy. After all, Dita would put the woman's name in the newspaper, and then everyone would know anyway, but she knew everyone loved being on the inside of a scoop.

Dahlia had started talking again. "She was a client. I sold her the Morgan house toward the end of last summer."

Dita knew the Morgan family, summer cottagers, had put their house up for sale a year ago, but she hadn't known it was sold.

Dahlia continued. "The one on the hill on the way to the school and the medical center. White, two-story, good shape..."

"Yes, yes, I remember it. In fact, I wanted my mother to look at it. So, the woman, what was her name?" Dita fished around her pack for her pen and paper. With all of Janie's things, hers were not easy to reach, but she managed to snag a small pad and a pen. "Where was she from? Did you know her well?"

"Bunny was from Westport, Connecticut. Fairfield County."

Dita knew Fairfield County was a wealthy enclave that housed mainly commuters to New York City. A substantial portion of the island's summer cottagers were from Fairfield County.

"She wasn't married, not now anyway; I think she was divorced or widowed," Dahlia said. "She thought she might retire here, sell her place in Westport."

"What's her real name?"

Dahlia opened her phone and searched. "Maryann Butler. We closed on the house the end of September, and I recall seeing her out here a few times afterward. In fact, she said she hired Josh Martel to do some work inside. Nice lady. I didn't know her too well, but I'd hoped to. How did she die, Dita? The chief wouldn't tell me anything."

Dita shrugged and responded in a flat voice, "She was murdered."

Dahlia covered her mouth with her hand. Her eyes, wide anyway, grew even wider. When she removed her hand from her mouth, she forgot to lower her voice, and she shouted at the volume and register of the ferry horn, "Here?! No, not here! Not again."

Janie emitted a newborn-sized shriek. Dita patted her and whispered some *there there's* to quiet her down. Dahlia apologized. Dita turned back to her.

"They found the body in the swamp across the street from the hardware store, by the clam flats," Dita said as she rocked Janie to and fro in her stroller, continuing to soothe her. "I think the chief will release more information after the family is notified."

Now Janie was pushing out a gurgle. These new babies were such strange little creatures, Dita thought. They cried, they gurgled, and mostly, they slept, but such sweet sleep. She reached down to stroke Janie's petal of a hand.

Dahlia attempted to lower her voice. "Dita, who found her? You probably know and can at least tell me that."

Dita nodded. "Blaze Connors," she said, explaining that the contractor was clamming on a day off.

"I didn't think he ate clams, let alone raked for them," Dahlia exclaimed, her voice rising once again.

Dita tilted her head as she looked at her acquaintance. She knew Blaze and Dahlia had dated when he first arrived on the island, but only for a brief dalliance. This was the first time Dita realized Dahlia still had feelings about him.

"He'd be at the top of my suspect list," the realtor huffed. "Aren't the people who discover the bodies on TV mysteries the guilty ones? I wouldn't put it past him. Clamming my eye."

"I need to go, Dahlia," Dita said looking at her watch. "You know more about Blaze than I do. Text me the last town he lived in before coming here, and I'll do some digging around on the Internet, but I have to get some groceries before my mother's boat arrives. I'll see you at your office at 11:30, right?"

"Right," Dahlia responded. "The news of this is really shaking up the island. People are frightened, but they're also afraid too much news about it will keep the tourists away. The season is just about to begin, and everyone needs money."

Dita rolled the stroller forward without replying. She couldn't help how people felt. News was news, and the *Island Gale* would cover Bunny's murder. She was more concerned with the immediate here and now. Janie was happy, if that's what gurgling meant, and this respite would allow her to cruise the aisles to shop. Then she needed to meet the boat to pick up her mother. She sighed. How would Caroline respond when she learned someone her age was murdered here? Instead of buying a house, she probably would demand that Sean and Dita move closer to her on the mainland.

The Gyp was almost empty, so strolling through the narrow aisles was a breeze. She checked out the groceries in her cart, almost glad there was a new European girl at the register whom she didn't know, so she didn't need to speak to her as yet. The European students came on short-term student visas and then disappeared, either melting into the greater U.S. to overstay, or returning home.

Dita zipped out the door, strapped Janie into the car seat, threw the groceries onto the seat next to her, and folded the stroller and pushed it into the trunk, an easier task than taking it out. Then she headed to the dock, where the *Emma Ann* was just steaming into port. Dita pulled into a parking space in the freight lot where they weren't allowed to park, but where everyone did anyway, and texted Caroline.

Mom, she wrote. *I'm in the freight lot. Look to your right as you cross the gangplank.* She watched the boat make its 180-degree turn as it approached the breakwater and then back into its berth. She waited for the hard knock as it hit the dock and watched it rebound. Then the vessel came to a halt, and the crew threw the ropes onto the stanchions, lowered the gangplank, and the car deck emptied. The vehicles snaked slowly through the parking lot and into the town. Foot passengers, who were kept impatiently waiting until the cars were off, disembarked down the staircases. Then came the deckhands.

Dita spotted her mother, despite her diminutive size, as she strode across the gangplank with a small knot of pedestrians. Dita was always surprised Caroline was not swallowed up in a crowd. She carried herself like a dancer, her head high, and always wore one piece of clothing that stood out, whether it be a white fluffy jacket, a red hat, or thigh-high boots. Her mother loved making a statement. Today it was her red hat.

The ferry had been far from full. That would change soon on the weekends. Once warm weather hit, the crowds would burgeon to standing room only on the upper decks. Then she would never have picked her pixie of a mother out, despite her élan and the spring in her step. Dita admired Caroline and rued the fact that she herself had inherited the height and occasional clumsiness of her father. Much as people often remarked on the similarity of other mother-daughter pairs, Dita and Caroline were remarkably different physically.

Caroline was looking around for her. Dita opened her door, leaned out, and waved. "Mom!" she called.

Caroline heard her, waved back, and strode toward the car, rolling an overnight bag behind her.

"Is this all you brought?" Dita asked.

"Yes, I need to go back in a few days and sort through my things. Does Dahlia have houses for me to see?"

Dita nodded, took her mother's bag, and attempted to squeeze it into the trunk with the Stroller, turning it one way, then trying another, finally giving it one last hard push which she figured would either make it fit or break it. It fit.

While Dita struggled with the suitcase, Caroline opened a back door and bent in to kiss Janie. "She's so beautiful. Hello, sweetie. Grandma's here," she whispered. She pulled herself away and said to her daughter, "She seems to be thriving. You're doing a good job."

Dita felt her whole body relax. She hadn't realized how anxious she was. It was then that she wrapped her arms around her tiny mother and said, "I'm so happy you're here."

"Me too," Caroline agreed, looking up at Dita and smiling. "This is going to work. I was lonelier than I realized."

Dita's father had died two years earlier, leaving Caroline widowed too early in her lifespan.

Caroline leaned over Janie again to give her a peck on the cheek. "Your father would have been smitten with Janie. We might have become island part-timers just to spend more time with her, and you, of course."

Dita knew that probably wouldn't have happened. Her father and mother had a full life on the mainland before his heart gave out. Now she would help Caroline make some friends among the older island women.

"Do you want to drop your bag at the house and wash the boat ride off yourself, or go straight to Dahlia's?" Dita asked.

"Let's go right out. The baby's already in the car, and I used the loo before we came into port," Caroline said, using the British "loo" for john.

"Still reading those British who-done-its?" Dita asked.

Caroline flushed for a second. "Oops," she said with a small smile.

They pulled out for the short drive to Dahlia's office. The turn-off, an unpaved driveway, was just past the Gyp on the other side of the street. When Dita paused to make the turn, she realized she was almost to the shellfish flats where Maryann "Bunny" Butler's body had been found. In fact, she could see the marsh from the street. Yet no one had observed the body being dumped. Maybe not so unusual, she thought, in the dead of winter.

Once they were in the driveway, Caroline leaned forward, trying to glimpse Dahlia's office.

"Is that it?" she asked, pointing to the white, ship-lapped cabin ahead.

Dita nodded.

"No cedar shakes," Caroline observed. "Not family-sized, but I like it."

"It was once an out-building of the large Victorian where we turned in."

"Yes, I can picture that."

Dita pulled into the turnaround. Caroline was about to get out and unlatch Janie, but Dita stopped her. "Let me go in and get Dahlia. We'll drive to the houses together. You sit with Janie."

A moment later she re-emerged from the office with Dahlia clattering in her cork wedgies behind her. Dita thought if those got any higher, Dahlia would need side runners to keep her from tipping over sideways. Caroline was now in the back seat of the car next to Janie. Dita directed Dahlia to ride shotgun and point out the houses. They drove to two places Caroline described as uninspiring, though she did the requisite walk-throughs.

"I like your tiny office better than these Hampton-style McMansions," she said. "These aren't the houses you sent me to preview on the internet. Is there anything more inviting? I don't really need a large castle."

Dahlia thumbed through her listing cards, "The next one will be better. Dita, drive to Hill Street. I'm sorry, Caroline. Two of those I sent you pictures of are already sold."

On Hill Street, Dahlia told Dita to slow down and park as they approached the house Bunny had purchased.

"I love that one," Caroline said. "That's what I'm looking for, an older Block Island 1½-story farmhouse with a wraparound porch. I can picture myself in a rocking chair there."

The house had a second floor, but it was a short story, not the full height of newer homes.

"Sean and I wouldn't like to live in one of those," Dita said. "We're too tall for that second floor. People were much shorter in the 19th century."

"I'm sorry, but it's not on the market," Dahlia explained. "It sold last spring."

She grimaced and said nothing further. Dita figured the realtor didn't want to taint her showing with an explanation of the purchaser's demise by murder. Neither did she.

"We're going to the one next door, similar though not identical," Dahlia said.

Caroline smiled as they approached the front porch, not a wrap-around, but deep. "I could fit a swing and a rocker out here," she said.

"And maybe a ping pong table," Dita added, because she knew her mother loved to play.

"This is a beautiful house. It even has a turret," Caroline said.

Dita smirked. "You've been watching too many British history dramas. It's a small bump out, not even a turret. There's no princess imprisoned in there."

Dahlia cleared her throat. Dita thought she looked a bit uncomfortable. On second thought, maybe there was a princess.

As Dita watched, Dahlia quickly shifted back to her sales pitch. "Even you and Sean could stand up on the second floor," she said to Dita. "It's not a one-and-½."

"Yard's a bit overgrown," Dita noted.

"Easily fixed," Dahlia answered, using the standard realtor reply.

Inside, a center hall ran alongside the stairs. Opposite the staircase, an archway opened to a living room with large picture windows in the front and a rose window on the side. The sun streamed in.

"This room is square," Caroline observed. "How remarkable. It makes furniture arrangement so easy." She glanced down at the oak flooring. "The floor's beautiful."

"The owner refinished them when they bought the house five years ago," Dahlia said.

"And they did the kitchen."

"Only five years ago?" Caroline asked.

"Yes," Dahlia replied. "Their company took a downturn, so they're selling properties. This is one of several."

"Come in the kitchen, Mom," Dita called. "It's a nice size with room for a table. You can even put Janie in a highchair here in a few years," Dita said.

They strolled through all the rooms upstairs, the three bedrooms, the bathrooms.

"I can picture myself living here, and it's only a few minutes away from you, Dita," Caroline noted.

"Longer in summer when there are crowds of tourists in town, but yes, convenient," Dita said. "I like it, too. I think you'd be happy here."

"There is something you should know about the history," Dahlia honked. Again, Dita thought she seemed to be uncomfortable. "You may have already heard the stories, Dita."

Dita looked at her. "No, I haven't."

"There isn't any princess in the turret, but in the 1800s a young woman who lived here disappeared during a Block blizzard. They never found her. Over the years, during storms, people living in the house have reported hearing someone crying her name and doors opening and closing."

Caroline looked at Dahlia in disbelief. "Are you saying there's a ghost?"

Dahlia shrugged.

Dita asked whether the price would be higher or lower due to the ghost, and then she also asked, "Was this ever used as a B & B? Sometimes innkeepers make up these stories to get notoriety, increase business."

"Not that I'm aware of," Dahlia responded.

Caroline was not deterred. "Well, I for one do not believe in the supernatural, and I'm not afraid of ghosts, especially ones you only hear during storms. The way the wind blows out here, rafters in Dita's house creak, and Addie's mother's house whistles. I was there once during a Block nor'easter. I do believe I like this house, and I'll make an offer. If an inspection doesn't turn up major problems, I'll move in as soon as possible. And by the way, what was the young woman's name, just in case I hear something?"

"It was Cora," Dahlia said. "Do you want to see the last house on today's list?"

"No," Caroline said. "I'm done. I love this house, Cora and all."

"Okay, call me later with an offer and I'll present it to the sellers." Dahlia held the front door open for them and they left, with Dahlia once again clattering over the porch behind them. "Wait! I need to tell you where Blaze used to live." She pulled a slip of paper out of her pocket.

Dita reached out and waited for Dahlia to catch up.

"Here," Dahlia said, passing her the slip.

Dita glanced at it and placed it in her purse. *This* would be easy, she thought. He's a Rhode Islander.

FOUR

Addie released a deep yawn as she drove up the hill toward the medical center. She hadn't gotten much sleep last night. Soon after the bars closed, she'd been called to the clinic to assist with two car accident victims, both of them islanders she knew. Fortunately, neither had died, but one was med-evacuated to a mainland hospital. Addie was tired, not so severely that she felt she might drift off, but enough that she hoped for a light workload today.

She was grateful that Sean and Dita had helped by watching Danny and getting him off to school this morning. Since Addie lived alone now and didn't have Mel to be with Danny when she took night calls, she had a temporary arrangement with them. Addie would take Danny out of the house cuddled in his blanket, trying not to disturb him too much, a feat not always possible as he was getting bigger. He hadn't hit his growth spurt yet, but when he did, she'd have to leave him alone in the house. For now, she walked him out, laid him across the back seat of the car for the two-minute ride to Sean and Dita's, then bedded him down on their couch without waking them. They found him in the morning, gave him breakfast, and sent him to school on the bus. It was the best arrangement she could cobble together. Addie was considering renting a room to someone just so she could leave Danny home without worrying when she was called out. A lot of islanders sublet to summer workers, but she thought she'd be able to find an islander in need of a home who she could trust with Danny. The extra money would also help pay her considerable mortgage. She was still trying to figure out how to pay her bills without Mel's share. He paid child support for Danny, but when he decided to make their separation permanent, he promised to quitclaim the house to her to get out from under those payments. True, he would forgo his part of the down payment and what they'd already paid, but she still would be left with a hefty monthly bill.

She was almost at the house Dita's mother, Caroline, had recently purchased. She could see Caroline outside trimming hedges along the front porch. Addie was a slow thinker this morning, but hadn't Dita told her last night was to be her mother's first time to stay there? And she was already out gardening? She stopped the car when she reached the house, rolled down the passenger-side window, and shouted a hello. Caroline looked over, laid her shears on the porch, and gestured to Addie to come in. Addie held up a finger and nodded but took a moment to call the clinic first. There were no early morning appointments scheduled. It was a paperwork morning, so she parked. She could conduct her official welcome visit while she was paying a social visit. Addie was not just the clinic nurse; she was also the island's visiting nurse and the island's school nurse. She was, in fact, the only working nurse. Her bag of medical gauges and devices was always stashed in her trunk. She paid each new retiree who washed ashore to the island a welcome visit, as well as seeing a number of laid-up and sick residents.

She grabbed the bag and met Caroline, who had opened the door. The scent of coffee brewing almost made her swoon.

"Most of my furniture came yesterday," Caroline said. "The rest is in storage, and I'll bring it over when I can rent a truck and Sean!" She laughed at that.

She brought Addie into the kitchen. On the counter were fresh muffins and scones from Books and Bakes.

"Were you expecting me?" Addie asked.

"I thought Dita might stop in, or Dahlia," Caroline said. "But I'm equally happy to see you."

"How was your first night?" Addie asked.

"Splendid. I did notice something next door, though. I thought Dahlia said the owner wasn't here, but I could swear I saw a face at the window opposite my living room several times last night. Dahlia mentioned there might be a ghost in this house. She didn't say anything about that house. Might the owner's family be here?"

Addie didn't know.

"There definitely was a face in the window," Caroline said. "The fact that someone murdered the owner, well, it spooked me to see the face."

"Dahlia should know," Addie said.

Caroline picked up her phone and called Dahlia to find out if she knew who was there.

Dahlia told her the woman's brother had inherited the property, but she didn't think he'd come to look at it. She hadn't heard from him, and as the recent realtor, she still had keys to the house. No one had asked to use them. She offered to call Bunny's brother and get back to her.

Addie queried Caroline more. "Were there any lights on over there? Could you see a man, or was it a woman?" she asked.

"There weren't any lights. I just saw a shadowy outline of a face and eyes. It made me curious as to whether someone was living in there. Dahlia told me she didn't think anyone had visited after the owner was killed. She didn't say whether the woman died in the house, though, so I'll ask you, did she? Not that I think she's haunting it. I'm just curious and, I admit, a bit frightened. Maybe that was her killer I saw."

"We don't know if she died here. The police went through the house after her body was found, but they didn't find any evidence of a murder there," Addie said. "It's so sad. She hadn't even moved in. Dahlia said she'd visited a few times, but her plans were to wait for better weather to start bringing her belongings over."

"Have they found her killer yet?" Caroline asked.

"I don't think so. Dita would know quicker than I would. She'd hear at the newspaper office. No one thinks it could be an islander, though."

"Why not?"

"Well, we all know each other, and there's no one who seems a likely suspect. What motive could a local have?"

Caroline furrowed her forehead. "No one would have thought your other friend, what's-her-name, would have been a killer either, or that there was a washashore drug gang."

Who could have forgotten? Dita had almost been killed, not once but twice. Addie had to admit that Caroline was right.

"Am I in any danger here?" Caroline asked, one hand on her hip.

Addie had one of those moments when she was not in the room. Some call it an out-of-body experience, others an absence. An image of Bunny lying on the stretcher, her back blown out, crashed into Addie's consciousness. It was an image she didn't want to see or think about, either.

"Well?" asked Caroline. "Addie, did you hear me? Are you okay? Say something."

"Um, sorry, I just drifted for a second. I think seeing Bunny affected me more than I knew. I hope you aren't in danger. No, no, of course you're not," Addie stated with a frown, trying to reassure Caroline and herself, too. "At least, I don't think so."

Caroline put her arm around her. "You've certainly had your difficulties," she said, referring to Mel's departure. "And here I am bothering you with mine."

"I have, but I think you have, too. You lost your husband not so long ago. My Mel is at least still alive, though sometimes I wish he were dead," Addie admitted, feeling guilty as soon as the words were out of her mouth. Never would she have dreamt she'd feel this way. She had a sudden insight into why spouses commit murder, and she was even more mortified that she could see herself in this group.

But Caroline did not reproach her or *'there, there'* her. She tried to help her understand what generated these feelings. "It's lonely after a long marriage to find yourself all alone, Addie. Yours was not so long, but long enough to make you aware that half of your being has been severed. For both of us at night in bed, there is no warm companion; at supper time, the table is way too large for one; and for me, my children were far away out of town. Yes, it's hard, but I'm strong and I know you are, too. I made some new friends, signed up for new activities, and then, presto, my rebel of a daughter gets pregnant. So wonderful for me. Of course I know her father would have been handing out cigars to the universe, but Janie has filled that hole for me also. Folding myself into family has been like an endless drink of the chocolatiest hot chocolate with whipped cream. And you still have Danny and your mom. I know you'll come through this and be even stronger than you were. For now, it's going to be hard."

Addie felt sad, and she didn't feel strong, but she appreciated Caroline's support. She set her vengeful thoughts aside and conjured up a picture of a bright-petaled violet-colored flower swaying in the breeze. Perhaps for both of them, she changed the subject. "Did Dahlia mention anything to you about the history of this house?" she asked.

"A bit. It was passed down in a local family for a number of generations until the last descendant left for the mainland. Then it was sold to summer people."

"People who've lived here reported seeing or hearing a ghost," Addie said.

"Oh, right, Dahlia mentioned the stories about Cora. That's what you're referring to, aren't you?" Caroline asked.

"Yes," Addie said.

Caroline smiled. "Hmmm. Whenever I hear these kinds of stories, I figure there's a more scientific explanation for knocks and moans and apparitions. In Connecticut there's a region that has underground rumblings easily mistaken for sounds of a ghost in the house at night. I'm sure it's the same here, especially with the wind knocking everything about on this island, although ghosts greatly increase tourism. But Addie, I didn't see a ghost next door. That was the face of a person. I'd like to know it wasn't someone who might have killed the woman who planned to live there. Forget about ghosts. It's real people that frighten me."

"The police are working on the murder, and Dita and I have been looking too," Addie said.

"Dita?" Caroline asked. "She can't be doing that again. She has an infant to think of."

"She's only doing online searching. We're not putting ourselves in danger," Addie said.

She finished her scone and coffee, and then she felt better. She was ready to take Caroline's blood pressure and a medical history, if she agreed, of course. Caroline thought it was a great idea. She planned to use the medical center for her health care since she now lived on the island. There were some questions about health that Addie thought important in lieu of Caroline's experience the night before. She felt disloyal to Dita even considering them, but as part of her job she had to assess whether Caroline might have been hallucinating due to a medication, an imaginative mind, or mental illness. Or was her vision impaired? She called the clinic and made Caroline an appointment for a physical with Dr. Bennett. He had, she recalled, wanted to meet her. She wondered should she warn Caroline about The Mustache, but decided Caroline might enjoy the attention, and she probably could easily brush him off if he got frisky around her.

Addie took her cup and plate to the kitchen and put on her jacket. It was time to get to the clinic. "I'm sure I'll see a lot more of you at Dita's. And do say hello to my mom. I think she'll be in the shop today."

"Definitely. I'll stop at The Lorelei," Caroline said. "I love your mom, and I love the shop. But Addie, I'm concerned about you. Given everything that's happened with Mel, with Loretta, and now with this woman Bunny, maybe you need to talk with someone. You know, not the couples therapist, someone of your own."

Addie was taken aback. Here she was wondering if Caroline was okay, and Caroline was worrying about her. Funny how that works. Addie took Caroline's hand.

"Thank you for being concerned about me. I've been wondering if I should do that. I just haven't had time," she said.

She was about to leave when Caroline's phone rang. She motioned to Addie to wait. Addie could hear Dahlia's honking voice even before Caroline put the phone on speaker. Dahlia reported back to them that as far as Dahlia's brother was concerned, no one had been to the house. She asked for Caroline to call the police if she saw anyone in there again. When Dahlia was done, Caroline followed Addie outside and resumed her trimming.

Addie drove up the hill the short distance to the clinic, passing the school on the way. She glanced over at the playground to see if Danny's class was outside having recess, but it was empty. She missed seeing him this morning and decided to pick him up after school. But first there was work. She needed to call the hospital on the mainland to find out how their patient was doing, and check on the injured accident victim who'd gone home, unless, of course, Dr. Bennett had.

Later that week, Caroline called Dita at 7 a.m., frightened. She told Dita she'd brought the trash out to the backyard earlier and seen a man slip out of the house next door. He was tall, but ultra-thin, what her plump friends called a "living X-ray," with sparse brown hair. His clothes hung off him, as though he'd dressed in someone else's. He was gone before she could speak, disappeared through a space between the tall hedges that only someone as thin as he or a child could squeeze through.

"And yes, I called the police," she told her daughter. "There's a cruiser pulling up now."

Dita was rattled. She told Caroline she'd be right over. She bundled up Janie and drove over with her. When she arrived, the cruiser was parked in front of Bunny's house. Her mother was waiting outside. Dita unlatched Janie and handed her to her mother. Then she went into Bunny's to find the police.

"Hello," she opened the door and called out. "Dita here."

It was her neighbor, Sgt. Karl Schultz, who responded. "I'm in the living room."

Dita felt disappointed when she heard his voice boom. He'd been lackluster as the policeman she'd been told to work with on the washashore murder case, and though she'd heard he'd improved, she hadn't yet seen it herself.

The entryway of the house was not unlike Caroline's, a short hall just big enough to contain a small coat closet before it opened out. There was a staircase and a room once called a parlor on the other side. Dita wondered what people used those for these days. In olden times, they contained a few overstuffed chairs or a small horsehair-filled sofa, once called a settee, that no one in their right mind would sit on because they were so hard. "Firm," a salesperson would say. Today the room was empty, as Bunny had not had a chance to furnish the entire house before her demise. The back two rooms were the reverse of her mother's. Straight ahead was the kitchen, then a sitting room with a more up-to-date, well-used couch. Its pillows sagged, but it might still be comfortable. Dita went through and saw Karl at a window. He wore rubber gloves and was dusting for fingerprints. She was glad he was taking this seriously. She thought perhaps the whole washashore gang affair had sobered him up. Chief Gomez had given him a talking to after the whole Loretta fiasco, from what Dita'd heard. For one thing, he wasn't at the pub all the time. Instead, he was at Sean's gym.

"Have you found anything?" she asked.

"Someone's been sleeping here," he said, pointing to the couch where a motheaten blanket and a yellowing pillow lay on the cushions. Karl sometimes slipped into the Rhode Island vernacular, dropping the r's in words and adding them where they normally wouldn't be, but he didn't do that today. "Otherwise, the place's been unoccupied."

Dita noticed he'd said 'unoccupied' rather than 'empty.' That would be part of his taking his role seriously, using officialese language.

Karl moved closer to the couch. Then he held his nose. "This stinks! Whoever couch-surfed didn't use the shower. Most likely one of the island guys who usually sleep rough. I'm searching for something left behind so we can identify him, but I'd bet it's Josh Martel. He fits the description your mother gave me, and he got kicked out of the room he was staying in at the boarding house. Plus, I think Bunny hired him as a handyman."

"Right, he would fit my mom's description of 'X-ray thin.' Isn't he at the Washashore Pub begging beers from Harry sometimes?"

Karl nodded, "A lot of the time. If it's Josh, or another of the folks without a room, he'll come back," he said, slipping into Rhode Island lingo. "He left his sleeping gear, and I don't think he knows Caroline saw him. We'll keep an eye out. If you spot him somewhere, call me. I think the victim's brother is coming over tomorrow or the day after, and it would be nice to have this wrapped up."

"Sure." Dita was impressed with the change in him. He was acting all official now. She hoped it would stick.

Karl promised her the police would drive by several times at night because they were still working on Bunny's murder. If someone was in her house, they would definitely want to catch up with them. Meanwhile, he would try to locate Josh so he could question him. Dita mulled this over. Maybe she would dig around too, starting at the Be Fit gym, right? Karl, better at detecting than he used to be, must have noticed her expression. He wasted no time to lecture her.

"Dita, I can tell you want to stick your nose in this, and I'm going to tell you, don't. You have a new baby to take care of. You don't need to be chased around the island by maniacs anymore. Leave it to us police. Hear me?"

Dita turned her back on him and headed for the door. "Of course," she shouted back. But she had no intent to leave anything to him. She gathered Janie from her mother and left for a visit to the Be Fit where she could discuss this with Sean. It was early enough that the realtors might still be there too.

FIVE

The Be Fit was located on the first floor of the iconic Double Ender Hotel. Two years earlier, Sean's friend Teddy had sold his technology company for mega-bucks to a global company and then invested a small portion of it in the purchase of the Double Ender Hotel. At the same time as Teddy hit the jackpot, Sean had reached a career dead-end, having exhausted all avenues to borrow the money he needed to start a fitness center on Block Island. Teddy offered Sean the opportunity to set up a gym in the Double Ender and become its manager for two years, after which he could lease the space from Teddy if it was successful.

Teddy had torn most of the first floor of the inn apart and rebuilt it. He left the cozy barroom with its curved red leather booths and polished wood tables, the dance floor, and the long bar with the curved leather lip along it. He installed the gym across from the barroom where the former formal dining room had been. The dining room would now be in a separate building behind the main hotel. Sean gave Teddy a description of how he wanted the gym to be set up, along with a list of the machines to purchase and where to place them. They built a small locker room in an old storage space.

The Be Fit was a success. The local realtors gathered there at 6 a.m. to exercise year-round, the older residents came in after them, sometimes overlapping to gossip, and the school's parents and shopkeepers stopped in whenever they could snatch an hour off. Sean supplemented memberships with training fees, and in summer, tourists poured in to sculpt their bodies. Sean even led a yoga group on the beach for tourists. Dita stopped in to give him some time off during the day, and she ran the gym on Sunday mornings.

Today, as she crossed the hotel lobby before reaching Be Fit's door, she heard Dahlia's honking voice. She was presiding over the other realtors, who were finishing up their workouts with some juicy gossiping. The news that Caroline had seen someone or something in Bunny's house was spreading, thanks to Dahlia. Dita thought they ought to be working for the newspaper instead of her. When the group spotted her, they went silent.

"What's going on? I heard you mention my mother," Dita said, directing her comment to Dahlia.

If Dahlia had been a redhead like Addie, she might have flushed, but she was not. She was shameless, so she just shrugged. Dita took advantage of this one time that Dahlia was speechless.

"Dahlia, maybe you can help us. Does anybody know where Josh Martel goes during the day? We think it might be him sneaking into the house next door to my mother's at night."

Genevieve, a realtor who brokered a lot of rentals, spoke up. "I've seen him in the library. He goes into the alcove with the magazines and newspapers and hangs out in one of the easy chairs."

"Right, but I've also seen him down at the harbor in a rusted van," Cathy Jones added. She was Dahlia's office assistant and also worked part time as a ticket taker for the ferry. "You know, it's one of those old vans that are almost colorless, faded, and rusted out."

"He looks that way too," a middle-aged woman sitting on a recumbent bike piped up.

It could have been a joke because he did. But they all knew Josh and felt sorry for him. One of the hoteliers had offered him a free room last winter because he was replacing the mattresses anyway. But Josh's poor habits, excessive drinking, and its aftermath, had proved too much, and he was evicted come spring with no return invitation the following fall.

He moved to the rooming house, but his habits propelled him out of there too.

"Do you think he killed Bunny?" Dahlia asked. "He seems like you could knock him over with a light tap."

They all agreed. Yet Cathy recalled a day at the docks when he got into a fight with a guy on one of the tuna boats and held his own. Cathy had watched from her perch at the ferry ticket office.

The realtors clattered and chattered as they gathered their belongings from the locker room and showered before heading out to their jobs. They were still lining up renters for summer vacation houses, and the length of time until the first week of real tourism was running short. On top of that, they had to allay any concerns potential tenants had about a killer running amok.

They all worshipped Janie on their way out, each pausing to whisper a word or touch her cheek. Janie seemed to enjoy their attention. She was gurgling on Sean's counter. He had a hand on her cradle, rocking her as he nodded goodbye to the realtors and talked with Dita, echoing Karl's warnings. As he spoke, Dita wondered if Karl had already called him.

"Dita, you need to sit this investigation out. You heard Addie describe that Bunny woman's body. You have Janie now. You can't afford to become a target."

Dita didn't argue with him. She put her pocketbook behind the counter and climbed aboard a treadmill, ramping up the speed to a good run.

"Hard to hear you over the treadmill."

"Really? I hear you."

Their argument was interrupted by the arrival of a man they recognized but didn't know. He was in his 60s, with close-cropped white hair and intense blue eyes. Dita tried to recall where she'd seen him before. He was shorter than her, but not by a lot, and he had a build that showed he worked out but not overly much.

"I'm looking for a summer membership," he said. "Do you have those?"

Sean did. Just last night they'd been debating what to charge this year and settled on raising the summer fee from $450 to $600 for three months. The monthly would go for $250, and a daily pass was $20.

"I do, but they don't start until June," Sean said, handing him the fee schedule.

The man looked it over. "I guess I could do one monthly until then," he said. "I don't have an address yet. I'm staying with a buddy until I can bring my boat over when it's a little warmer." He reached over to Janie, and she grasped his manicured thumb with her tiny pink hand.

Sean waited a second until she unclasped, and then he moved his little girl further away. "You look familiar, but I don't know your name," Sean said.

Dita was still huffing away on the treadmill, but she was listening. She heard a gruff note in Sean's voice. *Hmm,* she thought, *protective*. She glanced over to see if she recognized the guy. She thought maybe she did but wasn't sure.

"Carter Crane, but everyone calls me Artie. I keep my boat down at Dave's Dock in summer and come out weekends and days off or for jobs over here. I'm an electrician. In fact, Teddy had me update the wiring here."

"Yeah, that's where I think I saw you here," Sean said, seeming to relax now. "Welcome to the Be Fit."

"I have a couple of jobs lined up for the summer, so I think I'll be on the island more than usual this year," Artie said.

Sean had the paperwork going when Caroline, Rachel, and two other older women arrived.

"We're here for our seniors' easy moving class, Sean," Caroline called out.

Artie glanced over at them. Without looking up, Sean called out, "Just finishing up with someone. Be with you in a couple of minutes."

The women disappeared into the locker room.

"Hey, they don't look bad," Artie remarked. "Can men take the class too?"

Sean gave him a hard stare. “It might be a little too easy for you, but sure. It’s a few dollars extra per class, and the white hair may make them look harmless, but beware.” Sean waggled his eyebrows.

“Just kidding,” Artie said. “But I might stay and work out and watch for a while.”

Sean leaned in and lowered his voice. “I think they’re a bit self-conscious, so I wouldn’t stare.”

Artie went over to one of the ellipticals and started pumping the pedals while the women lined up for the class in the workout area. Dita, who was not far from them, heard Rachel whisper to her mother, “That guy’s kind of cute. Give him a smile, Caroline.”

She saw her mother wave Rachel off and roll her eyes. “I don’t have time for that. I’m going to be busy with getting settled, and Janie, and Dita. I need to help her, too.”

While they waited for Sean to start, they chatted. Dita climbed down from her treadmill and joined them.

“The man next door arrived yesterday with a woman,” Caroline said. “I’ll go over and say hello when I get home.”

“Bunny’s brother?” Dita asked.

“I assume so. If I had caught Dahlia here today, I could have asked her, but she seems to have left.”

“Now that there are people staying in the house, we should let Karl know so he can keep an eye out. Wouldn’t want whoever was couch-surfing there to bother them,” Dita replied.

“Or kill them like Bunny,” her mother retorted.

“Okay, everyone, time for class,” Sean had a microphone hooked up that he used to direct the exercises. “Dita, you’re on for counter duty and Janie time.”

“Yes, boss,” she said.

Artie was now lifting weights in the corner. He was pretty strong, Dita thought, deadlifting 150 pounds. He caught her watching and smiled as he dropped the weight to the floor. Dita thought he definitely was a flirt.

When the class ended, Sean returned to his post at the desk, and Dita took Janie and left with the group of women.

"Mom, he was watching you," she said.

"Really? Come on, he was watching all the women, and you too," Caroline said, laughing. "We know nothing about him."

"I'll ask Teddy," Rachel said, smiling as she always did when she thought about her boyfriend. "He did say he did the wiring for the Double Ender, right? I'll have Teddy do a computer search. He can do all that stuff."

"Don't bother doing it for me," Caroline said. "I'm just fine on my own. Don't need any guy. And Dita, don't forget to find out if they picked up that skeleton guy yet."

"I won't," Dita replied, waving goodbye and watching as the group went off to the Books and Bake to have their morning nosh. "Come, Janie, let's go home. Tuffy's waiting for us, and I have a computer search to do on Mr. Blaze Collins. I'm sure the clerks at Rhode Island's state court will help me. They've found files for me before."

But nothing turned up in the courts, and a search of the local news files yielded zero information, also. Not even a traffic ticket, she thought. She called a few reporter friends around the state, but no one could recall any negative news on Blaze Collins. Then she did something she did not ordinarily do. Knowing Sean's computer passwords, she switched to his browser and looked into his social media accounts for any messages with Blaze. He was a friend of Sean's in one account, and she spent a half hour reading through Blaze's posts and friends. Other than some angry remarks from Dahlia, there was nothing that would indicate he was homicidal.

SIX

As Memorial Day weekend approached, the pulse of the island quickened. It was as though the island itself woke from hibernation. Addie swore people walked faster, like they'd suddenly remembered there was somewhere they needed to be. Even the children were more active, their voices ringing through the streets, small gangs of them appearing as if from nowhere. The air, so dry in winter, began to absorb humidity as the temperature rose. It filled with spring light and radiated with anticipation.

Addie started preparing the clinic for the summer. She ordered more supplies: bandages, paper coverings for the exam tables and the patients on the tables, throat swabs, paper towels and toilet paper, frequently needed medications, hypodermic needles, tourniquets, soap. Soon the clinic would be swamped with people feeling ill, needing care for kitchen accidents, people in moped and car accidents, scraped knees, tick bites, dog bites, food poisonings, and the list went on. Addie and Dr. Bennett had to anticipate all the possibilities.

Today was Friday, probably one of the last when Addie would have free time after work. The Block Island School sports teams traveled to the mainland on Friday afternoons once or twice a month to play other schools, or for the non-sports minded, museum and cultural visits. Danny would meet Mel afterward and stay the weekend with him there. At four, Addie closed the clinic to patients but kept working, catching up on her charting and checking the medication cabinet since she didn't have to rush for Danny. When she had no more reason to linger, she drove down the hill toward her empty home, feeling empty herself. She was about to pass the Washashore Pub, but instead of driving on by, she hit the brakes to make a quick turn into the driveway and went around to the back lot to park. She somewhat surprised herself by that spontaneous *decision. Well, why* not, she thought. *I'll grab a beer and a game of pool, maybe even supper, hang out with other* people.

And suddenly it hit her that Danny wasn't the only one feeling the hole Mel's absence had created.

She entered the pub with a bit of trepidation, unsure that she really wanted to be there, and she sniffed before getting too far inside. No foul odors. The pub was passing her sniff test. The reek of stale beer and urine from toilet bowl overflow that used to greet her at the door was gone. Harry, the owner, had replaced the old wooden floor boards this winter, painted, and cleaned the place up. His efforts worked. She had to give it to him; he'd straightened out after the drug busts two years ago and made the pub, if not chi-chi, nice.

Addie glanced around to see who else was there. The place was pretty much empty. None of the usuals except for Harry himself. He was sitting at the long wooden bar alone, reading one of his car magazines. He heard Addie and turned around. She felt his smile.

"Come sit here," he patted the stool next to him. He'd recovered the worn and torn tops with new red vinyl. "Beer? Margarita?"

She accepted the invitation and thought how nice it was that Brenda, his longtime bar maid, would no longer come crashing out of the kitchen to interrupt their conversation. Brenda was serving a lengthy sentence at the state prison for the attempted murder of Dita and selling drugs with Loretta's gang two years ago. If she ever was released, it wouldn't be soon.

"I think a Margarita would be nice," Addie said. "And I thought I'd try playing some pool today, but it seems nobody else came."

Harry raised his blonde eyebrows. "Where's Danny?"

"At Mel's on the mainland."

He went around to the back of the bar and pulled out the tequila and the orange liqueur. "I always put in a bit of this liqueur," he said. "It's like floating orange blossoms in it."

He leaned over to get the lime and walked a few steps further to get a shaker. He poured in the spirits and the juice and gave the shaker a few good swings before he grabbed two cocktail glasses from the overhead shelf and set them on the bar.

"Salt?" he asked.

She nodded.

Then he fixed his unusual gray eyes on hers.

"So," he said. He poured the two drinks, keeping his eyes trained on Addie, not the glasses. "I think I can start your pool game off since nobody else is around. It's been slow all day. I suspect a lot of folks went off on the boat this morning to the mainland. Shopping day, or maybe even court cases. There's an 8 o'clock return ferry run tonight they can catch. Spring schedule started."

Addie glanced around the silent barroom. "Guess I'll play you then," she said, smiling in a way she hadn't in months. Harry was an old island friend, someone she felt comfortable with. She was almost glad no one else was around.

He set the shaker down on the bar and pushed a glass to her. "Glad to oblige," he said. "Taste it."

She took a sip. She nodded her head. He was still staring at her. She noticed the way his tats stretched over his biceps. She couldn't tell what the drawings were because they were so close together in a so-called sleeve. Their meaning was hidden, but his muscles were not. She noticed how square his shoulders were, how he didn't have an ounce of fat, unlike Mel, who had widened out over the years of their marriage, looking more like ranch livestock than the cowboy Harry resembled. That comparison sent a streak of guilt racing through her behind the electric current Harry was raising. Her body was noticing what she hadn't allowed her brain to do. Harry was buff, so pleasingly buff.

"How's that?" Harry asked, leaning closer.

Addie's cheeks reddened a bit. She was flustered, and it showed. Darn that red hair and see-through skin, she groused to herself. He'd caught her. He wasn't asking about the drink. Harry had been a friend for a long while, and rumors about the two of them had floated around the island now and again, but they had kept their friendship just that. Now with Mel gone, Addie felt a stronger vibe. He came around the bar again and put his tattoos around her shoulder. She felt warm. Did tats radiate heat?

They sipped a bit, and then he steered her to the pool table, took her drink, and set both hers and his on a nearby table. He handed her a pool cue. He even racked the balls and gave her the first shot. She tried to collect herself and concentrate on breaking. She aimed for the center of the rack and whacked the white cue ball as hard as she could. The crack resounded through the empty room, and the balls rolled around the table. A few dropped into pockets in staccato thunks.

"Good shot," Harry said. "Go ahead again."

That broke her concentration. She was thinking of him now. She aimed at a ball, missed, and the cue ball flew into the corner pocket.

"Oops, I think I'm out of practice," she said, laughing. She didn't want him to realize she'd been focusing on him instead of her shot.

"I don't recall you ever playing here," he teased. "I never once saw you practice."

Addie's flush crept up her cheeks again.

Harry shrugged. "Guess it's my turn," he said. He knocked off the balls on the table one at a time into the pockets as she watched, until finally the 9 ball was the only one left.

"Nice job," she said.

"Do you want to hit it in for me?" he asked, bringing it around the table to her.

She took the cue stick, aimed, and the ball hit the nine and knocked it into a pocket. When she looked up, he was standing right in front of her.

"Maybe we've had enough knocking balls around the pool table," he said, lifting her face to his.

She felt even warmer as he drew her to him; his lips touched hers, and a current surged between them. How long had she longed for this? She let out a sigh.

Finished with his macho pool show, Harry whispered, "Right, me too. I've wanted to do this for..."

She placed her hand over his mouth. "Don't say it." Then she removed her hand and kissed him again.

"Let's get out of here, Addie, before someone comes in. I'll take you to my place."

He went to the front door and locked it. She thought of all the reasons she should tell him she was going home, that she was not yet divorced, that they were good friends and shouldn't ruin their relationship, that someone might see her and it would be all over the island. But then he returned and put his arms around her and foxtrotted her out of the room, grabbing her coat on the way. Outside, they glided to his truck. He opened the door for her and motioned her in.

"My car is here. Everyone will see it." She stalled to try to talk herself out of going any further. She'd never been a one-nighter person.

Harry looked around and spotted the car. "It's in the corner of the lot where it's dark. No one will notice it."

"But Sean or Dita might come by on their way home and see it," she protested.

"We'll get it later. Make something up if they ask."

He pressed himself against her again, and her resistance melted. She climbed into his rusting, old model truck. He went around to the driver's side, hopped in and pulled her closer to him again. It had been so long, too long, since a man had held her like that, and oh, how she loved it. Could they just stay holding each other like this all night? But no, not out here in the middle of his parking lot.

"Look at that, you still have a bench seat," she said, trying to regain composure when he released her and started the engine.

But then he laid his hand on her leg and began to move it up, steering with one hand.

"Handy, isn't it, especially on a cool night?" he said, flashing a smile for her.

"Hm, very handy," she thought, but she was liking it too much to stop him. She knew his house was just a few blocks away, on the way toward the town hall, but she'd never been inside. It was a small fisherman's cottage built in the thirties, a bungalow with the standard graying island cedar siding and a picture window in the front. There was no water view in back, and in front, just the small yard, more a stripe than a swatch.

She stepped out of the truck in the driveway and waited for Harry to come around. He opened the front door, which in Block Island style was unlocked, and he gestured for her to go through first. She stepped into a living room dominated by a giant black leather couch that faced a gargantuan TV screen.

For games, she thought. *But doesn't he watch a slew of them at the pub?*

The floor was carpeted with an aging beige Berber. One other seat, a black leather lounger, was catty-corner to the couch, and a couple of end tables completed the furnishings. It was a typical single guy's living room, unencumbered by color and décor, except it was clean. No empty chip bags or beer cans strewn about.

It's like he doesn't live here, she thought, *or maybe he just uses it when he's expecting someone, like me.*

Now he was right behind her, his hands on her back, slipping lower, and she molded into them. She hadn't realized how much she missed being touched since Mel had stopped acting like her husband. Her skin almost rose off her back to meet his touch. The pleasure far outweighed any guilt the once-married woman part of her was feeling. He maneuvered the two of them to the couch and it was there that she engaged in her first post-marital sex. He dropped her clothes onto the floor with his. Any leftover restraint she might have had peeled away with her clothing. The words of an old rock love song played over and over in her head, and she wondered why she had denied herself for so long.

She fell asleep in his arms.

He woke her when the moon shone through the window. "Addie, when did you say Danny was coming home?"

"He's staying there."

She liked the fact he was concerned; she could sense his relief as he nestled into her again. Then he picked her up and carried her to the bedroom. When was the last time that had happened to her, she wondered, recalling how Mel's affections had faded over the course of their marriage until he finally drifted away without returning. How wonderful it was to feel wanted, to feel human again. She'd been beating herself up trying to figure out what she'd done wrong to make Mel leave. Now Harry was letting her know something about her was right. It might be only skin deep, but it was enough to make her feel alive after months of going through the motions of living.

Harry was caressing her again.

"Stay with me tonight," he whispered.

She knew she would. She caressed him in return. And this time, the sex was slower, deeper, melding them together, and there was no tomorrow or yesterday or today. Just this, just this now.

She woke to the scent of coffee and the sight of him through the bedroom door in a pair of sweats and no shirt, mixing batter for pancakes. She reached for her sweats, thinking it was a good thing she'd gotten out of her uniform at work, and joined him in the kitchen. He poured her coffee. She thought she must look a sight. He, on the other hand, was even more enticing than last night. Now she felt comfortable staring at his biceps, where she identified a dolphin, an angelfish, a blue tang. But staring at the muscles under the tats raised her temperature. If he came any closer, she thought they'd be at it again. But he stayed where he was and put a pan on the stove.

"I'm starving," he said. "How many for you?"

His face was open, relaxed; his mouth a small smile. His eyes twinkled. And, wait, she thought, they're marbled, an almost translucent blue with tiny swirls of gray. They're different. He noticed her face change as she stared, and he chuckled.

"You're noticing my eyes, right?" he asked.

She nodded.

"I took my contacts out. They're tinted, make my eyes look gray. Does that change anything?"

She liked him even better, and she told him so. "They're warmer. The gray is cold."

He nuzzled her neck as he placed her plate of hotcakes in front of her.

"Eat. Don't think I haven't noticed how thin you've gotten since Mel took off. I liked you before, too, you know."

They ate, side by side, and she felt the electricity build up in her again. She told herself she needed to calm down, go home, but when she put her fork down, he was pulling her to him, and she was on his lap, her pants around her ankles, engaging with him for the fourth time. She thought she might never leave, just stay here forever.

And then they were in the shower, still entwined, and she heard her cell phone ring. The spell was broken. She disentangled herself, wrapped herself in a large beach towel, and went to the bedside where she'd left her phone, thinking it might be Danny or an emergency at the clinic. Instead, it read "Mel." He almost never called, and yet here she was, having the most wonderful sex she ever could have imagined, and it was as though he'd been hovering, waiting for the moment to interrupt her.

"It's Mel," she said, pushing the off button.

"Okay, is that a coincidence, or are you two supposed to be meeting up?" he asked.

She shook her head. "No, we are so done. If it weren't for Danny, I'm sure he'd have forgotten my name."

"But not your number."

Harry was dripping wet. Was she imagining it, or was even his penis different from Mel's, perkier maybe? She wasn't an expert on the subject, although she was an expert on island gossip, which said he'd gotten around a lot. Still, he'd never come in to the clinic for sexually transmitted diseases. Whatever or however much he got around, he was a clean machine.

He unwound her towel and wrapped it around both of them. She could feel his breath, sweet and minty from toothpaste.

"How could anyone ever forget you?" he asked.

She smiled, but she pulled them toward the couch to reach for her clothes, which were spread out on the floor in front of it.

"Harry, I need to get home. I can't, you know, stay and..."

He unwrapped her. "I'll drive you home or back to your car, but I wish you could stay."

"Don't look at me, or I will," she told him. She hoped her face was not flushed.

In the truck, she leaned against the door, careful not to touch him.

"Do you need to duck down and hide?" he asked, laughing. "It's still early for anyone else to be out, not even six yet."

"I'm almost thinking of it. You know how rumors start here. I'm not ready for that." She shrunk deeper into the seat. The thought occurred to her that maybe she was trying to undo the night. Back in the daylight, she was a bit queasy about it all.

"Okay, then we'll keep this ours, for now."

The first thing she did when she got inside her house was to run upstairs to her bathroom and search for the morning-after pills she'd bought just in case. She found them and gobbled some down. She didn't know where this was going to lead, but she knew where she didn't want it to go.

Then she opened Mel's message. It was, as she'd expected, just instructions for picking up Danny. He was 11 now, old enough to ferry over on the *Emma Ann* without either of them, as long as he was dropped off and picked up. He was coming back tomorrow, not today. She had a whole day to herself. She looked around at Mel's things spread out around her house. Yes, she thought, my house. And she made the decision to start packing his belongings.

PART TWO

SHOULDER SEASON

SEVEN

Dita was folding laundry when her phone chirped. It was lying on the bed next to the laundry basket. She glanced over at the screen. It was her mother.

She turned the speaker on. "Hi, Mom."

Her mother's voice sounded like she was in the room with Dita when she responded, and she was, almost. "I'm at the door."

"Well, walk right in. Everyone else does."

Caroline did, and she took the moment as she pulled the door open to remind her daughter there was a murderer afoot and she needed to lock up.

Dita stopped folding and shuffled to the open staircase that overlooked the front door. She watched her mother sweep into the house. In a nanosecond, she was upstairs and swooshed past Dita to Janie, who was lying on a blanket on the bedroom floor next to Tuffy.

"Don't worry, Tuffy," Dita said. "She still loves us. It's just Janie is newer."

Caroline paused to admire the infant, who was trying to suck her own toe, then leaned down to give her a buss on the cheek and tickle her.

Finally, she acknowledged her daughter. "I'm invited to a gathering next door tonight, Dita, and I'd like you to come with me."

Dita thought her mother looked a bit nervous.

"Why? What's going on?"

"My new neighbors. They're very nice, by the way, though she's just his girlfriend, not his wife. They want to tell us about a financial opportunity they're involved with."

"They asked for me? Is that what you mean by us?" Dita was surprised.

"No, no, they never met you. They asked Dahlia and several of the older folks on the island. I just want you to come to hear what they have to say and discuss it with me afterward. Since he lived abroad when his sister was murdered, I am assuming he couldn't be the killer."

"What kind of financial opportunity?"

Caroline gave her one of her stern-mother looks. "I don't know. Maybe he inherited money from his late sister and found an enormous investment opportunity. That's why I want you to come. Also, they're my new neighbors, so I feel like I should go, but I don't want to get dragged into something I have no background to investigate."

"Okay. Not that I'm a finance whiz, but I can at least be the brakes if they get persuasive. Is that what you mean?" Dita asked. "If Sean can be home, sure. I can leave Janie with him and Tuffy. Let me just make sure he has no training appointments tonight. What time is this thing?"

"Dessert. Right after supper at 7:30."

Bernard Mallory and his sometimes significant other, Jessica Glen, seemed to have completely refurnished Bunny's house in no time at all. Bernard had not even set foot in the place until after Dahlia called him about the intruder a month earlier. Now it looked as though they'd lived there for years. Dita was astonished. She knew that new furnishings had to be shipped to Block Island from the mainland. Usually that took some time to arrange, and things arrived in an uncoordinated fashion, but Bernard and Jessica seemed to have trucked the furnishings to the ferry port and sailed the household over in one lot. Abbracadabra. Dita glanced around and leaned over to her mother, remarking on how the rooms had been transformed as though by a genie. Caroline nodded.

"And not to mention," Dita wondered, "how'd they shop for them all so quickly and get the retailers to supply them?"

"It came over in a huge moving truck, all at once," Caroline said. "I watched it from my porch. I'm still waiting for a rug for my dining room, and I've been here longer than they have."

The sagging sofa that Josh Martel slept on had been replaced with an emerald green velveteen settee and two fluffy white easy chairs, not island mode at all. Dita thought how they would wear quickly if people in wet bathing suits plopped into them, as normally happened at her house. A plush and expensive-looking oriental rug covered much of the floor in the living room, more a parlor than a modern sitting room. Dita thought perhaps the rug wasn't authentic, but looking at the paintings on the walls, the lamps, and other furnishings, she changed her opinion and guessed it probably was. The only thing plain in the room was the money that had been spent to furnish it. One, or both, of them were quite well-heeled and then some, Dita thought.

"Lots of money," Caroline whispered to her daughter, echoing her thoughts.

Bernard was pushing the fancy new furniture against the walls to make room for the extra chairs from the kitchen and porch that several helpers were bringing into the room and placing in a double-row semicircle. There was quite a sizable crowd gathered for the island on this spring night, mostly gray- and white-haired women and balding men. A long-haired white cat stealthily crisscrossed the space, occasionally rubbing against the legs of a guest. The guests were nibbling on small cookies and sipping martinis. Even the oldest woman on the island, Celia Rose, was there, circling through the crowd on unsteady legs, reciting her usual mantra, "all good," at three-minute intervals. Dita spotted Rachel with Addie and waved hello, but Caroline took her arm and led her to Bernard and Jessica.

"I'd like you to meet my daughter, Edith. She and her husband Sean have the Be Fit at the Double Ender Hotel, and she's a reporter."

No one but her mother ever called her Edith. Dita chose not to insult her mother by correcting her. Instead, she swallowed the word Dita forming in her throat.

"So nice to meet you, Edith," Bernard crooned, his voice as velvet as the furniture. "Martinis, ladies?" He turned sideways to the drinks cart and poured from a shaker, not waiting for their replies.

He was a bit older than Caroline, more toward his early 70s, with thinning and obviously dyed brown hair and a slightly paunchy physique. Dita thought he could use some workouts at the Be Fit. Had she ever seen Bunny, she would have noticed the resemblance of their facial features. Jessica was quite a bit younger than Bernard, more Dahlia's age, or even younger, Dita thought, probably early 50s. Typical for older men to want younger women, Dita groused to herself, and younger women to want older, well-off men. She stopped herself there as she realized she was making ungrounded assumptions, something her reporter-self tried not to do.

Jessica was what most people would describe as handsome—not beautiful, not stunning, but memorable in her own way. Her hair was bleached blonde for sure, Dita thought, and she wore contacts on her hazel eyes. Dita could almost always spot those. Her mouth seemed overly plumped. Dita could swear that the woman used collagen or some other filler. She wondered, did people with false mouths spread false narratives? If so, they ought not trust her as an investment advisor.

As Dita studied Jessica's looks, that woman's attention was focused on another guest. Dita recognized him as the man who had come to join the Be Fit a while back, Carter Crane. How nice to have a name that's alliterative like that, she thought, surprised that his nickname wasn't CC instead of Artie. Dita looked him up and down when she finished her examination of Jessica, but he didn't notice because his eyes were on Caroline.

Dita saw him nudge Jessica and heard him ask for an introduction. Jessica introduced her, and Caroline introduced Dita, whom he acknowledged he'd already met.

Dita took the opportunity to correct the Edith to Dita and then moved on to speak with Dahlia, leaving her mother to kibitz with Bernard, Jessica, and now Artie.

"Anything new on Bunny's murder? Still haven't caught up with Josh Martel?" she asked Dahlia quietly.

"I'm wondering if he got a ride off the island with someone since he hasn't turned up," Dahlia replied in her quietest voice, still loud enough for everyone around them to hear had the room not been so noisy.

Dita gave her a tiny nod.

Dahlia went on, "He couldn't come to the old couch that was here anymore, so maybe he left."

Dita shrugged.

"It must make you and your mom nervous to know they haven't arrested him, nor have they spoken of another suspect for Bunny's murder," Dahlia said. "I still wonder about Blaze Connors, the construction guy who found the body. Did you look for past arrests on the mainland? Has Chief Gomez questioned him? Maybe it wasn't such a coincidence that he was clamming there. He might have gone to see if anyone had stumbled across Bunny yet. You'd think Chief Gomez would call in the state police on this if he can't find the killer. Bunny didn't just get dropped out of an airplane. I mean, she'd have more injuries if she did, and according to Addie, she didn't."

"Yes, I agree," Dita said. "I did ask around and search court records on Blaze, but I didn't find anything sketchy."

"Hmm, no past. Maybe we should push Gomez a little more," Dahlia suggested.

"You mean I should, don't you? I could write an article on the perplexing lack of progress in the case," Dita said.

"That's a good idea. He'll be mad at you, though, you know," Dahlia murmured. "Hmmm, look at that Artie guy cozying up to your mother." She gestured toward Caroline with her martini.

"Don't know how I feel about that," Dita said, but she smiled and thought it wouldn't be such a bad thing if her mother had a beau.

"Oh, look over there. What's Bernard up to?" Dahlia asked.

Bernard was pacing, circling the room, tapping his glass with a spoon. When he reached the front windows, he asked for their attention. Celia moved in front of him. He took her hand and guided her to an empty chair.

"Not good," she said, in reverse of her usual chant, her head bobbing and her hand flopping into her lap, her voluminous black skirt flouncing around her spindly legs.

Bernard returned to his place in front of the windows. "You probably already know that I'm Bunny's brother. When she," and he paused, "died, I had been living in Spain, but I returned to take care of her estate. Jessica was her financial advisor and close friend. She was appointed executor of Bunny's estate, not me. But, I'm the heir. Now, though we were strangers, she and I have become close friends, too." He beamed at Jessica, who was standing right next to him, their bodies almost touching.

The room quieted down. He had their attention. Caroline had slipped over to stand next to Dita. She whispered to her daughter. "That's weird, isn't it? I mean, who makes a financial advisor an executor instead of a family member? I wonder if she left her some money, too."

Addie was suddenly standing next to Dita also. Addie whispered that there were still wonderful canapés on the table in the corner and did she think they could steal over there. Dita didn't see how they could get there without causing a stir, but she was thrilled that her friend was focused on food as she once had been before the Mel betrayal. She mouthed a no to Addie.

Bernard's voice was authoritative, and Dita turned her attention back to him. Dita suspected he was accustomed to issuing orders to underlings. "I asked you here tonight to get to know all of you, but also to let you hear Jessica," he boomed. "She's been an enormous help to me as an investment counselor. I understand she's made many clients wealthy, or should I say, wealthier. Now she's a new member of your community, as she and I are living in my sister's house part time," he paused to smile at Jessica, "and she would like to present this opportunity to all of you. Jessica?"

Dita turned to hiss a negative comment to Addie, but her friend had disappeared. Dita looked around and sure enough, Addie was at the canapé table, indulging in a shrimp puff. Dita smiled and turned back to Bernard and Jessica.

"Yes," she heard Jessica say, and the woman moved in front of Bernard.

"Hello everyone. I am Jessica Glen. I specialize in helping retirees with savings make investments that pay high returns. Often the products that people have been steered to by counselors don't pay a return that could make a difference between living on a budget and living well. Mine do. I could help you with your individual accounts, or we could form an investment club where we talk about our investments and research new ones, sharing information. Some clubs even buy stocks and options as a group. We could even dabble in cryptocurrency."

A burble of excitement filled the room.

"My office is on the mainland in Westport, CT, but as I will be staying here with Bernard quite a bit, he's offered to let us meet here. In fact, I think he'd like to join the club." She moved back next to him, and Bernard put his arm around her and beamed.

"Cozy, aren't they," Caroline murmured to Dita.

"Mom, I never realized where I got my reporter's skepticism before," Dita whispered back.

They looked at each other and smiled. It was an unusual moment for them. Dita thought that at last they might be entering into a more companionable relationship.

Jessica had come armed with a sheaf of brochures and information papers, all with her business card attached. They were neatly arranged like packaged napkins on a small side table next to her. She picked them up and handed some to Bernard, and the two of them circled the room in opposite directions, distributing them. Celia was out of her chair, weaving in and out, spouting, "Not good, not good." Jessica corralled her and moved her into another empty chair.

Dita spotted Rachel and moved closer to her. Caroline followed and leaned in.

"What do you think about all this, Dita?" Rachel asked.

"I don't know. I never heard of these clubs before. Of course, I have no money to invest anyway," Dita said, laughing. "Celia doesn't seem to like them, but she doesn't like anything anymore, especially people who are not from the island."

"I wish I'd brought Teddy. He has to look into this for me," Rachel said. "I'm not sure it would benefit me, though I'm quite sure it would benefit them." She lifted her chin toward Bernard and Jessica.

Dita thought that consulting Teddy would be wise. She knew Rachel had a small nut to last the rest of her life, and it wouldn't be a good idea to squander it. Teddy had had to learn a lot about investing when he sold his company for megabucks several years ago.

"I wanted to speak with both of you anyway," Rachel said. "Do you think we could go next door to your house, Caroline? Let's leave Addie here for the moment, though."

That surprised Dita, but a glance back assured her Addie was happy, nibbling on a small tart while she balanced a martini in the other hand.

"I'd love to. It's time to escape anyway," Caroline said, and the three of them slipped out the back door.

The two yards were separated by a privet hedge with a pass-through. Caroline led the way, and as she reached her yard, she let out a small, "whoops," and stopped in her tracks. A man Dita and Rachel would recognize as Josh Martel was about to leap over the hedge opposite them into the next neighbor's yard. Dita called out for him to stop. He kept going, but she almost caught up and reached out to grab the back of his tee shirt. The thin material tore as he managed to wrench loose and vault over the wall with a leap one wouldn't have thought that skeletal frame could manage. Dita was left with a swatch of discolored white tee in her hand.

"Yowza! Who was that, and why was he here?" Caroline said, as Dita shook the material to the ground in disgust. "Do you think he was in my house?"

"You've just seen Josh Martel," Rachel said.

Dita was already rushing to the street hoping to catch up with him, but Josh was gone. She called the police station to report the sighting as she returned to the backyard.

"Creepy," Rachel said.

Caroline was visibly shaken. "So that's him. I think his jump is as good as Nureyev's."

They proceeded inside her house, where she checked both her jewelry box and her money drawer. Nothing was missing.

"What in the world was he doing skulking around here?" Caroline asked again, her voice rising with her fear.

"Good question, Mom. It's time for him to be arrested," Dita said. "Now they have a reason to pick him up again and question him."

"I think we could all use a drink," Caroline said. "Let's sit in the kitchen." Her table had a round mushroom-style laminated top like the ones in cafes and student unions.

She brought out three wine glasses and poured from a bottle of Syrah.

"I like the idea of getting together with other people to talk about investing, but I'm not so sure I want to share how much I have or put money into anything with strangers, or even neighbors. Would we have to pay Jessica?" Caroline asked, downing her Syrah in one gulp. "I think we would."

Dita's forehead curled into a just-noticeable frown as she watched her mother refill her glass. She was realizing how shaken Carolyn was.

"I don't think he'll come back, Mom," she reassured her. "He knows we recognized him. If the police don't pick him up right away, he'll go into hiding until they figure out where he is. But he'll stay out of this neighborhood now that he knows people are here. There are plenty of empty summer cottages on the west side where he can hide."

"I agree," Rachel said.

"I'm a little shaken, but I'll be all right. I think he was hungry. I bought a loaf of Italian bread this afternoon and left it on the counter. It's gone," she said. "I think I'll have the locks changed."

"I don't think you need to. Just use the locks you have," Dita said. "You must have left the door unlocked."

"I did," Caroline admitted, nodding her head. "I was just going next door."

"If you're worried about him coming back, you can stay with me," Rachel said, sipping but not gulping her wine.

They sipped in silence.

Then, Rachel spoke again. "Are you okay now?" she asked Caroline, who nodded and smiled. "Because I wanted to talk with you about something else. I have an announcement to make."

She paused to make sure they were listening. "Teddy and I are going to get married."

"That's wonderful!" Dita shouted. Rachel had been alone for a long time. That love and companionship would come into her life after so much hardship—the loss of her husband and, more recently, her son—was spectacular. "You know I love you and Teddy, and I'm so happy you found each other."

Caroline, who was sitting next to Rachel, reached over and hugged her. "How nice for you both," she said. "When's the wedding?"

"Soon. We haven't worked out the details yet, but of course we'll have it at The Double Ender. I want to wait for Addie's divorce to be final. She's too upset right now for me to expect her to celebrate anything."

"I must admit I'm a bit worried about her," Dita said. "You've told her?"

"This morning. And I suggested something else. Please, this is just between us. Addie has been talking about finding a roommate to help her with the house payments. As you might guess, I'm not too keen on roommates after learning that mine was responsible for the murder of my son."

Dita saw Rachel struggle to even say that sentence. Loretta had been close to all of them, but Rachel had taken her in after she'd overdosed and almost died.

Rachel continued, "I suggested to Addie that she put her house up for sale and move into my cottage instead. You know that Mel is talking about quitclaiming the house to her instead of paying for her housing costs. If she sells it, she would have a nice nest egg, and she wouldn't have to pay any of it to him. That might sound conniving to sell it once she owns it all, but he was pretty conniving, and he deserves his comeuppance. And it will put an end to that louse staying at her house when he's working here and has Danny for a few days. Let him pay for his own room or apartment. This isn't a friendly divorce, not for her anyway. Having to see him all the time keeps the wound open for her. I'm moving into Teddy's house soon, so the cottage will be vacant. She can move in once he signs over ownership of their house."

Dita and Caroline both nodded. They liked the idea, but Caroline wondered aloud whether Mel could rescind his quitclaim by accusing Addie of fraud. Dita wondered to herself if Addie was angry enough at Mel to do something this underhanded. In her opinion, Addie was too aboveboard. Rachel told them she thought Addie could rent the house out in summer and bring in a lot of money, more than enough to pay the mortgage, then decide to sell it later if she felt too guilty to sell the house off right away.

"She'd be a little further up the street from me," Dita said, "but Danny is almost old enough to stay by himself when she gets called to work on emergencies at night."

"Yes, I think so too," Rachel said.

"Here's to the future, to Teddy and Rachel," Caroline said.

"And here's to your new life on Block Island, Caroline," Rachel toasted. "Don't let this run-in with Josh Martel ruin your new beginning."

"I think I'll get myself home to Sean and Janie now," Dita said with a yawn. She put her glass in the sink and started to the door. "Mom, do you want to come with me? I mean, in case Josh comes back?"

"No, I see there's a cruiser parked out front now."

"Oh, good. Goodnight, Mom."

"Goodnight, Rachel."

EIGHT

Addie had decided it was time to move Mel out of the house even before her mother suggested she move into the cottage. Addie was also moving the separation into a divorce. She hired a lawyer. She told herself it wasn't just because of a hot night with Harry. That might never happen again, and if it did, it might be just that, hot sex now and then. Or maybe...but she didn't want to think herself into pining for a relationship that might never be, although she did find herself yearning to be with him again. She called Dita to come over and help her pack up Mel's things. She promised her a leisurely Saturday brunch for the help. It was the Friday before Memorial Day, when tourists started arriving in hordes. Janie was at Caroline's, so of course Dita came, but she came with opinions. Addie expected them.

"I'm surprised you went to see the lawyer without talking to Mel about a divorce first," Dita said as she folded a sheet of cardboard to make a box.

Addie shrugged. Dita did not know about Harry yet.

"I told Danny. He's more important," she said, shaking her head so that her red curls fell in her eyes. "And Mel and I already hashed everything out in therapy, so it's no big deal."

"Of course," Dita agreed. Then she stopped folding the box and stared down at Addie. "But did something else happen to make you want to finalize the separation?"

Addie felt herself flushing. She wished she could stop every emotion she felt from showing. Transparency was not what she desired.

"Oh, I see the color coming," Dita was laughing. "Do tell. Who is it?"

"Nobody, Dita. Stop being a nosy reporter."

Dita scrutinized her friend and remembered that night a few weeks back when she noticed the lights never went on in Addie's house.

"What night was it? Yes, I think it was a couple of weeks ago, a Friday. I was watching the sunset, and I noticed your lights weren't on. Then before I went to bed, I glanced over once more from the living room, and your house was totally dark. Where were you?"

"Why were you watching my house?" Addie demanded.

"I wasn't snooping. I just happened to look out the window to watch the sunset and, later, the stars.

"If you must know, Danny stayed at Mel's," Addie snapped. She thought that might stop Dita's prying.

"And?" Dita pressed her friend as she started filling the box with books from the top shelf, which only she, and not Addie, could reach.

"And what?" Addie dodged.

But Dita was adamant. "Not what, where. Where were you? Running around the island in the dark by yourself all night?"

Addie didn't answer. She pushed a filled box to the corner and started putting books into another. "Mel sure had a lot of these sci fi books," she said.

Dita wasn't listening. She was thinking. Suddenly, it dawned on her. "Oh, I get it. It was Harry. You were with Harry, weren't you?"

Addie's cheeks turned bright red. Dita thought she looked like she had fifth disease, that childhood virus some call slapping sickness because kids' cheeks look like they've been slapped.

"I knew it!" Dita crowed, feeling victorious. "Tell me, I want to hear all about it, and before you tell me not to tell anyone, I promise I won't. What happened?"

She put down the books she was packing into one of the boxes and sat on the couch. She patted a cushion for Addie to come join her.

Addie stayed where she was. In her thickest Rhode Islandese, she warned her friend off. "Stop. It was nothing. You don't want to hear."

Dita gave her a look. "But I do want to hear."

"We had a drink and a game of pool."

"And?"

Addie gave up. Dita would badger her until she talked. She let out a deep breath. "Okay, we had the hottest sex ever, and that's all I'm going to say. We are not a couple and may never be. For now, that was all."

"The hottest sex ever and that was all?" Dita thought that was funny. She laughed. "It's never all."

"It probably was."

"Were you in the pub's kitchen spread out on the counter? Codfish on your butt?" Dita was having a fine time teasing her friend, recalling a girls' night out at the pub when Addie had disappeared into the kitchen with Harry. Later, Dita accused her of carrying on with him and Addie had retorted there was no codfish, the special of the night, on her butt.

"Were you setting up another blood pressure clinic like the last time you ended up in the kitchen?" Dita was relentless now.

"We went to his house, if you must know. Are you helping me or interrogating me?" Addie pushed her hair out of her eyes and handed Dita a box to fold. "Time to get off the couch."

"Just one more thing. Was the hot sex torrid? Sweaty? Or like a tidal wave?"

Addie threw a paperback at Dita, who ducked and fell on the floor as she broke up laughing. Addie started laughing too. Dita realized she hadn't heard Addie laugh like that in a long, long while. Whatever Dita thought about Addie and Harry not being a realistic couple, she was glad he was taking Addie's mind off her troubles. The sound of a car coming up the long driveway, or maybe a truck, interrupted their gaiety.

"Could Danny be home already?" Addie asked. "He was supposed to be at Mel's all weekend, and Mel was supposed to call me when he put him on the ferry."

But it wasn't Danny. When a truck came into view, they both recognized it as Harry's. "Were you expecting him?" Dita asked.

Addie shook her head, no. She motioned Dita toward the back door. Dita got the message and rushed to leave.

"Looks like I warmed the couch for him. It's ready for hot sex. I'll slip out before he sees me," she said, and she stepped outside.

She waited outside by the door until she heard the weight of his feet on the front steps; then she slipped around the side of the house and down to the driveway, running along the overgrown rosa rugosa vines and marsh reeds.

Addie watched Harry from the window while he parked on the far side of the driveway that formed a circle in front of the house. He went around to the driver's side of the truck and removed something from the front seat. It was a large paper bag, probably food, Addie thought. He looked like he'd just come from work in his faded blue jeans and a tee shirt under his unzipped motorcycle jacket. He wore a red baseball cap emblazoned with a B for Boston and walked with a slight swagger, not in a rush, but not tarrying. She'd never seen a man so comfortable in his own skin. She heard him come up the front steps as Dita tiptoed down the back ones. What had she gotten herself into, she wondered. And then he knocked.

She brushed that lock of red hair from her forehead yet again. Sweaty and disheveled from packing, she felt unattractive, but perhaps that was a good thing. She realized she had to push her needs, and his advances, back, at least for now. She opened the door and there he was, right in front of her. She stood unmoving, staring. She thought of all those summer girls, the workers, the young wives, who threw themselves at Harry every year; and yes, she knew why they did.

She gawked until he asked, "Are you going to ask me in or do I just hand you our lunch and run?"

His eyes were blue with gray speckles, and they crinkled up with his smile. He'd left the contacts out... for her?

She stepped aside, and tried to speak. "Of course, how nice, glad to..."

He leaned in and gave her a big smacker on the lips and held her tight.

"Here, sit down," he said, taking her to the kitchen table and lightly pushing her into a chair.

He put the bag down on the table. "I'll do the rest. Where are your plates? Just point."

She pointed to the drawer, and he opened a few more looking for the silverware.

"Got 'em," he said, and he unpacked the bag onto the dishes and sat himself across from her. "I didn't have time for flowers."

He'd brought blackened swordfish tacos with a tangy sauce, shredded salad greens and a handful of chips, all hot and ready to eat. She didn't quite know what to say.

"I figured you'd have drinks," he said. "Any in the fridge?"

She nodded as he strode over to it like he belonged in the house and took out a beer for himself and one for her.

She finally found her voice. "Harry, this is so very nice. You didn't have to..."

"I did. You haven't set foot in the pub since our overnight. I waited and waited, and I didn't want to call, so I came to you. If anyone notices, I can say I just brought your lunch order."

He was already eating and popped open his beer. He hadn't even taken his jacket off. She thought if men were in the middle of a meal on a ship when it was torpedoed, they'd probably finish up their food first.

He pointed to her plate. "Eat, you're getting thin."

"Harry," she started, "I, we, can't be, you know, right now. I lost control that night, but now I've begun divorce proceedings. I think Mel will agree to joint custody, or even cede it all to me, but I can't count on that until it's in writing. I need to comport myself as though the whole world is looking, as it is, really. I don't want to lose custody of Danny. He's the most important part of my life. Everything else, including you, has to wait. If someone catches wind of us and the island starts to talk, as it will, I could be branded an unfit mother. I can't risk that, no matter how dizzy, how overcome with desire you make me."

"Does that happen to you, too?" he asked, leaning over the table and touching her arm.

"Please, Harry, understand that this will take at least a month, maybe more. The groundwork has already been covered. We both went to required couples therapy for almost a year. It's possible we could iron out and ink this divorce in a matter of two months. Until then, I can't see you. I can't come near you."

"Addie, I don't think that stuff is true anymore, about not seeing anyone when you're separated. Mel's been seeing his lady friend for two years, and now he's moved in with her. If he can move on, why can't you?"

Addie felt faint. Instead of coloring as usual, she went white.

Harry reached over with both hands. "What's wrong? Addie, are you okay?"

"I, I didn't know that," she enunciated ever so slowly.

"I'm so sorry. I didn't mean to shock you. I thought you knew. Everyone's been talking about it. I mean, it's like everyone at the pub knows. Oh, my dear Addie, I'm so, so sorry." Harry went to her and knelt by her chair. He put his arms around her and drew her to him, and she lost every iota of embarrassment and shame. She sobbed as though she were alone. The defenses she'd built crumbled in the face of Mel's deceitfulness. She let Harry comfort her.

"Oh, Harry, it's not that he's the love of my life, but he was my husband, Danny's father, and we had a life together. It mattered to me more than head over heels, more than romance. It was a good life and we got along and it's gone, all gone. And my little boy is there with the woman who took it all away. My boy with a new mother."

"Addie, I thought you knew or I wouldn't have said anything."

"No, I needed to hear it from someone I trust and I guess I do trust you. I wouldn't have wanted to overhear it at the pub, or the gym. Even Dita must not know or she would have said something. I feel so broken."

She shook loose from him, took a deep breath and got up. She walked over to the bookshelves she'd been about to pack and slapped her hand across one filled with Mel's science fiction novels, pushing the volumes out so they flew into the air and cascaded down to the floor.

"These are his. I was packing up his stuff. Now I just want to throw them all out." She kicked them with gusto; they flew up and she kicked at them again, ripping the covers and the pages.

"Feel better now?" Harry asked. Now he was laughing.

"I do. And don't laugh. I'm serious. I hope the divorce comes through really fast. I never want to lay eyes on that jerk again. I wish divorces could wind backward and erase relationships from start to finish."

"What about Danny? He'd be gone along with Mel," Harry said. "We've been friends a long time, Addie. I hate to see you hurt like this. I'll help however I can."

"Thank you. I consider you a close friend, and I think we have something more than that. I want to see what happens between us, but I can't until my custody of Danny is secure. Mel is being so sneaky. I know now that I can't trust him until the court finalizes the divorce and our names are inked upon that paper."

He reached out to hold her. They stood in a silent embrace for a few minutes and then he leaned back and looked into her eyes. "I can wait, and," he delineated each word now, "I will never do to you what he did."

Addie thought that was all well and good if she was 25, but she was 35 with a child and a divorce settlement ahead of her. For now, his words were just words. Mel had made many promises, too. Addie felt cornered. She didn't know who she was yet and here he was pushing for a relationship on one night of good, well, great sex.

"But Harry, we don't know what we are yet. You don't need to make declarations you won't be able to keep. The season is starting up, and I don't want to hold you to a relationship that's just beginning to bud. Go find your summer ladies and enjoy yourself. I need to work a lot anyway once the island gets busy. By fall, who knows? Our spark might extinguish."

He looked at her with disbelief. "I swear I've never felt about anyone like I do about you, and it didn't just begin. I wished for you all the time you and Mel were together, but I settled for friendship because I didn't want to complicate your life. And I've been waiting for you to settle your relationship with Mel. We've always had an attraction to each other."

"Are you mistaking sexual attraction for deeper feelings?" she asked.

"Am I?"

Addie knew what island men were like. They professed deeply before the summer hit; then they were blinded by all the beauties fishing for fun. She thought Dita had been lucky that Sean was oblivious to the advances. Though he'd matured slowly as far as finding an occupational niche, he knew he wanted a relationship for life, and that was Dita, his wife. Many island men never matured out of a merry-go-round of adolescent crushes.

Harry thought for a moment before he answered, "No, we're not mistaken. We've been close for a long time. We've always been comfortable and happy with each other. I'll walk out the door right now if you want me to prove that sex is not the only attraction here."

Despite her doubts, she wasn't willing to let him go just yet. "Well, since you're here, maybe just this once," she told him.

Dita had escaped from Addie's house without Harry spotting her. She was now halfway down the driveway, sprinting toward the street. She loved moving through space, stretching as far as she could, sprinting in a rhythmic motion, her feet barely touching the ground.

Let her mainland friends frequent their fancy spas; the island brought the sea into her body with each breath. All the minerals touted in spa brochures—potassium, magnesium, manganese, and even the much maligned sodium—were suspended in the tiny, invisible droplets that floated in the sea-drenched air and swept into her as she moved and took deep gulps of air. The molecules coursed through her lungs and into her bloodstream without her paying some phony spa guru to mix exotic juice drinks containing them. At the end of the driveway, she turned toward her house onto Corn Neck Road. She slowed down to admire the brand-new buds emerging on the roadside brush. Small birds nestled near the thin trunks, perched on the even more slender branches. Spring was one of the seasons she loved most on Block Island. The birds were migrating back—wrens, robins, ospreys, American goldfinches—and of course the sparrows and gulls that lived year-round like her. She looked up to identify a flock sitting on the electric wires when she heard a large machine chugging along, closing in behind her. She turned around to see what was coming as it grew louder.

It was the yellow town dump truck with the sweeper on the front, and it was closing in, aiming straight at her. It brought her back to the moment two years ago when she realized someone was shooting at her in the dunes. Terrified, she leapt up onto the verge to save herself from being flattened, all the while trying to stave off a panic attack. She struggled for a brief moment to regain her balance when she landed, then headed across the lawn on the other side toward the patrol car parked in her neighbor Karl's driveway. She crouched behind it, laboring to breathe. She was out of wind and lightheaded. Her fingertips tingled. She placed her hand on her chest and tried to calm herself as she watched the sweeper truck lurch and grind to a halt. *What now?*The washashore gang members were all in prison. This could not be happening again.

The driver's face was covered by a black scarf, and an unmarked black baseball cap covered his head. She was unable to identify him. She broke into a cold sweat, reliving that night Brenda tried to shoot her. Then the vehicle's door opened, and the driver leaned out and shouted while he unwound his scarf.

"Dita? I didn't mean to scare you. I'm sorry. I was on my phone and didn't notice you at first." It was Billy Jenkins, one of the town public works employees. "Are you okay?"

She tried to catch her breath. Then she leaned out of her crouch and fell backward so she landed on the ground. She raised herself to a sitting position and stared over at Billy, now hanging out of his truck, the scarf loose around his neck. If she could stop heaving and shaking, she would say, *"No, no, I just had a panic attack because I thought you were running me over."* But instead, she forced the tiniest upturn of the tips of her lips to simulate a smile and waved him away. He drove off, rewinding the scarf around his face to keep out the dust from the beach sand that had blown onto the street. She sat there, her arms around her knees, her head down until her stomach stopped doing flip-flops.

When she looked up, Karl Schultz was standing over her, his hands on his hips.

"I saw that town truck almost plow you down. Who was that? Billy?" he asked. He watched the truck head down Corn Neck toward town. "What's goin' on? Are you doing any stories that put you in the crosshairs of anotha' gang? If so, tell me."

"No, I haven't been doing anything. I've been busy with Janie."

"OK, I'm going to catch up to it and pull him over. Move away, or hop in. I'll drop you next door," he said. "I hope you listened to me and aren't investigating that murder. Like I told you, you have a baby to think of now."

Dita sizzled a bit at his thinking he could tell her what to do, but she was glad he was there. He'd definitely improved his policing. Two years ago, he would've called someone at the station to go instead of following Billy himself. He'd slowed down on his drinking and gotten up to speed in his police work.

"No, you go and I'll walk home through our yards," she said, standing up. Her panic attack had subsided. "I think he was just looking at his phone instead of the road."

She straightened her clothes and walked toward home. Karl got back into his truck, took off, and disappeared down Corn Neck, driving at a clip he wouldn't be able to match later this afternoon once the tourists rolled off the boat in their big SUVs and crowded onto the roads.

After being scared out of her wits, Dita had forgotten to wonder what Harry and Addie might be doing across the street. She just wanted to go home and lock her doors, something she hadn't done since Loretta and her gang went to jail. But when she got closer, she saw someone sitting on the front steps. Tuffy's head was on his lap. It wasn't Sean; she knew it wasn't Karl, and Teddy was more rotund. Because she and Sean lived on the corner of Corn Neck and Scotch Beach Rds, she was used to people pulling into her driveway to visit or just to park when the beach lot was full. But after almost being rolled over by the town truck, she was in no mood for a confrontation with someone, whoever that was. Apparently, he had charmed Tuffy. Some watchdog!

When she could see the features of his face, she realized it was the police chief, George Gomez. She wondered if he'd seen Karl streak by in his truck.

He called to her, "I was just about to give up and leave to follow Karl."

"If you're waiting for Sean, he won't be home until later." He and Sean had become friendly since the gym had opened. George spent time there lifting weights and keeping his running time down, not to mention his waist line. Dita continued, "Go over to the Be Fit to find him."

"I'm not. I'm waiting for you. Sit down," he said, pointing to the space next to him on the step. "I'll find out what Karl's doing later."

She positioned herself on the step across from him, leaning on the railing posts, wary and curious. What was on his mind? Was she going to get another lecture on keeping her nose out of murders? He was not one of the men she could intimidate by looking down on him from her height. They were eye to eye. Now he turned to look at her, and she reciprocated, making this a standoff.

"I read your article," his voice took on a complaining tone. He paused before he continued. When he spoke again, his tone was no longer complaining, but commanding. "I thought when you asked me about Josh Martel you understood I couldn't talk about an open case, so I didn't expect to be criticized in the paper."

Dita felt a bit guilty, but she refused to be cowed into an apology. She'd been doing her job long enough to know how to stand up to criticism. She shrugged and reminded him how important this case was for her, personally.

"You do remember my mother lives right next door to the victim's house, don't you? George, I'm concerned that if it was Josh, he could hurt her next."

"And I'm aware of that too," he said. "We're doing the best we can with limited resources. We can't pin it on Josh without more evidence. Just because he was the handyman won't stand in court. It would help if someone could look into this woman Bunny's life. Why don't you make some phone calls to people on the mainland? Find out who she was seeing there—friends, boyfriend, business partners, whatever. Look into her police record."

Dita looked at him again. "Didn't you?"

"A bit, but you're good at this nosing-around stuff. Write an article on it."

This surprised Dita. He was asking her to help with the case? Ordinarily, she'd be thrilled, but now, not so much. "I have an infant. Some days I barely get myself out of the house with her."

"You think I should ask Karl to do it?" he asked.

Dita knew he was bluffing because that would never be her choice or his. Still, she grimaced and turned away. Even though Karl was better at doing his police work than he had been a few years ago, his detecting skills were lacking.

"I'm not asking you to snoop around the island and get into trouble with whomever did this. You only need to do the kind of phone research you normally do for background on your articles."

She really did want to crack this case and put her mother's fears, and her own, to rest. So, she faced George again and smiled. "You do know how to push my buttons, Chief. I'll make a few calls even though it's hard for me to believe it was Josh. What about Blaze? Have you looked into him? After all, he found her. Dahlia's convinced he did it. Maybe he was involved and he's covering up by claiming to have stumbled upon her. Just because he's 'one of us' doesn't mean he's innocent."

"Dahlia called me, too. We've questioned Blaze. He's still a suspect. I can't rule him out, though I doubt it was him. I can't uncover any motive. He doesn't admit to ever having met her, and he didn't need the jobs she was having Josh do. Blaze's crew works on bigger stuff. I think Dahlia's still angry at him for dumping her as quickly as he did. Josh had keys to Bunny's house."

"Right," Dita said. "The only keys on the island were that set and Dahlia's. Speaking of Blaze, I already checked out his background, and I didn't find anything. I'll poke around about Bunny," Dita said. "But you'll owe me. The minute you find Josh Martel, I want to know."

"Will do. Keep me informed." He stood up, brushed off his pants, and said, "So long."

"Wait," she called. "I know what Karl's up to."

He stopped. "Oh?"

She told him, and he let out a long sigh of exasperation. Almost to himself, he muttered, "I can tell this summer's going to be accident after accident—everyone laser-focused on their cell phones and not on the roads. A medical and policing disaster."

He walked away again as he spoke and waved behind his back to Dita. She waved and called her mother to check on Janie.

NINE

The island's official celebration of Memorial Day was mostly somber, with ceremonies honoring its fallen soldiers. A parade, a steak fry, and fireworks would be saved for the 4th of July. Still, the Memorial Day holiday marked the start of the summer season. All the restaurants took down their shutters and welcomed customers. Many of the shops opened, hoping to bring in enough money to buy more goods for the season. If the weather cooperated, Memorial Day brought cottage owners and tourists to the island for the three-day weekend. Not the hordes of July 4th, but enough people to refill the empty purses of the year-round folk with urgently needed cash. The island teenagers, energized by the expected arrival of fresh youth from the mainland, planned their first bonfire of the season.

Before Janie's arrival, Dita hadn't minded the noise of the crowds at the bonfires or even the shouting and drunken partying in the parking lot. The noise shot up to their windows, but she and Sean would bop down to join the fun. Now that they had Janie, and also the Be Fit, which demanded Sean keep early hours, people partying under their windows from midnight through 4 a.m. was not a pleasant prospect. They hoped this first bonfire would be mostly locals and not as raucous or late as the ones in July, although some of the graduating students from the state university who came over for a field day would stay over and crash the party on the beach.

At the Be Fit, Sean began signing up summer members, mostly

cottagers who would come out every weekend as well as for their summer vacations. Business was brisk, and Sean called Dita to come in and help. She was glad to go. She grabbed Janie and started the car, but Tuffy was standing on the deck watching. Poor dog was being left behind too much lately, so she got out and motioned to him to jump in the back seat next to Janie.

On her way, she passed knots of tourists meandering into the middle of the street. She made her way slowly in the traffic, which was moving at the pace of a funeral procession, and then she spotted Celia. The old woman's ubiquitous voluminous skirt flapped like a parachute as she toddled along the edge of the street, tapping her cane. Dita worried she might get hit by one of the cars. She slowed down,to the dismay of the driver in back of her, and opened her window. "Do you need a ride somewhere?"

Celia shook her head. "All good." She waved Dita away.

"Be careful of the traffic," Dita shouted, and she moved on.

As she parked there, Dita smiled at the crowd of cottagers outside the Double Ender. Inside the Be Fit, there were more. Sean was behind the counter looking beleaguered, fielding questions from this throng of future members. Dita made her way through them and joined him. He was so glad to see her that he threw his arms around her and lifted her off the floor. Then he shoved some forms at her and asked her to start signing people up while he showed them through the machines and class space. Tuffy curled up next to her feet. Dita placed Janie in the port-a-bed they now kept behind the counter and called for the next person in line.

At least for now, murder was not on tourists' minds. That was a good thing for the island and for Sean's business.

Addie thought the clinic should have stayed open for the holiday weekend, as she was called in for most of the day Saturday anyway. She was glad Danny was old enough to be somewhere with his friends and she didn't need to find a babysitter. He knew where to find her. The first patient was one of the college students. He had somersaulted off his moped going around the famous curve on Corn Neck Rd. that the locals named Dead-ped. This guy was lucky, only scraped and bruised. She'd seen way worse from that spot. As she cleaned his arm, she wondered if Harry was busy at the pub, and she wished she could be there. That, she knew, was not the way she should be thinking. She sent the boy on to Doc Bennett; he was soon patched up and on his way. As he went out the door, Bernard came in. He recognized her immediately.

"You're Rachel's daughter, aren't you?" he asked, and then he groaned and placed his hand on his back.

"Yes, Addie Morton," she said.

"I think I threw my back out doing some repairs," he told her in between heavy breathing and groaning.

"Dr. Bennett will see you shortly. You're in luck. He was here to see someone else. Have a seat while you wait. I'll fetch him."

When she returned, he was slumped in a seat but not groaning as much. In fact, he'd recovered enough to do a sales pitch. "Your mother ought to consider Jessica's investment group. It's going to make money for people on the island. And by the way, Addie, Jessica's only my business associate and friend. We're not married or engaged or even steadies." He leered at her and added, "I heard you're almost divorced."

The man had the audacity to wink at her. Dita's name for Dr. Bennett, The Mustache, leapt into her mind. Addie thought Bernard was probably as bad as The Mustache. She hesitated before responding, and then didn't need to, as a spasm paralyzed his back and he groaned aloud. Dr. Bennett, aka The Mustache, came out and sat down next to him. When Bernard could stand again, the doctor helped him into an examining room.

Why would I be interested in an old geezer like him? Addie thought, as she watched him hobble through the hallway. Odd that Dahlia seemed safe. She hadn't complained about him at all. Dita was wary of both him and Jessica, and their so-called financial business. She was glad that

The Mustache had come to get him. Twenty minutes later, she heard the doctor's voice saying goodbye, and Bernard hobbled through to the waiting room and out the door without speaking to her again.

She didn't hear Dr. Bennett sneak up behind her.

"He likes you, you know," he said. "Asked me about you."

"He's a hundred years old," Addie retorted.

"Not quite," the Doc said. "He's got some financial plan going. Invited me to join his club."

"He had my mother and a bunch of the older people over for a meeting. Some of them might join."

"Maybe I would, too, if I like what they have to say," the doctor said. "By the way, do you think I'm too old for you?"

Oh no, The Mustache really is back, she thought. She tried to be diplomatic, yet emphatic, spoke slowly, and stressed each word. "I am your coworker. I take orders from you, so I am off-limits. So stop, and I'll forget you ever said that."

"I was just wondering about our ages, not making a move. Go home, Red. I am."

Red? Addie almost jetted to the Be Fit to work off her anger. So this was what divorced life was going to be like, getting hit on by every guy on the hunt. She went into the now almost deserted hotel and found Dita stacking forms behind the counter, having worked her way through the line of applicants. She parked herself right in front of her friend and leaned forward over the counter.

"The Mustache tried to hit on me," Addie said. She saw Dita's shocked face and corrected herself. "A minor verbal pitch that I batted way out of the park, but still, I didn't like it." She couldn't tell her about Bernard due to patient privacy issues, but she wished she could.

"Why doesn't someone tell his wife about him?" Dita wondered.

"That's a good question that I can't answer," Addie hissed. "And how do you know no one has? And that reminds me, guess what Harry told me? Mel is living with that woman. Why didn't anyone else tell me, especially my best friend?" Addie glared at Dita, but then she could tell from Dita's face that she hadn't known. Her eyes were riveted on Addie's; her mouth had fallen open.

"No!" Dita shouted.

People turned to see what had happened. Dita started to pink up a bit like Addie and put her hand over her mouth.

"You didn't know either?" Addie asked.

"I did not. I swear."

"You and I must be the only ones," Addie said with emphasis on the only. "That day Harry stopped by, he told me, said everyone at the pub knew. I was so hurt I couldn't even tell you about it."

"Well, I haven't hung out at the pub since Janie arrived, so I didn't hear," Dita confirmed. "And if you're wondering, yes, I would have risked your wrath and told you. But, Addie, you're not even divorced yet, and he's living with someone?"

Addie nodded.

"Have you seen that lawyer?" she asked insistently. "You promised."

"Shush," Addie replied as she looked around to make sure no one was listening. "Yes, and she told me not to date or get involved with anyone until the divorce is final. Mel could use that against me, and I could lose custody of Danny."

Dita gasped. "So, it's okay for Mel but not for you? Quite old-fashioned, don't you think?"

"Exactly. You know how people are about women and sex. So keep mum about Harry, would you?"

"Of course," Dita said. "But shouldn't you be able to live your life and have some fun too? And speaking of fun, I'm done with my task here. The line of people is gone. How about if we stop at the Books and Bake for coffee? Janie and I can meet you there."

"I'd rather just come to your house," Addie said. "I don't feel like seeing people, Dita. I feel like everyone is looking at me now, trying to figure out if I know."

"Of course, I understand. I'll meet you at the house. I'll just pick up some cupcakes for us on the way. Would you take Tuffy?"

Dita put the membership applications on a shelf behind the counter, gathered up Janie in her portable car seat, and waved to Sean. *Going now,* she mouthed to him. He nodded back, and she left, Addie ahead of her.

She was saddened by Addie's revelation. It was hard enough on her that Mel had had an affair, but that he'd moved in with his paramour was worse. *Paramour*, she thought, what a word. It should be less lovely, like *festering obsession* or *animal attraction*. That was a good one, she thought, Mel's animal attraction. Had the new girlfriend known Mel had a wife and a boy on the island who needed him? Had Addie thought yet about the fact that Danny would be meeting the woman, and he might have to think of her as a stepmother? She knew she wouldn't want to share Janie with another so-called mother, let alone one who had broken up her family.

She stopped to put Janie down for a second. As she bent over, she caught sight of the ocean far below the grassy lawn. There was a speck of ferry steaming toward the island almost on the horizon and a small flotilla of fishing boats trawling toward the west side. She filled her lungs with the clean salt air, cleared her mind of those distressing thoughts, and felt the beauty of that view, one of the best on Block Island.

She was almost at her car when she suddenly felt watched. Her fear barometer skyrocketed, and she wheeled around. Josh Martel was almost upon her. He was a moving scarecrow. Her heart pounded, and she clutched Janie's travel seat tighter. Addie had melted out of sight, maybe walking through town or in her car already.

Josh called out, "Dita, Dita Redmond, wait. Please wait for me. I need to talk to you."

What was that when people shouted to you using both your names? She was the only Dita on the island. Josh was shouting like a cop arresting someone, and he was catching up to her. She wanted to interview him but on her own terms, somewhere with other people watching, and without her baby. She was unsure what to do: flee, flailing the baby seat as she ran, or continue doing what she had been about to do, which was to open the car door and place Janie inside? Maybe she would just stand there and be stupid as she was doing until he caught up. She opted to put Janie into the car with the window cracked open. At least her dear one would be safe. She was clicking the car seat carrier into place when she felt the man standing right behind her.

She startled and her skin prickled. "Back up," she ordered, as she closed the door separating Janie from their confrontation. At least the baby would be safe if he attacked.

But the man was not about to attack. He was out of breath from pushing up the hillside to catch her. She heard him struggling, huffing as he moved a few steps away from her again.

Dita turned toward him. His eyes were rheumy, his face sagged. Her fear subsided, and she thought, could this scarecrow of a man have killed Bunny and dragged her into the swamp? Probably not, though he had leapt over her mother's hedge.

Finally, he caught his breath. His voice was thready, and he paused to inhale between sentences. "I know y'all think I killed Bunny. I admit I was sleepin' in her house, but I didn't kill her, I swear. I'd never kill anyone, Dita, especially not Bunny," he insisted, wavering back and forth like a cattail in the wind. "You don't need to be afeared of me."

Dita hoped he didn't keel over before she could get him to a chair. She motioned for him to move away from her car.

"Let's sit down," she said, realizing she might not get a chance to interview him again.

"Someone might see me," he objected.

"We'll be far enough away from the path," she assured him.

She led him to a pair of green lawn chairs on the grass close to where her car was parked, and within hearing of people walking by, just in case she had to scream. He might have a gun. Though he denied killing anyone, he might be lying. Who, after all, would admit to murder unless coerced?

Dita texted Addie to tell her she was going to be delayed. When she looked up again, Josh was dropping backward into a chair. He needed to sit more than he needed to worry about someone walking by and recognizing him.

From her perch on the side of the hill, Dita noticed the speck of ferry was closer. Seeing the wide swatch of ocean calmed her as it always did.

Josh continued to plead his innocence. "She, Bunny, was payin' me to do repairs like fixin' loose tiles in the bathrooms and rehangin' cabinets in the kitchen, and I was supposta start painting. Then she disappeared. She was supposta meet me on the island to look over the work I already did and pay me more but, Dita, I swear, she never came. She still owes me the money. Why would I have killed her?"

"I don't know, Josh. That's something you would have to tell me," Dita tried to sound her reportorial best.

He shook his head, made a tight fist, and beat the armrest, repeating, "No, no, I didn't do it. You gotta believe me."

Dita's sense of alarm flew up again. The third time he slammed his fist, she shouted out what he wanted. "I hear you, Josh, and I'm sorry you didn't get paid."

"But I didn't do it," he shouted back, his face cringe-worthy, his body tightening, almost twisting into knots.

Several tourists on the path looked over at them.

"I believe you," Dita replied. "You need to calm down. People are looking, and you're scaring me."

He shifted in the chair and gave her a hangdog look. "Do you really believe me?" he asked, lowering his voice.

"I don't disbelieve you," she said.

His fists flattened out. Dita looked away from his hands and examined his face. The scary frown was gone. She relaxed a bit. Besides being frightened, she'd been worried he'd have a stroke. As he uncoiled from his rage, she looked him up and down. It hit her how extremely emaciated he was. He was less than a scarecrow. He was a skeleton. He really did need help. She felt sorry for him, but still wasn't totally convinced of his innocence.

"What were you doing in Bunny's yard the night her brother had the get-together there?" she asked. "And why did you sneak into my mother's house? You can't deny that was you. We saw you leaving."

"I'm sorry. I was so hungry. I took some bread, is all," he said. "I seen everyone at that party at Bunny's next door and spotted your motha' and all the food through the window. I couldn't go to the party, so I sneaked into your motha's. It weren't locked."

"You frightened my mother."

He looked down again, and against her better judgment, Dita felt sorrier for him than angry for that moment. But now she was angry at Caroline. She could barely believe her mother had left the door open like that with an unsolved murder at the house next door.

"You know the police have been looking for you, don't you? Mom's door may not have been locked, but it was closed, and you trespassed. And, Josh, it makes you look like the murderer, sneaking around like that."

He reiterated that he had no reason to kill Bunny and that when he heard they all suspected him, he hid. Dita wondered how anyone could disappear on this small island. That the police couldn't find him was beyond her. Josh shouldn't have been able to skulk around very long.

"Where'd you hide? This island's so tiny and gossipy."

Josh closed his mouth and stuck out his jaw, locking up like a clam. He folded his arms across his chest.

"You should really turn yourself in, Josh. Just tell the truth," Dita told him.

But, she realized, there'd not been as much suspicion about anyone else. No wonder he was hiding. "When was the last time you saw Bunny?" she asked, taking a less confrontational line of questioning.

"I only met her once. She asked Dahlia for someone to work on the house. There were a bunch of repairs she wanted done, and Dahlia gave her my name. Bunny called me, we set up a day to meet at the house, and I went. I think it was October. I remember it was still warm, not hot, though. We went through her list, and she said to give her a price. I told her I charge by the hour. She agreed to it and gave me a pretty nice deposit to cover materials and some of my time, said to start right away. I did."

"Was she aware you were sleeping there?"

Josh bobbed his head up and down. "She was. Said it was okay to take the couch. She'd call before she came so I could clear out for a few days."

"So that was you my mother spotted looking out Bunny's window at night at her?" Dita asked. When he didn't reply, she repeated her question, "Was it?" she demanded.

"Yes. I didn't think she saw me."

Dita leaned forward and just about hissed, "She did, Josh. You frightened her."

"Sorry," he seemed to slip further into the chair, drawing his body more tightly into itself.

Dita looked him straight in the eye. "And Bunny? When did you see her again?"

"She called once to say she was coming, and she'd leave me more money, but she never showed up. I tried calling her when I ran out of the money I'd already been paid, but she didn't answer, and she didn't call back. I didn't know whether to keep working or not. And, I couldn't get paint or anything without cash."

"When was that?" Dita asked again.

Josh took out his phone and scrolled through his calls. Dita marveled that even though Josh was literally disappearing from lack of nourishment, somehow he managed to hang on to his phone and maintain his account.

"Must have been sometime after Columbus Day, you know, after the tourists leave," he said, and he searched some more. "I tried calling and texting a few times after, but her phone went right to message. I even called Dahlia to find out if she knew anything."

"Can you find that call, Josh? If you do, I'll try to jog Dahlia's memory."

He scrolled again and found it. He showed her. She jotted down the dates and lengths of the calls. He was telling the truth about trying to reach her, but that still didn't prove he was innocent. He could have been inventing an alibi.

"Tell me what you thought about Bunny that day you met her," Dita prodded.

He hesitated. "She's okay. You know, rich lady, wants what she wants, but willing to pay lots, and, nice to me."

"You mean about letting you sleep there."

"Well, yeah. I liked her."

Dita thought for a moment. "Might she have said no, and you got angry?"

He started to get up and turn away while reiterating, "No, no. Dita, she said I could. I didn't get mad." By now he was totally turned and walking away, but he stopped to look back at her. "I thought you'd listen, but you're like everyone else." He stomped away.

Dita tried to follow, but with Janie in the car, she couldn't go too far. She called to him to come back, but he was already behind the buildings, into the lots above the Double Ender by the hedges that separated the properties. She'd bungled the interview. She knew better than to push people's buttons, didn't she? Yet she'd backed him into the corner she should have left for the police when they had him in lock-up. Television news anchors needn't fear her taking their jobs. Now she deliberated whether to tell the Chief she'd seen him. She never promised Josh she wouldn't. She called Gomez and reported to him. He promised to let her know when they picked Josh up.

It was time to go to the Books and Bake, pick up food, and meet Addie at home. She pulled into a space right in front. Mary, her editor, was just going in, so Dita snagged her to bring out some coffee and cupcakes for her.

TEN

Addie was sitting on the front steps when Dita pulled into the driveway. Usually, Dita admired her graying cedar-shingled cottage when she arrived, but today she noticed only her friend. Dita looked at Addie and thought how different she was from their former friend Loretta. Addie never sauntered into the house and made herself at home. She waited outside. Loretta would have been in the living room, stretched out on the couch reading Dita's latest *New Yorker* magazine while munching on Sean's trove of salted nuts or savoring the Belgian chocolates Dita's mother used to send. And when she realized how little she'd left the householders, she'd go to the discount store on her next mainland shopping trip and replace them with a cheaper brand. But Loretta was gone, and Dita needed to stop fretting over the days when her friendship was so quirky yet treasured. Still, she couldn't help thinking about how calculating Loretta had been. Was she as evil as Dita now believed, or had she been molded and fired like the clay that potters took from the island cliffs to fit into her family's criminal activities, unable to resist even if she so desired?

"What's wrong with you?" Addie wondered. "You're a thousand miles away. Did something happen?"

"Nothing."

Addie stood up. "Something happened that took you so long."

"Josh Martel happened," Dita replied. "He ambushed me on the way to The Double Ender parking lot."

She saw fear spread over Addie's face. "No, no, he didn't hurt me. He just caught up to me and wanted to talk, but he did scare me when he sneaked up behind me, and I had Janie in my arms. He says he didn't kill Bunny."

"Who would admit they did?" Addie asked, breaking into her Rhody dialect. "What's in the bag?" She reached out to grab it, but Dita whisked it away from her.

"You'll see when we get inside," Dita chided, but she was happy. This was more like the Addie of happier days, when her only concern was what she was going to eat next. Back then, Addie was quite a bit plumper, *zaftig* even, a Yiddish term for pleasingly plump. Since Mel left, she'd dwindled in size, both a good and a bad thing.

"Addie, he let me scroll through his phone to find calls he made to Bunny that went right to message, and to Dahlia to find out where Bunny was."

"Did you record the dates and length?"

Dita looked at her friend with disbelief. "Of course. I'm going to do an article. Why would you even ask that?"

"Since you had Janie, you've been preoccupied," Addie accused, thinking of all the times Dita had dozed off or not paid attention to what was being said.

Dita was insulted, and she said so. "Hmf, Addie, I could say the same thing about you. Since you mmmhmmed with Harry, you've been preoccupied." Dita felt smug, thinking she'd put Addie in her proper place, but Addie was a bit hurt.

"Mmmmhmmed? What is that? Oh, I should never have confided in you." Addie stood up and took a step down like she was leaving.

Dita bit her lip, and she laughed. "Just kidding. Don't get all insulted." She reached out to pull Addie back.

"You're tough to be friends with sometimes, you know," Addie said, but she smiled and let herself be turned around. "I got you, didn't I? You thought I was serious.

"Look, I started a spreadsheet on the investigation for us so we can keep track of what we know," Addie opened her phone and showed it to Dita. "We can plug those calls in."

They walked up to the porch together, went around the corner of the house to the kitchen slider, and let themselves inside. Dita set the infant carrier on the kitchen table and unbuckled Janie.

"Why don't you make the coffee, Addie, and put the sandwiches and dessert out for us while I feed her?"

"Certainly," Addie said as she opened the paper bag and looked in. "Yum, the special chocolate croissants. Now you are truly forgiven. Maybe we should eat these right now."

Dita realized how much she had missed that side of her friend. "They're for dessert!"

Addie took two plates out of the cabinet drawer and set one wrapped croissant on each. Then she unwrapped them. She made room for the sandwiches, too, but they had become the add-on instead of the main lunch course.

"Shall we go outside, Dita, when you're ready, of course? It's such a nice day."

Dita was around the corner on the couch with Janie, but she heard and shouted back a yes.

"The table on the deck or the Adirondack chairs in the yard?" Addie asked.

"The chairs," Dita responded. "I need about ten minutes, though."

"That's fine. I'm making our coffee, and then I'll come sit with you. On second thought, how about I make some margaritas, and we go to the beach when you're ready instead?" This was the old relaxed Addie, the one who was never in a rush. "I know you're not supposed to drink, yadda, yadda, yadda, but I'll just pour you half of one, okay?"

Dita liked that idea. "Nurse Addie, shame on you, prescribing a bit of fun." She laughed. "It's a wonder anyone wants to have a baby these days with all the restrictions during pregnancy and nursing. In the old days, mothers were allowed to enjoy life and their new babies. What happened to 'a little bit of beer helps them sleep'? Now you're only supposed to stick the kid in day care and go back to work. Well, I like my extra naps and visits with friends."

"So, I guess that's a yes, and I'm the naughty nurse," Addie answered.

She got out the beaker and began pouring. She knew where everything was kept in her friend's kitchen. As she shook the cocktail, she took a moment to enjoy the view through the slider. The dunes were in full rosy bloom. The pink-petalled flowers wound in no particular pattern up and down the dunes, mixing with the grasses, which now looked alive instead of like winter hay. It was the most beautiful time of year, at least in her opinion. As she watched, a truck turned off Corn Neck Rd. and dropped to the washed-out beach road with a loud bang. Its load of stacked wooden pallets that she knew were taken from the ferry freight yard rattled in protest. Most drivers always forgot when they turned into that track, no matter how many years they'd lived here. The pallets were used to fuel bonfires for parties or clam bakes. They were a sign the summer season was about to begin.

"Looks like there's something going on at the beach tonight," she shouted to Dita.

"Have you forgotten it's Memorial Day weekend? Probably the local kids celebrating," Dita replied. "They always have the first party, and it's not too loud or late."

"And, Dita, a wedding party just drove in behind them," Addie said, still gazing out the slider. "Maybe there's a clambake."

"Could be, but it's a bit early for that. Still a bit of a chill in the air for adults to be hanging on the beach when the sun sets. The teenagers go out because they don't feel it."

Addie watched the wedding party go by, dressed in the finery they would wear for the ceremony. She admired the lace on the bride's bodice. She wondered if it was hand-tatted. The group laughed and chatted in loud voices as they marched toward the dunes at the entrance to the beach, the spot that their photographers usually preferred. At the end of their procession, a photographer with equipment—a real camera instead of a cell phone, bags for large lenses, an umbrella, and stand—straggled along, sharing the load with an assistant.

"I'm going upstairs to watch," Addie said. She would have a bird's eye view from up there. "I'll tell you if it's anyone we know."

"If it was someone we know, wouldn't we already know?" Dita asked, laughing.

"Not necessarily. Remember that presidential family member? And that movie star? We knew who they were..."

"Okay, but we didn't really know them."

"Very cute couple, but not from here," Addie called down. "The groom is gorgeous. Great biceps. Come look."

"I can't. I'll take your word for it." Yet again, Dita felt relieved that Addie had come alive. "Are they full of tats like Harry's?"

Addie continued to spy on the group as the photographer took pictures and moved her subjects around on the dune. As Addie watched, her thoughts drifted back to her own wedding day. She'd chosen a dress with lace also. How hopeful and happy both she and Mel had been—at least, she'd thought they were. Don't all divorces start with weddings? She tried to stifle a sigh, determined not to ruin the day by diving into depression. Still, she hoped the vows of the couple on the beach lasted longer than hers and Mel's.

Dita called to her. "Stop standing in full view in front of the slider and ogling them. I know that's what you're doing up there, even though I can't see you. They're going to refer to me as the nosy neighbor who keeps an eye on every move out there. Besides, I'm ready. Let's go outside," Dita said.

"No one looked over here," Addie retorted. "No one."

Addie carried the drinks, two plastic cocktail glasses, and the food in a basket, and balanced the folding beach chairs on the other side. Dita cradled Janie in her arms, Tuffy trailing along in the hope of grabbing some crumbs of both food and attention. The wedding party and photographer left, not quite as noisily as they had arrived. The two women spread out and sat in silence while enjoying their sandwiches and the peace. The only sounds were the occasional wind gust rustling the sea grass, the soft shush of the surf, and the trills of the songbirds.

"Hear that?" Dita asked. "Those are robins. They made a nest in the outdoor shower. There's a space between the top of the wall and the floor of the deck and they snuggled in there in a corner. They're lucky it's still too cool to go swimming and we aren't using the shower yet or their babies would die of fright." Maybe this was a good time to tactfully bring up Loretta. "Addie, this woman Bunny...her murder made me start thinking about Joel and Loretta again."

"Me too, a bit," Addie admitted. "How could she have sent those guys to kill my brother and still act as though she was my friend? And let my mother take her in after her overdose? I just can't wrap my head around the friend we knew..."

Dita finished Addie's sentence. "And the friend we didn't know. I've never been religious, never thought there was really evil, but if Loretta wasn't evil, what was she? How could she have inserted herself so fully into our lives when she only meant harm unless she was, well, evil."

Addie sagged in her seat. "I don't know the answer to that. I only know she damaged my family, my mother, my Danny, and me. I thought Mel also, but now I would place him somewhere on the continuum between good and evil. Not a killer like Loretta, but not a good guy either. Maybe he was play-acting like Loretta."

Just then they heard a truck enter the beach path. It was Harry, his pickup bed loaded with cartons of beer. He had taken the drop-off with care and there was no crash. He looked over at the house, spotted them and waved, and continued on his way up the beach.

"Hmm, has the thrill worn off?" Dita asked. She laughed as Addie began to blush again.

"Apparently not for you."

"Stop. You know I asked him to cool it," Addie said, pushing a lock of hair into place.

"I didn't think he would."

Voices drifted up from the beach, snippets of conversation. The soft wind carried them away before Addie and Dita could string together sentences or clauses to construct any meaning. Not long after, a larger truck with a grill and coolers came through. Then they heard Harry's truck again and he pulled up close to them. "Guess there is still some thrill," Dita murmured under her breath just loud enough for Addie to hear.

"Looks like he's coming here."

Addie swatted her friend's arm, and Dita tried to stifle a guffaw. Then Harry was standing right in front of them, smiling and saying hello. He looked a tad uncomfortable, out of his element there, inserting himself into their bubble. His forehead was dappled with sweat beads from unloading the truck in the sun, his shoes were encrusted with beach sand, and his work clothes clung to his body, wet with sweat like his forehead. Dita looked him over, and like Addie had said the other day, she knew why the young women who wandered into his barroom fought over him, even or especially when he was drenched from laboring. She turned to Addie, who was gawking with no shame, and she understood just how smitten her friend was.

Harry seemed almost shy. "Just thought I'd say hello," he said. "Got to get back to work in a couple minutes. Looks like you two are enjoying the afternoon. I didn't think it was Margarita time until 5."

Dita stood. "Harry, do I have to tell you what the song says?"

"Umm, no." He smiled and folded his arms over his chest, making Dita aware he was still sweating and didn't have a drink in hand.

"I can run back to the house and get you something cold to drink if you don't want a cocktail—I mean, not beer, you just dropped off plenty of that. A Coke? Lemonade? Water?" She also thought she should give the two of them a few moments alone.

"Any kind of soda would be good," he said, acknowledging his thirst after unloading the truck. He sat on the sand in front of Addie. When Dita's back was turned as she trotted to the house, he grabbed Addie's ankles. "How are you?" he asked, looking up at her.

"What do you think?" she answered, putting her hands over his. "But remember what I told you."

He looked up at her. She noticed he was wearing his gray lenses, and she was glad, because she knew if he hadn't been wearing those, she'd have been unable to resist him. He stood up and walked to the water, nodded to Tuffy, and threw a stick into the surf for him to chase.

In the kitchen, Dita fussed as long as she could before she reappeared and tried to look casual. "So who's that party down the beach for?" she asked, having decided not to acknowledge the rising tension between her friends.

"The high school kids," he answered. "You know, the first of the season, so the parents got together and paid for the food and the cook."

Addie gave him a big nurse look, and he quickly explained, "The workers bought the beer for later. Not for the kids."

He chugged the soda down. Dita'd never seen him so flustered. Addie seemed super flustered herself. An awkward silence ensued, and then they all tried to speak at once. Harry won.

"I didn't want to interrupt your lunch, so I'm going to go back to work. Thanks for the drink, Dita," he said, turning to get to his truck. His hand went up in a backward wave. "See ya, Addie."

Dita threw her hands up. "You're just going to sit there, Addie? Not saying goodbye, not going after him?"

"I don't need to remind either of you that my custody of Danny's on the line here."

"Addie, anyone who sees you two in the same room, or passing each other on the street, can feel the current zap between you. It's no secret."

But then Harry came running back. "I actually need to tell you something. That's one of the reasons I stopped before. The skinny around the party crew is that Josh Martel is being arrested for the murder of that lady."

"That lady meaning Bunny?" Dita asked.

He nodded.

"Right," Dita said. "I just spoke to him, and he insists he's innocent. I let Chief Gomez know I saw him, so he must have sent someone to pick him up while he was out of hiding."

"And I forgot something else." He lifted Addie to her feet, took her in his arms, and kissed her. "Surely you trust Dita."

"But not if Mel's lawyer subpoenas her to testify in a custody hearing," Addie whispered.

"He wouldn't dare," Harry said. "This whole island would go after him. Do you not know everyone loves you?" Harry said. "We all have your back, sweetie, and I'm not letting that happen. But right now, I've gotta get home for a shower and then back to work." He turned and left. Both Addie and Dita watched him walk away. What woman wouldn't?

"Did you ever get close enough to decode all those arm tats?" Dita asked.

"Never telling," Addie said, and she gathered their dishes and trash and brought them into the house. Dita followed, but not all the way. Instead, she slid into one of the Adirondacks in the yard where they originally were going to go. Janie was still asleep, and she put the carrier in the grass next to her. Tuffy laid his face on her leg.

"Oh, you're wet," she chided, but she petted him anyway.

She heard the slider again and looked up. Addie was waving goodbye. As Dita waved back, she wondered if Addie was going to get Harry to wait for her divorce to come through. Maybe he wouldn't be able to wait and would wander off to someone else first. She understood her friend's determination not to get drawn into an affair that could endanger her custody, but she also thought Addie would be smart not to rush into a relationship with Harry even after the divorce. He'd been, up to now, a man who often seemed adolescent in his personal life. Did he even have a clue about the anguish Addie would feel if she lost Danny? Far greater than any anguish he might have by not satisfying his sex drive, Dita thought. For that matter, did Harry ever look ahead beyond running the bar and sliding through the winters, keeping the bar open for what amounted to some local friends?

But that's Block Island, she reasoned. Maybe she and Sean would have to get other work, too, in the winter when the newness of having an island gym wore off and fewer islanders joined. She needed to keep her job to supplement their income. With that in mind, she texted the chief to follow up on Harry's information about Josh. He texted back that the handyman indeed was under arrest, but it was a bad time for a conversation, as the island was busy, and that meant the police department was busy. That was okay with Dita. She didn't want to talk to him. She wanted to interview Josh again in jail as soon as possible. The chief said they couldn't take him to the mainland for arraignment until Tuesday, so there'd not be a bail hearing until then. Since Josh had nowhere to live anyway, he was not averse to free room and board for a few days, so she had time.

It was quiet out there in the yard now, just Dita and Janie, and of course, Tuffy. Dita drifted into alpha rhythm, watching a flock of feathery white clouds cha-cha by in the wind, dancing their way to the open sea where they would draw up more moisture and grow into a storm. She inhaled the scent of the early flowering lavender she'd planted just a few paces from her Adirondack chair. And then she allowed herself to drop off into a deep slumber, a state every new mother yearns to reach, even if only for a few blissful moments.

"Dita!" The voice penetrated and reverberated over and over like a clapper ringing a bell, Dita, Dita, Dita.

Her eyes refocused. Caroline, yes, her mother, stood on the deck calling. Dita shut her eyes. Maybe if she didn't answer she would leave. She should have been happy to see her, but she would rather have had her nap. Was this what Caroline's move to the island was going to be like? Surprise visits whenever, just like Dita's friends? But she realized she didn't resent her friends and she did resent her. She felt guilty for her selfishness at the same time she felt encroached upon. Why couldn't she be more like Addie, who had a close relationship with her mother and appreciated her? Would Janie resent her someday? But now Caroline had spotted her and was approaching. Dita's nap was ruined.

"Hi, dear," Caroline crooned.

Dita did not feel like a dear. In fact, she knew she wasn't.

"Did I wake you? I'm so sorry." For a moment, Caroline looked penitent. She'd once been a new mother too, and she told Dita she remembered what it was like, how her body had ached with the need for sleep. And, she said again, this time with feeling, "I am really so sorry I disturbed you." She leaned down and kissed Dita on the forehead.

A small smile unfurled, just a bit, on Dita's face. She stretched her arms next to her ears and repositioned herself, sitting up as straight as one can in one of those deep Adirondack chairs. "It's okay, Mom," she said at last between two yawns.

Caroline was carrying a folder and she waved it in front of her daughter. "I came to discuss this with you. It's from Jessica, my neighbor."

Dita yawned again. "What is it?"

"Our group met again last night and we're all investing together," she said, ignoring Dita's yawns. "It's a prospectus, she told us. I thought I could spare a small amount of money for her fund."

"Really? How much did she get you for?" Dita had no idea what a small amount of money would be for her mother. A few hundred dollars? A few thousand? More?

Caroline frowned. "Nothing yet. I brought this for you to look at first." She waved the prospectus at Dita again. "It's the terms and all that."

Dita grumbled. She didn't really want to read a financial document, nor did she want her mother putting any money in an account with someone none of them knew. She especially didn't want to read boring legalese terms. Did anyone ever? They could just as well write one cover sentence as all that garble. "Can you leave it on the kitchen table? Sean and I will read it tonight. Right now, even though I forgive you, I really want to finish my nap."

Caroline felt a pang of disappointment. Would her daughter ever grow closer to her? She had moved here hoping that they would develop a better relationship, but she acknowledged to herself now that that might never happen. But at least there was Janie.

"Okay, I'll hold my granddaughter instead. She likes me." She swallowed her disappointment and reached down to pick up Janie. Then she sat in the chair Addie had just vacated. "By the way, I have a date tonight."

"You do?" Dita's voice was soft and disinterested, as her mind was still far away.

Caroline nodded. "With that guy who lives on a boat. What's his name, the one that was at Jessica and Bernard's? Carter. He called and invited me to dinner."

"Hmmf," Dita responded, more awake now. "Be careful. There's a murderer on the island, and you're going out with a man whose name you're not sure you remember."

Caroline looked closely at her daughter, who, for the moment, had just reversed their roles, acting the worried parent. Maybe things would look up between them.

"And please don't wake Janie up," Dita said. "If you do, she's all yours, if you know what I mean." And with that, she shut her eyes. Tuffy curled up on her feet again.

Caroline cuddled Janie and smiled like a kid with her hand in a cookie jar. She whispered to Janie, "As if you being 'all mine' would be anything less than sublime."

ELEVEN

The alert woke Addie at 3 a.m., an hour past the bar closings; there were critical injuries at the beach bonfire. She threw cold water on her face, jumped into her scrubs, dashed out the door to the car, and roller-coastered over the potholes in her driveway to the beach parking lot in micro minutes. The lot and the beach entrance were blocked by vehicles escaping from the scene to avoid the police, who were sure to come. The escapees were mostly off-islanders who had active warrants or kids carrying drugs.

Addie ditched her car in Dita's driveway and tried to run, her least favorite pace, her breath heavy from the acrid smoke that covered the whole area. Sparks crackled overhead. The bonfire flamed ahead near the water. Shadows moved about in its flickering light.

She found Sean there. He'd arrived just before her, his headlamp beaming. He shouted questions to the last of the partyers driving off and the few stragglers warming themselves by the fire, hanging there as they were too inebriated to leave or be of help. They pointed down the beach towards town, and Sean broke into a run in that direction. Addie followed as best she could.

The escaping vehicles disappeared, and an eerie absence of noise settled around them, broken only by the sound of the waves breaking on shore. But it lasted only a minute or two, for then, without the grinding of motors and tires, Addie heard faint shouts.

"Over here," a male called from a distance, his voice thready. Other voices joined his.

Addie felt the wind on her back. "They're closer than they seem. The wind is carrying the sound away from us," she yelled to Sean.

"Let's move," he shouted, running faster.

A light flashed far down the beach at the foot of the dunes. Addie tried to sprint, but the soft sand caught her feet and slowed her pace. She fell behind. They must have spotted Sean's headlamp, because the cries grew louder, and people flashed cell phone lights to guide them. Sean shouted back to them, his booming carrying on the wind toward the scene.

"We're coming. Keep your lights on so we can find you."

Addie hoped this was just going to be someone with a sprained ankle or too much to drink. She never really liked emergency duty and was always glad she wasn't usually the first on the scene. She often met the ambulance along with the doctor at the medical center. Her real forte was supporting people through their illnesses to regain their health and providing preventive care, but these emergencies came with the job. Maybe, she thought, it was time to move elsewhere in her career. She steeled herself for however gruesome a scene might be waiting.

She spotted shadows now, specters moving about in the wan light, and she pushed toward them. Sean was already out of sight, unidentifiable, somewhere ahead of her. When she reached the outer knots of people gathered in a ragged semi-circle, pointing, crying, and grasping each other, she threaded her way through. It was a large crowd. Most of the partiers had gravitated to the trouble. She didn't recognize most of them and surmised they were new to the island, summer workers letting off steam after their first busy night tending tourists.

Suddenly everyone wanted to talk at once. "Help her...she's not breathing..."

Addie's heart sank. This was not a routine call, and she and Sean were the first of the responders to arrive. The kids, summer workers, told them they'd heard the roar of a large vehicle followed by high shrieks. No one was close when it happened. They'd all been by the fire, and the screams stopped before anyone found her.

"I almost stepped on her...she hasn't moved... We tried CPR, but she's bleeding too much...we couldn't stop it."

Now the spot the cell phone lights pointed to was not far ahead. A few people clustered near her. They seemed stunned, in shock, as they stepped aside to let Addie through. A body lay sprawled out upon the sand, stomach down, head turned to the side. Sean was bending over. Addie leaned in with her flashlight. She looked closer and pushed her unfastened hair out of her eyes. There'd been no time for a cap tonight.

"Noooo," she moaned. "Not Cathy Jones." She'd seen her only two days ago when she bought Danny's ferry ticket for the school trip.

"Yes, it's Cathy," Sean said under his breath as he felt for a pulse. Cathy was a fitness center member. "I saw her just this morning working out."

Then he looked up. "Got it, but faint, very faint," he said.

Addie ran her flashlight above Cathy's abdomen. "She's bleeding out. Her abdomen, ribs are crushed. She's crushed." Addie ticked off what she saw, then her voice rose with alarm. "What's taking the ambulances so long? We need a pressure compression tourniquet." She took off her hoodie and tried to stanch the bleeding, but it seeped right through.

Sean sounded desperate. "She's having trouble breathing."

Then she heard the whine of truck engines. She knew the police and the ambulance had pulled into the parking lot and were about to roll onto the hard sand at the top of the beach. The beach warden arrived in his special vehicle with large tires and a rack on the back. More emergency personnel drove in in their own trucks and SUVs, spreading out across the beach, pointing their headlights toward the crowd.

"Fast, her pulse was faint," Sean called to his comrades.

Addie was already on the phone to Dr. Bennett, who had arrived at the medical center to await their arrival.

"He says to get her to the medical center pronto," Addie ordered. The facility was but five minutes away.

The EMTs stabilized Cathy, then lifted her onto the beach stretcher and rushed to the ambulance. They slid her into it, and two of them hopped in.

"I'll meet you at the medical center," Addie called.

"Of course," a voice on the vehicle responded.

The driver had already started moving. Sean stayed behind. There could be others out there in the dark.

"Is there anyone else hurt?" Sean called out. "We need people to search."

A group of volunteers strafed the area with their spotlights to search for more victims. Addie needed to get going so she could meet the ambulance at the clinic. Sean was not needed anymore since there were enough without him, so he offered to stay with Danny at her house. He didn't want to risk waking Dita and Janie, or Danny, by moving him. The two of them slow-jogged back toward the driveway, Sean pausing twice to let Addie catch up so they could get there together.

"Who did this?" Addie asked, not expecting an answer. "Everyone loves Cathy."

"Apparently almost everyone. We'll talk about her later," Sean said. "Do what you need to at the medical center. I'll leave a note for Dita and then go be with Danny. I'll sleep on your couch."

"Thank you. Poor Cathy," she choked up. "She's so young, she's really just past a girl."

Addie sped through town and up the hill past Caroline's house and the school to the medical center. At this time of early morning, the streets were empty, and she was only minutes behind the ambulance. When she arrived, Dr. Bennett was standing outside the clinic emergency doors, waiting for the drivers to remove the stretcher and roll the patient in. She saw him take a quick look at Cathy as the volunteers wheeled her through the doors. Addie rushed into the building behind Dr. Bennett.

"I know her," he said as they entered an examining room along with the stretcher. "But I can't recall her name."

"Cathy," Addie said, bristling with impatience. How could he not recall her name? "Cathy Jones, who works at the ferry ticket office. You see her whenever you buy a ticket."

Almost everyone on the island worked two or even three jobs in summer to cobble together enough money to pay their bills through the winter. Cathy worked two part-time ones in the winter as well.

"Yes, yes, of course, I remember now," he admitted.

"Did you call for the helicopter?" she asked.

"No," he said. He hesitated, and then he told her. "Addie, she passed in the ambulance. They tried, but she was too severely injured. She lost a lot of blood on the beach."

She realized that's why he had been standing outside, and why Cathy was still on the stretcher when she arrived. Her eyes welled up as she faced the realization that Cathy was gone.

"Poor, poor Cathy," she wailed. "Who did this to her? I'm sorry. I can't be professional right now." She broke into tears.

Dr. Bennett wrapped her in his arms and let her cry. When she finished, she shook loose and thanked him. She reached into her bag and wiped her face with a tissue stuffed inside.

"Come," he said gently. "We have work to do. Do we have a chart on her with contact information?"

"We do," Addie said, snuffling and wiping away a tear. Thank goodness the doc had a heart after all. "But I think I hear her friends in the waiting room, and Chief Gomez is there, too."

"I'll go talk with them first."

Addie stayed behind. She knew her task: to unhook Cathy from any life-saving equipment she'd been connected to in the ambulance. She hoped she wouldn't have as strong a reaction to the deceased woman as when she'd been confronted with Bunny's torn body. That had been her first death since her brother Joel's demise.

And so Addie gazed down at Cathy, and not having any beliefs about death, sent her heartfelt love. The young woman was crushed from sternum to knees, a most disturbing sight. Addie clutched her hand to her heart. She was rocked with grief as she stepped closer and tried to think of her as a body now, not a human Cathy. She willed herself to remain calm and not to flip into a panic attack as she disconnected the IV. When she finished, she reached over to gently sweep Cathy's hair from her face, as she would were it her own child, then stepped away again out of the room to wait at the doorway for Chief Gomez and Doctor Bennett.

What had happened out there on the beach, she asked herself. Overdoses, drunken brawls, burns, all of those she'd seen in other years. But this? It looked like Cathy had been run over by that truck, repeatedly. She knew the girl was a fairly recent washashore who came for summer work several years past and stayed on with a group of friends when she finished college. She blended into the island's heartbeat so well that most people forgot she hadn't been born there. She worked part-time with Dahlia's real estate agency answering phones and doing paperwork, hoping to train as an agent as well as supplementing her income as a ticket agent at the ferry office. Almost everyone knew her. She had always been so pleasant. Addie couldn't imagine how her parents would feel when they were told. And Dahlia. Dahlia would be devastated.

She felt her shoulders sag and she realized she was tired. When the doctor came back, she went home.

And at her house, Dita had slept through the arrival of the police and the ambulance. They didn't turn on their sirens in the middle of the night, but when the partygoers began to leave the beach and congregate in the parking lot, their loud voices and vehicles roused her. Sean was missing. He was no longer snoring next to her, so she realized something must have happened to break up the gathering and he'd been called there. She threw on a robe, checked to see that Janie was still asleep, and went outside on her deck to call down to the crowd and ask what had happened.

"There was an accident at the beach. Big crowd at the bonfire tonight and a girl was run over," someone said.

Dita drew in a breath. "Who?" she asked. "Does anyone know who?"

"Cathy Jones," a voice from the dark called out.

Now Dita couldn't breathe at all. Cathy, whom she'd seen only a few days ago at the Be Fit. "Oh no! Is she okay?"

"Barely alive."

They were not aware Cathy's heart had stopped.

"What happened?" Dita cried.

She was met with silence, as often happens when someone is injured at a party with young people drinking and doping, no one wants to break code. Dita went back inside. She found the note from Sean.

"I need to go down there," she said to no one, but she couldn't just leave Janie alone, and she wouldn't wake up Caroline.

Quickly, she grabbed a pair of jeans and a sweatshirt. Unlike her good friend Addie, she didn't need to look official. Her tools of the trade were a pad and a pen, and of course, a flashlight to be able to see. Once outside again, she tried to find someone she knew and spotted Harry sitting on the fender of his truck. Dita almost smiled. He looked like he belonged on that fender. She was surprised he was alone.

"Harry, Harry," she called. "Would you stay with Janie for a half-hour while I run down to the beach? Sean is over at Addie's watching Danny."

"Sure, no problem." He slid down and walked toward her.

"By the way, you wouldn't happen to know what happened down there, would you?"

"I answered the call that came over the police radio. I wasn't there. I was cleaning up the bar, so I joined the guys searching the beach. We didn't find anyone else. I was just sitting here collecting myself before I went home."

"There's beer in the fridge if you want one."

He held up his hand to show her he already had one. "This one will do."

"Thank you," she called, already running to the accident site.

"Find Mike Palmer if you can. He was standing next to her when I got there," he added.

"He's her boyfriend, right?" Dita said.

He nodded and shrugged. "Sometimes. Watch yourself."

"I will. I have my phone. I'll record people."

"I'll text you if Janie wakes up," he told her.

"Thanks again," she said, thinking how ironic it was that her husband was at Addie's and Addie's heart throb was at her house. Oh, well. It laid a coating of humor onto a gruesome dawn. She watched him go into the house, just to make sure he did, and then, unlike her friend Addie, she burst into a full run, loping like a deer, headed to the fire and the crowd that now clutched around it. Everyone gathered earlier by the ambulance was now back at the fire or on their way home. She found someone she knew and began questioning him. He hadn't seen what happened. Had he seen Mike Palmer? Yes, but Mike was at the medical center now. He'd followed the ambulance. She spoke with a girl she knew who was good friends with Cathy. Cathy and Mike had argued, and Cathy had gone off by herself down the beach. Was Mike still by the fire when they heard Cathy's screams? The girl wasn't sure, just as she wasn't sure what they were arguing about.

A small group had gathered around Dita. None of them had noticed the truck or the person behind the wheel. They weren't paying attention, and they didn't know why Cathy had walked off in that direction. There were fireworks, music, and passing the dope around, so Cathy and Mike arguing was not a priority. Besides, that couple fought a lot, and they saw other people. Neither of them was true to the relationship. Was Cathy meeting someone? Dita knew she'd need to speak with Mike. One thing she was sure about: Josh Martel was locked up in jail. He couldn't have killed Cathy. The idea there might be two murderers on the island, well, she did not think that was feasible.

TWELVE

Sean yawned, got out of bed, and stretched. He ambled over to the bedroom slider, opened it, and closed it again. He'd returned home when Addie finished at the medical center around 4 a.m. and slid back into bed with Dita for a couple more hours of shut-eye.

"Still acrid out there from the fire," he said. "Breakfast?"

Dita glanced at the clock and asked, "Aren't you late for work?"

"Caroline opened for me. She has her yoga class, and she's sticking around all morning. I'm really glad your mom moved here," he said, emphasizing the I.

Dita yawned. "Your best friend, I guess."

Sean frowned. "And yours, though you don't seem to know it."

Dita gave him a smack on the butt to let him know that hit home. "Make coffee, please," she said, "and hand Janie over before you go down to the kitchen. And, before you go downstairs, did you talk to Addie last night when you came home? How was Cathy?"

Sean felt the levity of their morning dissolve. She didn't know, and he had to tell her. Dita snuggled back under the covers with the baby next to her, but Sean got back in bed close to them, and then he told her about Cathy. They held each other, devastated, and wept. Dita felt her heart tremble. She asked herself how this could be real.

And in her kitchen, Addie pushed the lever on the one-cup capsule coffee machine, which she'd purchased after Mel left, filling her mug before she sat down at the table next to Danny.

"I heard you when you got called out last night, Mom," Danny said as he shoveled cereal into his mouth.

The amount of food he'd been eating recently astonished Addie, but when she noticed how much he was growing, she knew what the food was fueling.

"What happened?" he asked.

"You didn't speak to Sean?"

He shook his head. "You know you don't need to bother him when you get called out. I'm older now."

She knew, yet she worried. "Soon," she said in reply. That her little boy was growing up was not a subject she wanted to think about this morning. Last night had stretched her coping abilities to the limit, and now she had to tell him. She didn't want to overly alarm him, especially because of his Uncle Joel. He'd been so close to Joel. She struggled to put last night into words.

"There was an accident at the bonfire. Someone," she couldn't even say, Cathy, it was too terrible. "Someone we know wandered off along the beach without a flashlight, and a truck ran her over." She didn't know whether or not Cathy had a light with her, but she assumed she did not. "We think it was an accident."

"That's bad. Who was it?" he demanded to know, his mouth still full of cereal. "A someone we know must have a name."

Now she spoke in almost a whisper. "Danny, it was Cathy Jones." There, she'd gotten it out.

Danny stopped chewing. His face contorted. "Cathy? Not nice Cathy at the ferry? Surfer Cathy?"

Addie reached out and took his hand. "I'm afraid so."

"Who did it?" he asked.

Addie thought he looked as stricken as he did when she told him Mel wouldn't be coming home anymore.

"Danny, we don't know. Whoever it was drove off."

Danny's face turned as red as his and Addie's hair as he repeated, "They just drove off?" over and over. He stood up, and Addie stood, too. She wrapped her arms around him.

"Mom, that's awful. Who would do that?" Tears spilled from Danny's eyes, but Addie had no more tears to shed.

All over the island, the same scenario was playing out as people passed the news to each other about Cathy Jones. Her loss rippled through her circle of friends, the community who knew her at the ticket office, the realty businesses, and the surfer community, as Cathy had been one of them, eager to suit up and catch a wave, even travelling with them to Costa Rica to tag bigger waves.

This, Addie thought, was not an auspicious way to start the summer season. Her phone rang, and Addie saw the medical center phone number. Danny saw it, too.

"You look tired, Mom. I hope you don't have to go in again."

She considered letting it go to voicemail, but obligation won out. It was Dr. Bennett. He'd spoken to Cathy's parents and sent her body to the mainland where they would go to identify her. They had no intention of coming to the island, and her funeral would be held in their town on the mainland. Addie was relieved but wondered why he couldn't have waited to tell her that until after the weekend. And she already knew that students, residents from the mainland medical school, and from the nursing school would handle emergencies at the clinic for the rest of the holiday weekend, which meant she probably wouldn't have to return to work until Tuesday, but Dr. Bennett felt compelled to remind her anyway. She hurried him off the line, and then she felt guilty because he was human too. Maybe he needed someone to console him after being thrust into the worst kind of human tragedy.

Danny left to go fishing with his friends, so she crawled back in bed for a few hours of denial before facing the day.

THIRTEEN

Was Cathy's murder connected to Bunny's? Dita needed to collect herself and pick up her investigation. First, she'd speak with Mike Palmer. She knew where he lived, just a few blocks away, so instead of calling him, she decided to pay him a visit. If he was grieving Cathy's death, seeing Dita in person would be more amenable than receiving a cold phone call. If he was the killer, she might catch him before he patched the deed over with alibis and lies. She could walk, or even indulge in a run to his house. Sean was still puttering around the house, so she parked Janie on the couch and left her with him.

This was one of those island days that inspired poets and artists. The wind was soft, the sun warm, and the ocean calm. Spring daffodils burst in clumps along the stone walls that edged the road, their yellow heads swaying in the occasional gusts of wind. Songbirds returning from their winter homes dotted the power lines like tightrope walkers, then swooped off to find food. Flocks of grackles stretched across the lines, then cartwheeled away only to return moments later to repeat the cycle. Even the brambles along the yards on the other side of the stone walls were alive. Dita could hear the rustle of the tiny new leaves as the field sparrows hopped through them. Clearly, the tragedy last night was but a tiny speck in the fabric of the universe, but not for her.

She ran at a good clip and reached Mike's rental in minutes. He lived in one of the tiniest cottages on the road. In exchange for doing repairs, in addition to his monthly rent, he was allowed to live in the house year-round, something few year-rounders on the island had the luxury of doing. The cottage had been built as a vacation getaway by a family from Connecticut who no longer came. It sat on a plot of land that was sectioned off before zoning enactments dictated building lot size. The house had a flat roof, and its shape resembled a cube. The walls were constructed of concrete blocks stuccoed over in white. Mike had added green shutters and painted the front door green. It looked to have maybe one bedroom, if that. Mike's work truck was parked in the short gravel driveway. He was probably home.

Dita knocked on the front door and waited. She tried again. This time she heard footsteps approach, and the door swung open. Mike, a tall, burly construction worker, filled the entire doorway. Dita was not accustomed to feeling small around men, but she felt like he could pick her up with one hand, like a giant with a Lilliputian.

Burly as he might be, she thought Mike was usually known as even-handed, not a brawler.

He looked down at her with bloodshot eyes, bed-head, and clothes that still held the slight stench of smoke from the bonfire. Clearly, Dita thought, he hadn't slept well or changed out of last night's shorts. She launched into her spiel, and as sometimes happened, blurted it out.

"Hi, Mike. I'm so sorry for your loss. We all loved Cathy and are truly shocked. I know you're grieving, but I wondered if you would take a few minutes to talk with me. Do you have any idea what happened out there last night?"

He stood aside and motioned for her to come in. Dita was surprised. She'd half expected him to shut the door in her face rather quickly, but then, he and Sean had bartended at the BeachDune years ago. And though they'd not been close friends, they were friendly workmates. She was comfortable around him, having waitressed at the bar at the same time, and apparently he was equally at ease with her.

She stepped inside to a trailer-sized living room furnished with an aging leather recliner and a matching love seat. A TV sat kitty-corner across from them as the front window took up most of the other wall space, and a wood stove the other corner. She couldn't see the rest of the cottage. He flopped into the recliner, and she sat down on the couch, placing her bag on the fake wood flooring after she removed her pad and pen.

"We didn't go to the party together," Mike said. "I wasn't expecting her to come. She was supposed to be at the ticket office this morning before the 8 o'clock boat, so she said she wanted to go to bed early. None of us show up for these parties until at least 10 or 11, even later, when people get out of work. But you probably know that, living right by the parking lot, and because you used to go to the parties also." He paused and stood again. "I made some coffee. Want a cup?"

She nodded.

"Milk and sugar?"

"Just milk," she said, relieved that this would not be an antagonistic interview.

The kitchen was behind the living room through a doorway. There was no other opening between the two rooms, so Dita held her next question until he returned bearing two chipped mugs. She wondered if she should feel frightened of him, but she wasn't at all. It was hard to imagine this seemingly mild-mannered large man she once knew, who was now bringing her coffee, as an enraged killer.

"Thanks," she said, as he handed it to her. "What time did you get to the party? Was Cathy there?"

"I got there about 11:30. Cathy and I, we weren't exclusive or anything. I mean, we, I saw other people. I'm not sure about her. When she said she wasn't going to the bonfire, I asked one of the summer girls from the Double Ender to come with me. I never expected Cathy would have changed her mind and be waiting for me there."

"Was she waiting for you?"

He ran his hand through his hair. "She was with a group of girlfriends, the ones she surfs with, and a couple of the guys. I saw her before she saw me, and I tried to stay out of the light so she wouldn't notice me. I mean, I didn't want her to see me with this Jeanne, but then again, she lied to me about staying home, so..."

"Did she lie or change her mind?"

"If she changed her mind, I figured she would have let me know, don't you think?"

"I guess."

"Maybe someone already told you, but when she saw me with Jeanne, she got mad, and we started to fight. She said she was waiting for me, but it didn't look that way to me. One of the surfer guys was hanging really close to her. Anyway, she stalked off, and that was the last I saw of her. I went back to Jeanne for the rest of the party."

"Do you recall what time you were arguing with Cathy?" Dita was trying to establish a timeline.

"No, I was there about a half-hour or so before we ran into each other."

"So, Mike, people told me you were her boyfriend, but you're saying there were no commitments. Were you her boyfriend?" She asked this question as non-confrontationally as possible. She didn't want to make him angry.

Mike let out a long breath of sadness and slowly formed an answer. "Sort of. She didn't want us to be a couple in that way. She said she wasn't sure I was the one, but we did a lot of stuff together. She stayed over here a few nights a week, and we seemed to like each other a lot. I kept hoping."

So it was Cathy who kept the relationship from moving forward. Dita thought that was puzzling, and she sharpened her inquiry a bit. "But not enough to not date when Cathy turned down an evening with you?"

He turned toward Dita and seemed almost to plead with her. "Look, I'm a guy. If I see a chance to have a one-nighter, I take it."

With that, Dita knew why Cathy wouldn't commit to him. He was an island guy, like Harry, and he would probably never be monogamous.

"But you were angry that she might be interested in that surfer guy," Dita said, prodding.

He threw up his hands.

"You didn't follow her in your truck when she stalked off?" Dita asked in the quietest of voices, trying to seem non-confrontational.

"Of course not. You can ask Jeanne if you want. She cleans rooms at the Double Ender. I was with her all night."

His phone dinged then. He picked up the call. "I have to go. The police want me at the station," he said. "I guess they want to give me the third degree next."

"Okay, thanks for your time, and again, I'm really sorry about Cathy. I get that you cared for her a lot," she said. "If you remember anything else, please text me."

He ushered her out, got into his truck, and backed out to the road without offering her a ride.

On her way home, walking and thinking, she decided not to rule him out. Her gut told her he was innocent, though. She would contact Chief Gomez later toward evening to get his statement, but this afternoon she'd head to the Be Fit and try to find this Jeanne in the hotel. Then she called Addie to catch her up. Addie also wondered if Bunny's murder was connected to Cathy's, because if they weren't, it would mean the island's tiny population of 1,000 or so people harbored two murderers, not just one, a prospect that frightened both of them.

FOURTEEN

The Be Fit was deserted. Not even the regulars were around, Dita's mother had gone home, and Sean had Janie laying on a yoga mat while he worked out with weights on the leg machine.

"I guess we should have hoped for rain this weekend," she said, looking around at the empty fitness machines.

"It's always... deserted... right after... lunch," he bleated out between leg pushes.

She was already leaning down, tickling Janie. "Did you hear that? She giggled! Janie giggled."

He set his weights down and climbed off the machine. Dita tickled Janie again, and this time he heard. He grabbed Dita and danced her around in a circle.

"Do you know a Jeanne who works for Teddy here as a chambermaid?" she asked when he stopped.

"Black hair in a ponytail, pretty, young? That one?" he responded. "Comes in here a lot to work out but doesn't hang with anyone."

"Could be her. Mike Palmer says he was with her at the bonfire when Cathy took off down the beach. I want to talk to her."

She picked up Janie, sniffed her bottom to make sure she was not harboring a load, before placing her in the waiting stroller.

"I'll go out to the desk and ask if she's here," she said.

"I think Teddy's hotel manager, Darlene, is on the desk today," Sean said. "By the way, Teddy was telling me about his wedding. Did you know about that?"

"Yeah, didn't I tell you?"

He shrugged. "I don't remember, but now I know."

She smiled, but for sure she'd told him. *Men. Do they ever listen to what we say?* She waved to him, pushed the stroller out of the gym, and proceeded to cross the lobby to the front desk, where she asked Darlene for Jeanne.

The young woman was on the second floor cleaning the hallway. Darlene texted her, and two minutes later she appeared, looking as Sean had described, only not just pretty, strikingly beautiful! Dita realized she would not have liked it if Sean had used the word beautiful. He'd been wise not to tell her that.

Darlene pointed Jeanne to Dita. "She wants to ask you about last night."

Dita watched the young woman stiffen and close her mouth.

"Glad to meet you, Jeanne," Dita said, reaching out to shake hands. "I'm Dita Redmond from the *Island Gale*. I'd just like to talk to you a bit about the bonfire party. I heard you were with Mike Palmer."

"I'm never going to live this down," the girl blurted out. "I didn't know Mike had a girlfriend when he asked me to go to the party with him, or I would have said no. I met him at the Washashore Pub, he seemed nice, and I thought it would be fun to go with a local. I'm new here. Came for this summer job."

It was interesting to Dita that she didn't express sadness or horror over Cathy's death but, instead, put forth a defense for being with Mike. She probably didn't know Cathy, being new here herself, but still, shouldn't her first reaction have been for the girl, not herself?

"Of course, you wouldn't have known," Dita said, smiling and trying to radiate warmth. "I'm not here to berate you for being with Mike. I'm just trying to piece together how and why Cathy died last night. Can you tell me when you got to the bonfire and what happened there?"

"We had dinner first at that restaurant at the dock, the seafood one, and a few drinks afterward. He didn't want to go to the party until eleven-ish, so we got to know each other a bit more before we headed over. When we got to the beach, someone had a playlist going from their truck, and we hung out at the fringe of the crowd dancing to the music. Then I guess he spotted Cathy. At the time, I didn't know who it was, and he left me to go say hello. I started to follow, and he didn't introduce me. She asked who I was, and they started to fight. I don't like that kind of stuff, so I hung back and searched around to see if any of my coworkers were there. I found one and hung with her and her friends until Cathy screamed."

Dita pressed her. "So you weren't with Mike all night?" she asked, because Mike had been quite adamant that he was with Jeanne the whole time.

"No, he ditched me, and I never saw him after that until we all ran over to where Cathy was. He was standing near her saying her name."

"Did he run over there with everyone else, or was his truck there?" Dita asked.

"I don't know. I was upset when I saw what had happened. I stayed until the ambulances and police came, and then I left with the other Double-Ender workers. I haven't seen or heard from Mike since then. The person I had dinner with, I wouldn't have thought, would be capable of running her down, but the guy who had the argument with her was furious. I can say I don't want anything to do with him."

She didn't seem upset, but then, she probably had had a lot of young men – too many even – hovering over her. Dita knew that those beautiful young girls had a lot of difficulty filtering out the ones who liked them as arm candy from the ones who had more depth and cared for them.

"Thanks, Jeanne. I'm sorry you had such an upsetting introduction to Block Island."

"I won't be going to any more late-night parties, that's for sure."

"Don't be surprised if the police contact you. They brought Mike in earlier today."

Dita returned to the Be Fit and called Addie again. "Addie, the summer worker, Jeanne, who was with Mike at the bonfire, says he left her after the argument with Cathy. He says he was with her all night. One of them is lying, and I'd bet it's Mike. Did he have anything to do with Dahlia's real estate company? Did he do any contracting work for her?"

"I don't know," Addie replied. "We'll have to ask Dahlia."

"I'm trying to find a link between the two murders," Dita said. "I'll ask Dahlia, but I'll give her a chance to recover from this first. She was quite fond of Cathy."

"Let me ask Dahlia. I want to help, and you have enough to do with Janie."

Dita was happy Addie volunteered. "Have you heard anything yet? Did the police determine Cathy's death was murder? Last I heard, it was still possibly an accident, a hit and run. Although the way you described the body, I would conclude someone ran her over and then did it again."

"And that would be a hit and rerun, not an accident at all," Addie replied. "You follow up on the official report, and I'll catch Dahlia. Talk to you later."

Sean had been on his phone, too. "That was Teddy," he said. "There's going to be a paddle-out for Cathy. Not sure when yet. The surfers are checking the tides and the winds."

Not being a surfer, Dita had to ask. "What's a paddle-out?"

"Sort of a surfer funeral, a memorial service," Sean said. "Everyone brings their boards and jumps in the water. They form a circle, bring flowers, sing, or pray or both. It's a solemn send-off. It'll probably be across the street from the BeachDune, near baby beach where the surfers always go."

"I guess we'll watch?" she asked.

"We can go in with our boogey boards and be part of it if we want."

"I wonder if my wetsuit even fits. I'm still pouchy from Janie."

"You're not a kangaroo. I'm sure it will fit."

"We'll see," she said, and turned to her laptop to do some work.

She noticed a new email from Mary, her editor, with an attachment. Cathy's parents had left information for an obituary with an announcement for the paddle-out, and they wanted someone to write it for them, and Mary wanted Dita to do it ASAP so they could run it in this week's newspaper. Dita read through the information. She hadn't known Cathy was born in Ohio. Dita wondered what had brought her here, an out-of-the-way island, especially year-round. A boyfriend, now an ex? Word of a friend? Or maybe surfing, though there were better places to surf, especially in winter.

FIFTEEN

June is wedding month on Block Island, and this year was no exception. Everyone was busy working with the wedding tourist trade from Wednesday mornings through Sunday nights, and even then, the cleanups continued. There were huge weddings and small weddings, ceremonies in the churches, the hotels and restaurants, rites on the beach, and others under tents. Relatives and guests filled the hotels and rental houses, some even for the entire week of their event. The wedding planners were busy, photographers were busy, caterers were busy, and flower arrangers were busy. Realtors were busy cleaning houses and fielding problems. Even the Be Fit overflowed with exercisers. The ferries were booked solid. The buzzword for June weekends was BUSY, or maybe, more appropriately, MONEY. Weddings brought millions of dollars to the island.

Cathy's paddle-out needed to be in June before the larger influx of tourists in July. Her friends planned it for a Tuesday, the one day of the week with few tourists and wedding chores, and therefore the day most workers had time off. They chose one when the tides were right, and the weather forecast was good.

When that Tuesday arrived, it turned out to be one of those rare golden days that make islanders realize why they chose to live on a rocky clutch of land surrounded by miles of often turbulent sea. The sun beamed down, diamonds of light danced upon the water, and the breeze was sweet, as though someone had whispered, "Be good for Cathy." It seemed warm enough to swim in just a bathing suit, but only if you didn't know the ocean would be in the low sixties, still not over the cold winter chill, so everyone looked like shiny black seals in their wetsuits.

All the island surfers turned out, and those who didn't surf either jumped in anyway or lined up along the beach to watch. It seemed the only one missing was Cathy. Even Mike Palmer was there, as was Josh Martel. Dita realized she had not followed up with her second interview of Josh, but then he had not been charged, and neither had Mike.

"Lack of evidence," Dita whispered to Addie. Dita noted the two suspects were not together. Did they even know each other? Was there any connection between the two murders? It was a hundred-year event for anyone to be killed on the island, or it was before Bunny and Cathy, and Joel, of course.

Cathy's brother came, suited up, ready to surf. Her parents, he'd told her friends, were still in their car parked along the road, watching. They'd all ferried over, reluctant, because they didn't want to be on the island where their daughter had been murdered, but they came to try to move the investigation along. Dita wondered if there'd be trouble when they spotted Mike. Addie leaned over and wondered about that aloud to Dita, saying she hoped there wasn't any trouble so no one got hurt. Dita knew she meant she didn't want to have to spend the evening at the medical center, and she understood.

At 6 o'clock, Father Dupree arrived, dressed in his robes. Cathy's parents had contacted him to do a short ceremony, and they joined him when he reached the beach. He was new to the island, having been sent to get the parishioners in line, the parishioners who lived together in unholy matrimony and apart in divorce, some with new paramours, and even engaged in unsanctioned practices such as birth control and abortion. The island's congregation was out of control, and the holies on the mainland wanted to round them back up. At least that was everyone's unofficial belief.

Although Father Dupree seemed to be young, almost no one looked critically at the priest as they would have anyone else arriving on the island. Those few who did noticed how handsome he was despite his priestly vestments, and they whispered about it behind the congregation's back. Addie told Dita that Dahlia was smitten, and some of the older women who'd stopped going to church when services were led by the dour Father Maloney had begun to attend again.

Cathy's parents left their car to join the priest. Dita noticed they both looked tired. Her mother had dark circles under her eyes. Her father had several days of stubble on his face. The priest motioned for everyone to come close, and he spoke about the solemnity of the occasion, of Cathy's horrific demise.

"We are here to honor the life of this young woman, who was beloved by almost everyone whose path she crossed. She was an honored member of this community and was taken far too early, in the most despicable way. She will be missed." Cathy's parents moved closer to him, and they prayed together, her mother holding an armful of flowers. The priest spoke of the tides as a symbol of the life cycle. The paddle-out would be a fitting tribute, he told them. When he finished his prayers and they said their amens, to the astonishment of the crowd, he dropped his robe. The good father was suited up for the paddle-out just like the others. A church choir boy ran to him with his surfboard.

"Are we ready?" the good priest called, swinging his incense container to bless the swim before he took hold of his board.

"We are!" the crowd shouted back.

Dita heard Teddy, she was sure it was he, shout, "Amen!" Cathy's brother threw his board into the water to lead them. His mother laid her armful of flowers onto it, and he pushed out to sea, the others behind him. Dita ran into the water past Addie, who plodded along step by step, unbalanced by the cold-water gear she'd never worn before. Strands of red curls stuck out from the hood like tendrils of an anemone.

Even Danny, who'd begun surfing lessons the previous summer, and Tuffy, who didn't need lessons or a board to surf, joined in.

When she hit the water, Dita felt like she was in an ice cube tray. Her fingers and toes were numb in no time, even though she had the whole getup like the surfers and everyone else did: a suit, booties, gloves, and a hood, and her hair completely tucked in. She decided never to try this again until the water warmed up in July. Still, she waded out until she was in deeper, and then she stretched out on her boogie board and began to paddle further into the sea with everyone else. She felt a sharp shock of Arctic cold as the icy water trickled into the wetsuit at her ankles, wrists, and neck. It was at those points that the gloves, booties, and hood weren't connected. The water seeped in and formed a layer of cold water between her skin and the neoprene. She wished she had a dry-suit underneath like some of the surfers, but in seconds her body heat warmed the water, and the wetsuit did its job, at least for a little while. Now she, Dita, Sean, Teddy, and Tuffy were swimming together. They linked to the others to form a circle around Cathy's brother, who spread the flowers over the water: red roses and yellow daffodils, and lastly, blue forget-me-nots picked from one of the marshes. They floated with the current. Tuffy chased the roses, retrieving them to Cathy's brother, and then Danny. Members of the island's Universal Choir started singing a song that Cathy loved, and they all joined in. The ferry had sailed from its berth to the outlying water, and as the singing faded, the captain blew the horn three times as a final sendoff for Cathy.

Despite the wetsuit, Dita was totally numb. She caught Addie's eye, and the two of them left the circle to return to shore. Dita positioned herself next to her board to wait for a wave large enough to ride but not too big to handle, then rolled onto her boogey board and let herself relax for the ride. She so loved flying up and over the crest of the wave until she crashed and scraped along the shallows. All else disappeared as she went with the thrill, and, she thought to herself, when she was splayed out unceremoniously on the sand, "I'm back. I'm me again. My body's mine again!"

Tuffy returned to shore when she did, landing next to her, but with much more grace. He spread out on his back, his face turned toward her as wet dog and human shared their joy. Until, that is, he stood up to dry off, shaking water drops mixed with sand and sending Dita running.

Then Sean, who'd landed down the beach, was there, whispering in Dita's ear, "Maybe it's time to learn to surf." All Dita craved at this moment was a towel.

The cosmos kicked Addie in the butt, so to speak, landing her right next to Mel, who she hadn't even known was there, jolting her out of the reverie of the ride. Instead of taking a moment to gather herself and rip off her hood so she could push her wet hair from her face, she jumped up and tried to run, but he shouted, "We need to talk," grabbed her wrist, and attempted to yank her back.

"Let go of me," she protested, feeling like a flounder on a hook.

"We need to talk," Mel shouted again, not letting go.

Addie broke loose and saw Harry watching, sleek in his skin-tight wetsuit. She held up her hand to stop him from rescuing her; then, like a robot in heat, reached up and ripped the hood off so she could fluff her hair. Like Dita, what she needed was a towel. When she looked back, Harry was standing right next to Mel, blocking his path toward her, arm on Mel's shoulder, deep in conversation. Then Addie saw Teddy with Rachel, Caroline, and Dahlia, and she streaked over to them at a pace she normally didn't adopt. The three women had watched from the beach, keepers of the supersized beach towels that would warm their families when they came out of the water. When Addie caught up with them, they were debating whether they were too old to surf.

Teddy was telling them they could indeed do so and was offering lessons. Rachel wrapped Addie's shaking body in a towel. Dita joined her, and they grabbed their clothes to change in Teddy's van.

The BeachDune had food ready for them, a picnic on the beach. Some of the surfers changed in the vans that filled the parking lot, peeling off their suits and throwing on shorts and tops. Then they all returned to toast Cathy. Even Father Dupree came, still in his wetsuit, joining in a tipple with Cathy's parents. Addie found the food table and chose a lamb chop lollypop to quiet her rumbling stomach. Dita watched and approved.

Soon Cathy's father spoke. "Thank you all for this circle of love for our daughter.

We appreciate how much you cared for her, as we also did. Now we ask anyone who was on the beach that night and saw or heard anything to come forward to the Block Island Police. And even if you weren't there, if you've heard rumors, whether you believe them or not, please pass them on to the police."

His face was covered with tears, his voice filled with rage. "We need to discover who so brutally crushed our daughter underneath their truck, ran over her and backed up and ran over her again, and left her in anguish to die. We can't let this go unpunished." Her mother, leaning on her husband for support, added, "Please help us. If you were a friend of Cathy's, help us find her murderer."

Chief Gomez, still in his wetsuit as he had stayed in the water the longest, reiterated their pleas. The crowd shouted back at him. They all wanted whoever had done this rounded up before July.

Dita searched the faces in the crowd, hoping to see someone's memory spark. She found Mike among his friends, but his expression was impassive. He was still her prime suspect, and she was sure he was the chief's. Josh was now almost off the list. She didn't see Jeanne, but she wasn't surprised. She bet Jeanne had already left the island.

"Time for you to be a mom again," a voice crooned in her ear. Caroline stood next to her, Janie wrapped in her arms. "I can't feed her."

And Dita was reminded that her body was not totally her own, not yet.

"Thanks, Mom, for letting me do this today. You know, I was anxious about you moving here, wondering if it would work, but now I am so happy you're here." Dita reached out to hug her mother and took Janie back. "By the way, how was your date?"

Caroline shrugged her shoulders. "So, so. If he asks again, I guess I'll go, but no biggie."

Dita could tell she wasn't over-enthused with Artie, or was his name

Carter? "I see. Meh, hah? Well. It's time to go home, isn't it? I'd better find Sean and Tuffy again. They seem to have wandered off."

"Check the table with the food," Caroline said. "Your guy always seems to drift there. And your friend Addie."

SIXTEEN

Maria, the owner of the BeachDune, promised Danny a few bucks if he cleared the beach with them, so Addie drove home from the paddle-out alone. When she arrived, Mel's SUV was idling by the steps and he was sitting in it, apparently waiting for her. Then she remembered. She'd locked the house, something they never used to do. But now that she lived alone with Danny, she felt it was important.

He got out of the vehicle as she pulled up in back of him. She noticed again how much stockier he'd grown since he walked out on her. His new lady must feed him a lot of carbs. The weight didn't become him. She had stopped letting Mel stay at the house when he worked his weeks on the island. Apparently, he didn't have a key anymore, and that, she thought, was a good thing.

"You locked me out," he complained, an undertone of anger in his voice.

"You don't live here anymore, remember?" Addie said, slamming her car door. "Just why are you here?"

"You wouldn't talk to me at the paddle-out, so I had to come over."

"Hmmf," she growled. "We have lawyers for those discussions, but since you're here, take your stuff with you. It's all boxed up in the basement."

"Is it?" he asked, now leaning against the truck's fender, his arms folded across his chest in a gesture of defiance.

Addie wasn't going to be bullied. She couldn't help comparing his boxy build to Harry's sleek frame. Perhaps she was completely over Mel.

"Yes, really," she said. "It's time for us both to move on, although I heard you already have." She threw him a disdainful glance, wondering if he was doing the same thing she had just done, compared her to his new love. She didn't even know what the woman looked like. She felt his eyes drill into hers. It was a steely gaze. She thought she'd never seen that look from him before, and she realized how far out of his orbit she'd fallen.

After a pause that made Addie feel quite uncomfortable, he said, "So my lawyer tells me he got a call from yours with some demands, like shared custody may be off the table since I've, in their language, strayed."

"As if you haven't," he added, his voice as chilly as the water during the paddle-out.

Thank goodness she hadn't let Harry into her life yet. "So this is what you wanted to talk about. Search the house," she said. "You won't find anyone or anyone else's belongings but mine and Danny's. You, on the other hand, have been living with someone all the while I thought we might get back together."

Addie's face flushed. She felt the beet red creep up from her neck to her hairline. It was hard for her to believe that this man who'd been her lover and friend and father to their child, who'd been so comforting when her brother was killed, could be so cold, so hateful to her. He didn't acknowledge that he was cohabitating.

He cleared his throat and spoke in a flat voice as though he was reading from a teleprompter. "I'll be leaving my job here in a month. I'm full time on the mainland now, so I won't be bothering you anymore. Like I suggested before, the house is yours if you don't make me pay any more of the mortgage. I did the numbers, and over the years, it'll even out."

They'd both contributed to the down payment and the monthly payments, but by turning the house over to her, he didn't need to worry about repairs and maintenance. She knew he'd done the math. That was, after all, part of his planning job. Was that a good deal for her, taking responsibility for the whole mortgage? Once again, she considered taking a roommate to help pay for the place. Without Mel to help carry it, she'd need someone else, or she would have to take Rachel's suggestion to sell it and move to the cottage. She needed to run the idea of moving by Danny first. He might object.

"And Danny, your son?" she purposely used the pronoun 'your' to emphasize that the boy was not to be pawned off like the house.

"Danny can come visit me when the lawyers finish working out the custody agreement."

"You mean Danny can visit you and what's-her-name. I'm not happy about that." She started up the steps, and when she got to the door, she turned back to him. "Come to the basement door. I'll let you in to get your junk. I think it'll all fit in your SUV."

She unlocked her door, went in, and relocked it from the inside. She didn't want him to come into the house, her house. She shuddered, thinking that she'd been intimate with him, coddled him in bed, cooked his favorite dishes, given him a son, carried all the duties when he was off-island at his other job, and not known who he really was. She decided not to tell him she'd probably sell the house once it was hers. It was worth far more than they'd paid when they bought it. She didn't want to split the profits with him. Keeping the money would be her revenge. She went downstairs and opened the basement door for him. She didn't want to jump on his offer too fast and make him wonder if it was too much in her favor and change his mind.

"I have to think about the house before I give you an answer," she said, trying to look calm. "I'll let you know. And if you agree to visitations every other weekend and two weeks in the summer, we can sign the divorce papers as soon as they are drawn up. I had thought we would share custody and be flexible, but you know what? I don't want Danny spending a lot of time in your house with the woman who broke up our marriage."

As he started down the steps, she added, "You can check the box on the feelings form that says 'Addie is bitter.'"

She turned her back on him and stomped away. "I'll be upstairs. Text me when you're done." She was glad Danny was helping at the Beach-Dune instead of witnessing their hatred for each other, because that was what had happened to their relationship.

A half-hour later, Addie watched him drive off. She was surprised to feel relief that he would soon be out of her life, and she was glad she'd drawn a line with Harry until the papers were signed. She went upstairs to her bedroom and glanced over at Dita's house. She saw Mel pull into their driveway. He was not gone. What was he doing there? Did he think they'd still be friends with him after what he did to her? She saw Sean come out the front door. They stood on the deck talking, and then Mel went back to the truck and drove off. Addie checked her watch. The last boat should be leaving soon. She hoped Mel would be on it. She waited a few minutes, and then she called Dita.

"What did Mel want?" Addie asked, trying not to sound demanding.

"To see if Sean would buy his SUV," Dita responded. "They were friends, you know. He could have stopped just to say hello to Sean, although I think Sean is almost as hurt as you that he's leaving the island totally."

"Are you buying his SUV?" Addie asked, hoping they wouldn't. She really didn't want to see it going by anymore, reminding her of Mel.

"No, we're not. Of course not, Addie."

"Good."

"Why was he at your house? Were you expecting him? I noticed his SUV was loaded," Dita said.

"He came to bother me, but since you and Harry helped me box up his stuff, I used the opportunity to make him clear it all out. He was angry. He doesn't like my lawyer's divorce agreement," Addie explained, "but I do, and since he wants to get rid of me as fast as possible -- that much is quite evident -- he's going to sign."

"You know we're on your side in this," Dita said.

"Yep, I do," Addie choked back a few tears. "And thank you. This has been so hard, but I think I'm finally getting through it. I'll talk to you later."

"Wait, Addie, remember, um, we're working on solving these murders together? Did you happen to notice if Josh Martel and Mike Palmer hung out together at all at the paddle-out?"

"No, I never saw them near each other. Josh left early, right after the paddle-out," Addie recalled.

"I think it's time we made some progress," Dita said. "Don't you? I'll have a sit down with the chief again for another article. I know you're going to speak with Dahlia, but maybe you can also check around with your patients when you see them. We don't need victim number three."

"Don't even think that," Addie gasped. "Why would you?"

"Because I never thought there would be two, or even one. You did say you'd help."

"I did, and I will," Addie said.

"And I am going to have another sit down with Mike, only this time I'll bring Sean along, not that I believe Mike did it, but he was with Cathy enough to know if someone was hanging around her or threatening her. We just have to jog his memory."

"That's a good idea," Addie said. "I'm sorry I've been distracted. My mind has been on my divorce. I've made my decisions, though, and the papers should come through soon."

Dita couldn't resist needling her. "And soon you can have fun with Harry."

Addie hung up.

SEVENTEEN

Dita and Sean were just sitting down for breakfast when Dita's phone buzzed. Her mother was texting, "Call me."

Dita was annoyed. "Why didn't she just call instead?" she griped, adjusting the knot in her penguin robe, hoping her mother hadn't changed her mind about watching Janie this morning.

Sean said that if Caroline had called, Dita still would have been annoyed. That was the nature of her relationship with her mother. She gave him a look that could only mean now she was angry with him, and she did as Caroline had asked. She called her. "What's up, Mom?"

Sean whispered, "Speaker."

"Mom, I'm putting you on speaker phone. Sean's being nosy. He wants to listen."

"It's okay," Caroline said. "Dita, you'll never guess who approached me when I got home."

Dita was not in the mood for a guessing game. "Either Josh Martel or the ghost of Cary Grant."

"Oh, how you mock me. My neighbors! They invited me to dinner. Dita, they are fabulously wealthy. You never told me that some of the wealthiest people in America come to Block Island."

"Are they that wealthy? And no, I never told you because I never cared," Dita said, surprised that her mother was so easily impressed. "Obviously, you do."

"It's not every day you get a chance to know someone like that, except, of course, for Sean's Teddy, but he's a genius, not the same as the landed rich and famous."

Sean was very obviously trying to stifle himself. Dita could not believe this was her mother.

"You sound like you're from Podunk, Nebraska, Mom, instead of Milford, CT, which I might remind you is part of that tony Fairfield County, one of the richest in the country," she said. "We're eating breakfast. We're dropping Janie off with you soon, remember?"

The instant she clicked off the call, Sean laughed out loud. "Fabulously wealthy," he mimicked his mother-in-law, wagging his shaggy eyebrows.

Dita was amused too. "I never knew she was so shallow," she said.

"I wouldn't say shallow, just very vulnerable, or suggestible right now," he said, careful not to say anything negative about Caroline. "You'd better keep an eye on her and keep her from investing too much with them. We don't know where their wealth came from."

Dita agreed. She knew he was right. "And that guy Artie, short for Carter," she rolled her eyes. "He's been sniffing around her."

"Your mother, whether you know it or not, is still a catch," Sean said.

"Really?" she asked. She'd never thought anyone would look at her mother as a possible partner except, of course, for her father. Caroline was, to Dita, just her mom.

Sean nodded. "Like mother, like daughter," he said, and he reached out for her.

"Uh, uh. Not now. We're going to see Mike today, remember?"

Mike Palmer was evicted from his cottage when the landlords learned he was a suspect in Cathy's murder. He'd had to find other digs. He now lived in the attic apartment of a house atop a hill, just past the business district. It was best described as a house in shambles. Once a grand dame, the house belonged to the members of a family that had left the island

and were suing each other for ownership. Meanwhile, no one attended to the upkeep. It was painted white like the old hotels, but the exterior was peeling and decaying. One outer wall was blackened, a remnant of a gas propane explosion at the house next door. It had occurred when a workman took a break on the upper deck and lit a cigarette, unaware of a gas leak.

The former grand dame had been divided into apartments which were rented out to island workers. They packed themselves into every corner like plush carnival animals stuffed together in cubbies. Given the shortage of available rentals for workers and year-rounders on the island, the tenants were, if not happy to be there, relieved to have a roof, albeit there was a mishmash of people with varying housekeeping habits and the landlords never fixed anything.

Dita shuddered as she went into the front hall. "I hope I'm not smelling dead bodies."

Sean sniffed. "Dead something. Maybe mice."

"This is like the House of Usher," she said.

"We're lucky we had a down payment saved and only had to live here a short time," Sean said, reminding her that they too had sought refuge in the house. "Seems much worse now, though."

"Amen to that," she agreed. There were times when they were totally in sync and this was one of them. Living stuffed into almost a cubicle with no sound-proofing was far from ideal. They climbed the worn steps to the third floor and knocked. No one answered. Sean cracked the door open and called to Mike.

"Not home, I guess," Sean said, shutting the door. "I'm good with that. Let's get out of here. This place is creepy."

"His truck was outside," Dita pointed out. "He might be sleeping."

"If he is, he might not want us to wake him up. He works at night at the BeachDune, remember?"

"Maybe we should have a look around," she suggested again. "I could go in and you can be my lookout."

"Not. You can't just go in and go through things. Maybe he walked somewhere. He might come back."

"He might be sleeping, Sean. We should at least try to wake him up." She reopened the door and shouted for him again.

"No, definitely not home," Sean said, pulling her away from the door. "We're not Bonnie and Clyde. I'm not going in if he's not home, and I'm not your lookout."

She thought Sean was being too careful. "You're no fun. I should have come alone.

Please, please, just be lookout and let me go in for a minute," she pleaded.

"What are you looking for? Cathy was run over by a truck. The murder weapon was the truck. What could you find?" he asked.

"Just in case he doesn't hear us. I don't know what I'd be looking for besides him. Go downstairs and let me know if he comes back. Go." She gave him a gentle shove.

Sean grumbled. "This cannot be good. Be quick."He went down the steps and waited on the porch. She went inside. The front room, a combination kitchen/sitting room, was not very neat. Dirty dishes filled the sink. Grinder wrappers were strewn on the couch. The floor was sticky. She hadn't planned to touch anything, but now she was too grossed out anyway. Compared to the shipshape manner he'd kept the cottage, this was a disaster. Obviously, he was depressed. She moved to the bedroom, the only other room, as quickly as she could. The bed was unmade, but Mike wasn't in it. A bra hung over a straight-backed chair. Cathy's? Jeanne's? A mess of laundry piled up across the floor.

Dita's phone chirped. Sean.

"He's coming up the street. Get down here fast," his voice shrilled. "Do you hear me? Get downstairs. He's almost here."

"I just started to look around. Can't you delay him?"

"No."

Dita could hear panic in his voice. Why didn't she feel it? She realized she felt safe because Sean was there, and he was way stronger than Mike. It didn't occur to her that he did not want to fight with Mike.

"Dita, get down here."

Now Sean sounded angry and panicked. Dita sighed. He wasn't very adventurous. She ran from Mike's apartment and zipped down the stairs, landing outside just as Mike approached Sean.

"Mike," Sean said. "We were looking for you."

Dita felt Mike's cold stare. That didn't work, she thought.

Mike belted out, "What do you want? I already talked to you, Dita. I said everything I know about Cathy. I don't want to talk about her anymore. It's bad enough the police questioned me, and then her parents gave me a hard time. I lost my housing and had to move to this dump. I can't put up with this anymore. Go away before I lose my temper."

Dita thought he already had.

Sean cleared his throat. "I," he said with emphasis, "wanted to talk to you, Mike. It's not about Cathy. I wondered if you could help out at the Be Fit desk. It's getting hard to find anyone who isn't already working three jobs. I thought you might have a couple of afternoons or evenings you could work for me. And also, I know you're good at fixing things. I need someone I can call if there's a problem with the exercise machines and I can't fix it by myself."

Dita thought Mike looked surprised. The anger in his eyes faded, but only for a few seconds as he seemed to be thinking.

"I don't have a lot of time this summer," Mike said. "I can come help you out with a problem, maybe, once in a while, but I already have prepping and bartending for Marie at the BeachDune, I drive the garbage truck a couple mornings a week, and do the unloading for the Gyp Grocery. I think you already knew I'm pretty busy, so no, I can't work your desk. I'm not your guy." Then he demanded, "And what made you ask?"

Dita could hear he was fuming again.

"Me," Dita said, thinking as fast as she could. "I noticed you were pretty broken up about Cathy, so I thought if we kept you busy, you might not dwell on what happened."

"I'm fine. Don't need your help," Mike said as he pushed open the front door and stomped up the stairs.

"That was too close," Sean said. "Don't do anything like this again. You hear? He was this close to hauling out and punching me."

Dita felt Sean's temper now. "But Sean, yes, okay, he almost lost it. He was always known as mild-mannered, but look how quick his temper rose and he almost attacked us. I think he could have killed her."

"All the more reason to stay away from him. Hear me? Stay away."

They retreated down the front steps. They hadn't been able to ask the questions she'd prepared. Dita was disappointed. All they'd done was get Mike angry and Sean upset.

"Look, The Sisters is open," she said, trying to calm Sean down. "Sandwich?"

The Two Sisters was a summertime island favorite. It was the tiniest cottage, like a child's playhouse, with a grassy yard surrounding it. Inside, there was a back burner and a counter with storage below. The refrigerator was outside, as were all the tables, picnic tables, some with triangular sails strung between trees for shade.

"Let me get some breaths of fresh air before I think about food. I was hungry before we went into that hallway."

Dita waited, but it was only a few minutes before Sean started across the street to the The Sisters. Sean, as Dita's mother had pointed out, was always ready to eat. They entered through the front door, placed their orders to the "sister" manning the counter, and then exited out the back. While they waited, they chose an empty picnic table. When their names were called, Sean waved, and the sister brought the basket of food outside to them.

Dita handed Sean a bag of the potato chips that came with their orders. He had already taken two giant bites, and his grinder was half gone, while Dita was still unwrapping hers.

"Why did you agree to go with me?" Dita asked. "I know you didn't want to."

"I can't believe you asked me that," Sean said. "I didn't want you going alone, and I knew I couldn't stop you. Dita, I'm worried about you getting involved in these murder investigations. This isn't a case of graft or a guest house cheating the tourists. Someone is killing people." His voice grew deeper and louder as he reached the end of the last sentence. His eyebrows almost reached his hairline.

"I know that, Sean."

He glared at her, and she squirmed on her bench. "It could be you, Dita, and I don't want it to be you. Karl called me all worried, and I agree with him. Why do you feel compelled to put yourself in danger, especially now that we have Janie to think about?"

The fact that he inserted Janie into his argument made it difficult for Dita to counter, but that was him fighting dirty.

"I've thought about that, too," she admitted. "I want justice for Cathy, and I guess for that woman, Bunny, too. Addie was so upset after they brought Bunny's body to the medical center. A poor defenseless grandmother, she had called her. She said she understood why I pursued her brother's case and wanted to help find Bunny's killer. I said I'd help, but Sean, doesn't it bother you that we have a murderer, maybe two, walking among us?"

He stopped eating for a second. "Of course. That's why I don't want you in pursuit. Report on something else. Write up some houses, or just work in the fitness center. You don't need to be a reporter."

"Of course I don't have to, but I love being a reporter, and this is the kind of story that I love."

"Maybe you don't care enough about us," Sean retorted, glaring at her. He fought dirty again by leaving her no chance for a reply. "I need to get back to the fitness center. I'll drop you home."

Dita rewrapped her unfinished sandwich in the paper it had come in and took it with her.

Was what Sean said true? Did she care more about her investigations than her family? Surely he couldn't be serious. He was walking away at a clip, almost running away from her. He said nothing more as she joined him in the truck.

He started it up and drove the short distance in pregnant silence. He pulled into the yard and put his hand on her arm.

"Don't be angry. I'm just worried," he explained.

"But you implied I don't care about you and Janie."

"I didn't really mean that. I just, how would we get along if something happened to you?" He leaned over so he could hug her, as much as one can when separated by a center console in bucket seats. "We love you."

Dita's eyes teared up as she stepped out and watched him drive off.

Addie spent her day at work in the clinic. She didn't have to query her patients about Cathy's murder. They were all talking about it and asking her questions. Still, none of them had seen the truck that ran Cathy over, and no one could pinpoint whether Mike Palmer was missing at the time. Addie was disappointed. She had hoped someone had seen something.

When she had arrived on the scene that night, Mike Palmer was bent over Cathy, yet no one recalled seeing him head over there. They remembered the argument the two had had, but only that Cathy walked away from the fight and didn't return. That was not unusual for one of those bonfire parties. People drifted in and out all night.

Was Mike with Cathy at the scene because he had killed her? But his truck wasn't there.

Could Mike have run her down and driven off the beach using the exit by the BeachDune? Would he have had enough time to drive back down Corn Neck Rd., park in the lot by Dita's house and hoof it up the beach to her before the rest of the crowd caught on? Doubtful, as everyone said Cathy's scream and the sound of the truck engine had sent them racing toward her. Unless someone had been in the truck with him, Mike couldn't have done it. Addie also wondered why Mike hadn't called 911 when he found her. Sean's call was the only one logged in to the station. She or Dita needed to ask him why.

Then to her surprise, almost as though she'd conjured him up, who stepped through the clinic door with an injury but Mike himself? He'd cut himself on a mandolin while slicing up cabbage for coleslaw at the BeachDune, where he still worked in the kitchen helping to prep food as well as tending bar. His hand was wrapped in a dishtowel, bleeding profusely. Addie wondered why he'd been cutting by hand instead of using a food processor, but then she remembered how particular Marie was about the size of the shreds.

Doctor Bennett took him right in and Addie attended, handing him the sutures and bandages when needed.

"How'd you do that?" the doctor asked.

Mike told him how distracted he'd been since Cathy's death. "It's not just that she's gone. It's how she was killed," he said. "And everyone, the cops, her parents, seems to think I did it. Dita keeps bugging me too, like I'm her only story right now. She and Sean were at the house waiting for me this morning. In fact, I think they were in my flat. The door wasn't shut. I was distracted today, and I cut myself."

Addie stood by as the doctor worked and Mike talked. She watched Mike's face and searched for signs he was lying, a change of color, a slight upturn of his mouth, an alteration in the original story he'd told. But there was nothing she could detect. She actually felt a bit sorry for him. Maybe he wasn't guilty.

As he slipped off the examining table to his feet, ready to leave when Dr. Bennett was done, Addie asked the questions she'd been holding in. "Mike, after you and Cathy argued, did you see her leave the party with somebody else? The story from everyone is that you both were angry. Was she with another guy?"

"No," he said. "She disappeared into the dark, but I didn't see anyone else go with her. I wasn't jealous, if that's what you're implying. If anyone was jealous, it was her because I was with Jeanne. Like I told the cops, I didn't kill her. I was at the bonfire when everyone heard her screaming. I ran toward her and got there first, is all."

Addie didn't want to rile him, so she framed the more important question carefully. "Did you call 911?"

He replied immediately, "Of course I called."

She did not confront his lie by telling him she knew he hadn't. She watched him leave, and then unpinned her cap, washed her hands, and left also. He was still in his truck, talking or texting on his phone. She got into her car and called Dita to tell her that Mike had lied. It would soon be all over the island that Mike was wearing a big bandage on his hand anyway, so she didn't feel she was breaking his privacy.

"Sean and I went over to his house. I wanted to reinterview him," Dita said, and she related their encounter with him. "I still suspect him."

"He's pulling out. Maybe I'll follow him just to see where he's going," Addie said.

Dita tried to discourage her. "I don't think that's a good idea. He almost came to blows with Sean this morning."

Addie was adamant, so Dita just cautioned her. "Be careful. Not too close so he spots you."

"I know how to do this, Dita. I watch TV too," Addie retorted, a bit annoyed.

"Of course," Dita said. "Keep your phone on and I'll stay on the line. Which way did he go?"

"He's heading down Payne Road, not toward home. He's driving with one hand, you know.

The other one's all wrapped."

"I've had my own run-ins with a mandolin," Dita said.

"Yes, I know. I helped bandage you up, remember?"

"Oh yes, I do, Nurse Addie. By the way, take your cap off so he doesn't spot you in his mirror, though I don't know which is more identifiable, your cap or that red hair."

"I'll have you know I'm wearing a scarf, and I'm quite far behind him. Wait. He's stopping."

Addie stopped, too. She pulled over in case anyone else was coming, but the road was clear.

"He's at the Taylor's house. He beeped his horn."

"The Taylors? They're not even here yet," Dita said.

"Maybe they're renting it to someone," Addie suggested. Then she was excited. "Dita, a young woman just ran out of the house to the truck. I don't know who she is—black hair, and I would say beautiful, yes, not pretty, but beautiful."

"Medium height?" Dita asked.

"Yes."

"Sounds like Jeanne. So she hasn't left the island after all," Dita said.

"The one he was with at the party? Oops, he's on the move again," Addie said. "And if he's distracted, it's not over Cathy. Jeanne just leaned over and gave him a big smacker on the lips. He's a liar."

"So is she. I thought she said she wasn't seeing him again. I wonder where they're going."

"Keep following them, Addie."

Payne Road was a long stretch, unpaved in places, and even the paved parts were deeply rutted from island storms. It was one of those back roads with few houses and nothing else, so it didn't rank high on the town's repair list. Addie turned right at the end of the road, just as Mike had. She trailed him at a distance until she noticed he was circling back toward the medical center.

"Is he bleeding again?" she wondered aloud.

But then, as he started to climb the hill toward the school and the medical center, he pulled alongside the road to park right before he got to Dita's mother's house.

"Dita, he's almost at Caroline's!"

"At Bernard's?"

"Yes."

The two exited the truck and, hand in hand, knocked on Bernard's door, then entered the dwelling.

Dita wondered what he was doing there. "My mother said they invited her to dinner. I forget which night."

"If they don't come out soon, I'll have to leave. I can't wait forever, Dita."

"That's okay. Go home. Now we know Jeanne lied to me, too. She's still here, and she's still seeing Mike, and he lied to you. I wonder if the two of them teamed up to kill Cathy. But why?"

An hour later, Addie was home prepping green beans for supper at Dita and Sean's, snipping off the ends and chopping them into shorter sections, she heard a truck pull into the yard. Her heart began to race with expectation. Was it Harry? She was so sure she didn't even look out the window. She still had her knife in hand as she rushed to answer the knock on her door. She opened it, and there was Mike Palmer, bandaged hand and all. His face was a menacing scowl.

"Is something wrong, Mike? Is your hand bleeding through the bandage?" she asked, concerned he might need help. "Shall I look at it again?"

"No, nothing's wrong with it except it hurts like hell. I'm here because I want to know why you followed me before." His legs were splayed across the doorframe, and he leaned forward, hulking over her, almost touching her, his face purpling with fury.

Addie felt her knees weaken. She stood there, trembling, her mouth agape, her heart still pounding, but with fear, not expectation. She gripped the hilt of the knife tighter and concocted a lie, that she'd been concerned he might start to bleed again, but knew instantly it was too flimsy to use. Mike backed off a step or two. She began to breathe again.

"I don't know why you followed me. Don't ever tail me again," he said in his low growl. "I know people think I killed Cathy, but it wasn't me."

He stared down at her. "That doesn't mean I couldn't hurt anyone else."

Then he turned and stomped down the stairs, yanked open the truck's door. He left rubber as he sped away. She heard the vehicle bouncing as he flew through the driveway ruts toward Corn Neck Road.

Addie was still shaking moments later when Danny came into the kitchen. "Who was that, Mom? Mike?"

"No one," she said, trying to pull herself together in front of him.

He started to protest, but she gave him her Big Nurse look, the one she normally used with her cap on, and he shrugged and went back to his video game. But if she thought he forgot, she was wrong. Later that evening when they had brought the green beans and salad to Dita's to add to the fish Sean had bought from "Artie" Carter that afternoon, Danny brought up Mike Palmer's visit; or, as he put it, Mike's scary visit. That boy on the cusp of adolescence addressed Sean directly as he told his version of what had happened. As she listened, Addie realized he'd been there spying from the corner of the staircase the entire time.

Dita felt Sean's eyes drilling into her, and she knew he was conveying, *Now do you see why I told you not to mess with Mike by yourself?* He turned to Addie and asked, "Do you want me to pay him a visit?" Then added, "On second thought, I'll bring Karl with me."

Addie was horrified. Might that make it worse? She wouldn't be safe anywhere if Mike thought she'd sent the police after him, so she said no. But Dita knew Sean would go regardless of whether Addie said yes or no.

"Don't, please don't," Addie pleaded. "He'll really be furious if he thinks I sent the cops after him. He was brutally clear about me staying away from him. Dita, don't let him do that. I wouldn't have even told you."

Danny piped up again. "Sean, she had the paring knife behind her back the whole time, ready to use it."

Sean's eyebrows raised. Dita asked why she didn't grab a carving knife.

"I was prepping the beans. It's plenty sharp," Addie said. "And Danny, enough about it already."

"I think Danny's done a good job. Don't worry kid, we'll take care of this," Sean told him.

"We'll let him know we're furious that he would threaten your mom like that."

Addie pushed curls from her forehead, stood up, and leaned her hands on the table. "I'm telling all of you, back off. I'll handle this myself. I don't need protection. That little knife would've sliced open his bandage and reopened his wound. He'd have bled all over. If he thought it hurt the first time, the second is worse."

"Oh my god, Big Nurse is here. Do you hear her?" Dita asked. "And she's not even wearing a cap."

Eager to change the subject, Addie used her Big Nurse voice. "All of you, stop."

Then she added, "Dita, how about some dessert? Danny has school tomorrow. It's getting late."

Dita couldn't help herself. "We should have 'just desserts,' I guess."

EIGHTEEN

Danny told Addie he missed Mel. The divorce was not yet final, but the custody arrangement and Mel's visitation schedule had been agreed upon, so Addie had Danny call Mel to set up a visit for that weekend. Just to make sure Danny wasn't stranded when he left the ferry if Mel forgot, Addie went to the mainland with him and took the day for a shopping trip. She was borrowing the old car Dita and Sean kept in the mainland ferry lot. It was a common island practice for those who could run two cars to keep one on the mainland and allow their friends to drive it when necessary.

Mel stood at the corner by the dock's fish market waiting for Danny when they landed, and Addie got her first glimpse of his not-so-new lady. She watched, angry and envious, as the woman bent down to hug Danny. She thought that the woman was quite ordinary, and as she sized her up, she called Dita to report to her.

"Dita, I think she's mousy. I expected someone glamorous, but she's just someone who could fade into a crowd: brown hair, medium length, bangs, a big mouth, a bit dumpy. In fact, I would call her downright dumpy."

"Meow," Dita replied.

"Okay, okay. But he didn't replace me with a raving beauty. It's not like someone like Jeanne came along. That makes it hurt even more," Addie said. "And my son will be her son for a few days."

Dita knew how painful this was for Addie, so instead of commiserating with her, she tried to cheer her up. "Don't be sad. Think of it as free babysitting. Go over to Locks Attracts and get a haircut if Sandy has time. That'll make you feel better."

"Maybe. Thanks for letting me borrow the car, by the way."

"Of course."

Addie wasn't in the mood for a haircut, but retail therapy might help. She poked around in the discount box store near the ferry but was unable to get interested, not even in the activewear section. So she left and headed over to her favorite grocery store to shop. She'd brought a cooler with an ice pack so she wasn't concerned about perishables. She found she was happier at the grocery, especially in the fruits and vegetables section where they stocked ripe red tomatoes from a local hothouse in fall and spring. She was debating between two types of apples, granted they were not from the fall harvest but still passably good, when she felt hot breath on her neck. An arm wrapped around her like a serpent, a man's arm in a navy peacoat. It lifted her feet off the ground. She recognized Mike Palmer's voice in her ear.

"Just so you know," he growled in a low whisper, "I can find you and follow you just like you followed me. Maybe even better because you didn't spot me."

Addie turned as red as her hair. He released her and moved on to the yellow squash, but then he turned and winked. Suddenly she felt like she needed to shop elsewhere. She dropped the apples she'd chosen and walked as quickly toward the doors as she could without drawing attention to herself. Mike moved behind her and shoved her so she lost her footing and fell into a bin of tomatoes. To her good fortune, they weren't the luscious and soft hot house tomatoes that would have burst open and squirted all over her face. They were the unripe winter-pink tomatoes from a southern state, the ones she usually abhorred. Today she considered herself lucky as they were firm like pickleballs and didn't squish under her weight. A bony arm reached out to steady her and a spindly voice crooned, "Not good," as the person helped her stand straight.

Addie recognized the voice. “Celia! Thank you.” She reached out to give her a small squeeze.

“Not good,” Celia crooned, pointing and nodding to Mike’s back as he left the grocery. “No, he’s not,” Addie agreed. The woman made sense.

Celia’s companion, a youngish island woman who helped older folks, appeared and took Celia in hand. She greeted Addie, then shooed her charge on.

“Sorry if Celia’s bothering you,” she said over her shoulder. “Sometimes she fixates on someone.”

“She helped me. Not a bother at all,” Addie quickly responded, wondering who had decided that woman was an appropriate caregiver.

Addie understood Celia’s warning. She wondered if people underestimated Celia’s grasp of the undercurrents swirling around Block Island. She made a mental note to warn her mother again about Bernard and Jessica’s financial offerings, recalling that Celia had circled the room the night of the cocktail meeting, uttering “Not good,” until Bernard corralled her and led her away.

Addie stayed by the tomatoes and watched Mike get into his car. She kept her eye on him until he drove off. Could she finish her shopping without worrying about him returning? She needed to bring home a load of groceries before the onslaught of tourists arrived in the week before July 4th. Once they came, the clinic work would be non-stop all day, every day, and on many nights for emergencies as well. She plucked up some courage and continued through the produce to the meats and canned goods. Cereal and snacks were super expensive on the island, so she grabbed some of those as well. Her hands shook as she unloaded her cart to check out, and she watched out the front windows for Mike’s truck in case he returned. She didn’t see him, but she was waiting for the wrong person. As she passed through the automatic doors, she almost crashed into Jeanne, who was hovering just outside.

“Hello, Addie,” Jeanne scoffed, and she smiled malevolently and nodded. “Surprise! Did you happen to run into Mike in there? Better hurry, he’ll be back to pick me up soon.”

How, Addie wondered, could someone so beautiful be so ugly inside? Trembling, she willed herself not to run. She strode as fast as she could to put distance between herself and Jeanne, repeating to herself a mantra, 'first one foot, then the other,' until she was midway through the parking lot. But instead of making a beeline to Dita's car, which she desperately wanted to do, she turned toward the shoe store instead so Jeanne would not know she had Dita's car—that is, if she hadn't already seen her pull into the parking lot earlier.

Had both Mike and Jeanne been on the morning boat coming over? Addie didn't recall seeing them, though they might have stayed in Mike's truck for the trip. More so, had they teamed up to kill Cathy? But, why? Mike could have just stopped seeing her. Addie didn't understand why they were so angry about her following Mike that day.

With a glance over her shoulder first, Addie zipped inside the tiny sneaker store and pretended to browse; even tried on several pairs of new sneakers, while keeping one eye on the parking lot to see if Jeanne had followed her. She was so tense she could barely tie the laces. She saw Mike drive up and Jeanne jumped into the truck. The two of them advanced to the driveway and disappeared down the street. When they were gone, Addie felt her whole body decompress. She chose a pair of shoes, tore out to Dita's car, and locked herself in. She tapped her fingers on the steering wheel, thinking. Why were they pursuing her? Yes, she'd followed Mike that one time, but did he think she knew something she didn't? Should she take him seriously, or was he just pulling a prank? She could hide in the movie theater, take in a matinee, but what if they looked for her there? Could they know she was using Dita's car? Was it just accidental that she and Mike were in the market at the same time, or had they followed her from the ferry lot? She looked at her watch. There was a boat returning to the island in a half hour. She could just make it, or should she go across the street to the used furniture and tchotchke shop and see if they turned up again? But even if they didn't, they'd probably go back to the island on the late boat with everyone else. Could she risk being trapped on the ferry with them? There were lots of spots on an off-season boat that would be deserted and unseen, spots where someone could push a being over the railing, undetected. Was she exaggerating? She couldn't risk finding out. She might be able to fight off one of them, but not both.

With that, she turned the car around and headed back toward the dock. When she got to the parking lot, she called Dita and hotfooted it across the street while she brought her friend up to date. Dita agreed she should come right back home, but emphasized Addie needed to make sure Mike wasn't going home now, too.

Addie looked around the dock. It was nearly empty now, as everyone else had boarded.

Sean's friend Joe was taking tickets at the gangplank. He called to her to hurry; they were about to push off. She picked up her pace and, after she stepped aboard, asked if he'd seen Mike. He hadn't. Addie was relieved, and she asked Joe not to tell anyone that she'd asked, especially not Mike.

"He's still a suspect in Cathy's murder, you know," she said.

She climbed the stairs to the ferry's cabin, and when she got to the open doorway, she scanned the rows of green seats lined up in the center of the cabin just to make sure he wasn't aboard. Joe could have missed him, but she was reassured when she looked around and didn't see him or Jeanne. The seats were almost empty, as were the picnic-style wooden tables and benches along the sides. Only one was occupied with that guy Carter "Artie" who had asked Dita's mother to dinner, and a couple of men in suits, probably lawyers coming to town hall on business. She didn't think Mike would bother to go to the upper deck, and if he had, he wouldn't see her down here.

It was a calm day on the water, the waves barely licking the shore next to the docks. *Calmer than my state of mind*, she thought as she queued up at the lunch counter to wait for it to open. She heard the winch on the deck groan, and she knew the boat had begun to move. The kid behind the counter also heard. He pulled up the wooden shutter and took her hotdog order. She slid into one of the picnic benches by a window and watched as they transited the 'no wake' zone along the seawall. Several men were fishing from the rocks. A small boy with one of them waved. Every few minutes, she found herself checking over her shoulder just in case Mike had followed her and gotten on, though she knew once the ferry was underway, there was no way for him to do that. The boy at the counter called to her, and she picked up her order.

Dita called her back to remind her she'd warned her not to follow Mike. "Okay, I'm not as good at that as I thought," Addie admitted. She couldn't keep herself from firing back at her friend, "But at least he didn't shoot at me."

"Touché," Dita said. "The washashore gang did try to kill me. That said, please be careful. Mike might have better aim."

Knowing Mike couldn't be on the boat nor on the island, Addie relaxed a bit when they landed, and she ambled across the empty lot, the one used only in summer to line up cars waiting to load onto the ferry. It felt good not to have to run, and today she didn't even mind having to cross that space to get to her car. It did always strike her, and a lot of other locals, as odd that they were not allowed to park there in winter when no one used it, but were forced to walk through it to the other end of the area where they could park. But soon none of the lots would be empty anyway as summer traffic ramped up.

She drove through town and spotted Dita's car in front of the Washashore Pub. It had been a long time since they'd met for drinks there. Before the washashore murders, they'd hung out with Loretta in the barroom to gossip at least once a week. It would be nice to have a drink with Dita for a change, so she pulled in on impulse without even thinking Harry would most likely be there. She spotted Dita and made a beeline toward her, but stopped short when she realized her friend was working. She had her reporter's pad on the table and appeared to be interviewing the new school principal, who sat across from her. Addie couldn't interrupt, so she took a stool at the bar instead. It was almost empty except for a new summer hire behind the bar with Harry, who had his jacket on. She figured he was about to leave. The new summer hire caught her eye and started to approach for her order, but Harry grabbed his shoulder, stopped him, and sent him into the kitchen. Suddenly, Harry was right in front of her, leaning his elbows on the bar, staring into her eyes. Despite her decision to keep her distance until the divorce papers were inked, she had to admit she felt safer with him close by, so instead of shooing him away, she smiled.

To his "how's your day," she dropped all pretense and spilled about Mike. She and Harry had, before their dalliances, been good friends, in some ways confidants, and he reacted at once.

"Mike's always been a bit of a bully. He had a rep for being mild-mannered, but he always had a temper if you pushed the right buttons. I wish you hadn't put yourself in his crosshairs." He was silent for a moment, and then, having thought on the situation, he blurted out, "Someone needs to make him back off. Sean was in here earlier with Karl talking about him. I'll get in touch with them. That said, I don't think you should sleep home tonight," he said.

"And where do you suggest I go?" Addie asked, her heart quickening.

Harry smiled and put his hand on hers. "I think I know a place."

Addie was thankful that he had those gray contacts in. She couldn't have resisted his naked eyes.

"Harry, Mike wasn't on the boat," she said. "He was with Jeanne, and they may stay on the mainland tonight."

"He's coming back later. He's working the bar at the BeachDune. Maria stopped in here earlier and told me."

"Okay then, I guess he's coming back, but I don't know if I should be at your house, in your bed."

Addie's divorce papers were not yet signed, but they were agreed upon, and the attorneys were drawing them up. Was it still too soon to get involved with Harry? Maybe yes, maybe no.

"Come on," Harry urged. "You can bring your car home, grab some things, and I'll come get you. Then no one will see it here. I know you went over to the mainland to drop Danny with Mel."

Her fear of Mike was greater than her fear of being caught with Harry. She reached across the bar and placed her hand over his.

"Okay."

"Do you want to wait for Dita to finish, or go now?" he asked.

"Now. Wait a few minutes before you leave, please." She hoped he couldn't notice the flush that was creeping up across her face.

She turned quickly and marched out without waving to Dita, hoping she wouldn't notice. But Dita did notice, and she also noticed Harry slip out a few minutes later. Ten minutes later, she wrapped up her interview, and on her way home saw them heading down Corn Neck the other way, toward town. She wondered if they were going to Harry's house. She sent him a full-handed wave as he passed, as was the custom on Block Island. Friends got full waves, acquaintances a couple of fingers, and tourists either none or a middle finger.

Harry waved back and looked over at Addie, who was shrinking into her seat.

"She caught us," he said, grabbing her hand with one of his.

She sighed. "We live in a fishbowl."

"Literally. Lots of fish swimming out there all around us."

"Please turn around and drop me at my mother's, Harry. I'll spend the night there."

"You're sure?" he asked.

Addie realized her body could not be in control of her life. "I am," she told him. "She's not home yet, but she'll be there later."

It was a beautiful, almost summer day on the island, not just in the water where the fish lived. The sun seemed to be sending out sparkles onto the tips of the spartina grass and onto the faces of the people walking along the road. Addie and Harry hadn't noticed; they were too caught up in their own melodrama. But Dita did, and she itched to get outside for a run. When she got home, she put off picking up Janie from the Be Fit. Instead, she changed into her shorts and took off for a run down the beach with Tuffy, who was always willing to sprint with her. She grabbed a tennis ball and sent him chasing into the water after it. This was one of the last days that she would have this stretch of sand to herself. Soon, blankets and chairs would cover most of the stretch between her house and the beach pavilion. Summer was on its way.

She loved how thoughts, sounds, memories, and illusions floated into consciousness like the faces of Harry and Addie as they passed her car—the flash, or flush as it had been, of guilt across Addie's cheeks, the startled widening of Harry's eyes and mouth—were all there in retrospect, though she hadn't registered them when she was driving. She hoped Addie got those divorce papers signed pronto. She did not want to be called to any court proceeding by Mel. But would he really do that? After all, he left her. She had heard, however, island gossip that Mel thought Addie was sleeping with Harry for a long time before he walked out. Addie could see how that might have happened, given the chemistry between those two whenever they were near each other. Was that enough to send a spouse like Mel into retreat and into someone else's arms? Maybe Addie and Mel had silently been drifting apart?

If Sean were drawn to another woman, would she automatically feel betrayed? Innocent flirtations were normal, but an outright affair? Unless she was ready to give up on Sean anyway, she'd stay and fight for his affections. Or so she thought.

She was enjoying her time alone so much she went back to the house and got into a bathing suit, fixed herself a margarita, and returned to the beach with a chair, a towel, and the drink. She took a few sips and dashed into the water, running until it was up to her knees, then jumping in full body. The sea was salty and cold, exhilarating. She floated on her back, then dunked under, washing away the doldrums of motherhood, because there were stretches of time when the joy wore off and the tedium set in. It was nice, just for a little while, to be her former self, Dita Redmond, free woman. She let the waves wash her ashore, and then sat sipping her margarita, watched the dusk descend and send the birds into the air, flying home to their nests. The swifts were silent, but the crows squawked as they flapped.

When she finished her cocktail, she gathered her things and went home. It was time to go to the Be Fit and become Dita Redmond, mother, wife, reporter, and murder investigator again.

NINETEEN

Harry pulled up in front of Rachel's cottage. Addie loved the familiarity of the leaning building, hunched over like an old woman perched on the edge of a cliff above the sea. She had grown up spending summers there, running the beaches with the other kids on languid summer days. Right where Harry parked today, she had shared her first salty teenaged kiss with an island boy. Such happy times.

Harry's voice brought her back to the present. "Aren't you going to invite me in...maybe for coffee?" he asked.

She nodded. She didn't want to spend the night with him, but she wanted to keep him close today. Being at her mother's should quell any flame igniting between them. They hung their jackets on the hooks in the hallway leading to the kitchen. Then in one swift swoop, Harry enveloped her in his arms and pulled her onto the living room couch with him, the couch that was still relatively new and still unstained by food or drinks. She didn't resist. They shed their sweaters and jeans and locked together so fast that Addie couldn't have said no if she'd wanted to, which she didn't. So much for the idea of her mother tamping their passion. Whenever she and Harry were close, there was just now, no past, no future, just this need, no matter how hard she tried to deny it. They stayed in each other's arms and time evaporated. She wondered if meditation and yoga were just poor substitutes for good sex.

Later, hearing her mother's car pull in, Addie nudged Harry and they threw on their clothes as best they could in the brief time before Rachel would walk through the door, but the mussed clothing and their guilt gave them away. Rachel was greeted by their pretzeled bodies on her almost new couch, and the scent of recent sex.

"Hmm," she said. "I see you're breaking in my sofa. When you did that as a teenager, you at least jumped off onto the chairs. It's ten o'clock. How long have you been here? What's wrong with your own houses? Did you even have dinner?"

Addie flushed. Harry looked at her. Did he expect her to answer?

"Um, no, Mom, we haven't."

Rachel chided her more. "And you don't look hungry."

Harry knew when it was time to go, and he did. He fetched his coat, said his goodbyes, and slunk out the door.

"Well, well," Rachel said, looking at her daughter. "That was interesting, I guess. Why were you two here and not at your house or Harry's? And why are you still here? Are you staying over?"

Addie filled her in.

Rachel tsked, her hands on her hips. "I could have told you where Mike was. He's at the bar at the BeachDune. And I know where Jeanne's been. She got off the ferry with the groceries for Bernard and Jessica's dinner, went to their house, and prepared and served it. I know because Teddy and I were invited."

"Did Teddy go right home?" Addie asked.

"He couldn't come. He's in Massachusetts meeting some people. I think he might have started a new company. It's been quite a night, not just for you. Are you sure you know what you're doing? Harry's quite the ladies' man."

"And I know why," Addie replied with a mischievous smile. "And you know, you said the word quite twice. Quite, quite trite."

"All right, all right, enough, I get it. I'll stay out of your business, but keep your business at your own houses from now on, okay?"

Addie laughed. "How was the dinner?"

"Disturbing. That's the only word I can use to describe it, much more disturbing than finding you and Harry on my couch like a couple of teenagers."

Her mother's choice of the word disturbing to describe a should-be-boring dinner piqued Addie's interest.

"Why? What happened?"

Rachel put her off. "I'm going to get comfortable first. How about making us both a cup of tea while I change my clothes?"

When Rachel returned, they settled into their chairs, put their feet up, and let their tea steep.

"It wasn't a big gathering like the last time," Rachel began. "There were Caroline and me, Doc Bennett, that Artie guy, and of course Bernard and Jessica. I don't know what Artie's relationship is with them. He seemed comfortable with both of them, but even more so with Jessica. He might be from Darien or Rowayton; you know, those tiny towns in Connecticut that really ought to be areas of a larger town, not have town halls and governments of their own, not to mention railroad stations. Do you know there's a string of small stations strung across Fairfield County like bus stops? Rowayton is only 1.4 square miles. Darien is 12.9 square miles of land, and they are less than 10 minutes apart. Yet the big cities like Bridgeport and Stamford only have one stop."

"And this has what to do with the dinner?" Addie asked, amused and happy that since her mother's relationship with Teddy had grown, Rachel had recovered from the depression that plagued her for years since Addie's father had died, and then again, when Joel had been murdered.

Rachel laughed. "Maybe I'm just using it as a metaphor for how indulged the lives of these people appear to be. And I figured out that even though Artie and Jessica are from different towns, they actually live right on top of each other and might know each other very well indeed, though they don't admit to."

Addie thought about how appearances can be deceiving. Her mother's evening was beginning to sound interesting. She placed an elbow on her armrest and rested her chin on her hand. "Okay," she said. "Go on."

Rachel took a sip of her tea and sat up a bit straighter. "They sat Artie next to Caroline, and he spent the evening attempting to charm her."

"Attempting?" Addie asked.

"Yes. She seemed not to be enchanted. I could tell from her body language. She leaned so close to the other edge of her chair, the one away from him, I thought she might fall off."

Rachel laughed as she pictured Caroline trying to get as far from Artie as she could in her chair. "She didn't pay attention to him, but that made Dr. Bennett happy. He was across from her and quite willing to talk it up with her."

Addie thought her mother was enjoying her rendition of dinner at Bernard's. She couldn't keep herself from commenting on Rachel's choice of words again. "Hmm," she said. "There's that word *quite* again. I guess it was quite a night."

Rachel laughed. "Yes. Oh, and I don't want to forget to tell you about Bernard and Jessica. Those two are so pleased with their self-proclaimed killing on the stock market, smug you might say. And to clinch it, Artie said he invested after their party and has already doubled his nut. He's putting more in."

Addie nodded. "I figured this evening was a sales pitch."

"But wait, I haven't told you the big news yet. The dinner was also to announce that they have gotten married."

"Um, who got married?" Addie asked.

"Jessica and Bernard. After all his patter about them not being a real couple, they are now married," Rachel said.

"What? To each other? And you didn't tell me that first thing? No big wedding or anything?" Addie was flummoxed. "Married? Not long ago he tried to gussy up to me, saying they were just friends."

Rachel shrugged. "People, you never know. And to top it off, Bernard was as much of a flirt as ever. I guess the ceremony doesn't really change anything."

"Except that without Bunny, Jessica is legally his heir, right? Unless they have a prenup," Addie said. "Would this have happened if Bunny hadn't been murdered?"

Rachel shrugged again. "I don't know. Presumably he wouldn't have moved here."

"Wait until Dita hears," Addie said. "That's quite convenient for Jessica. First her client dies and leaves most everything to her brother, then she marries the brother. Seems contrived."

"Or the brother sees an opportunity for himself. I keep reminding you Jessica is independently wealthy. She's a successful businesswoman," Rachel said.

"What about that Jeanne?" Addie asked. "I told you I had a run-in with her earlier. What was she doing there?"

"She was serving and doing kitchen work, but she spent a lot of time listening from the kitchen door. What surprised me was that Artie concentrated on Caroline, when Jeanne was around. She's stunning. Have you noticed?"

"Yes, I did, but it seems the focus of the evening was to sell you and Caroline, and Doctor Bennett, on the investment opportunity. Maybe Artie was in on that," Addie said.

"Like I've said before, I have Teddy checking on their financial offerings. I'm not jumping in, and neither is Caroline. Your boss, Doc Bennett, who knows? He might throw some money in."

"Well, he's got more to spare than we do," Addie said, as she took her teacup to the kitchen.

Rachel yawned. "It was a long night. I'm going to turn in now. I trust Harry won't be sneaking in a window like some of your old boyfriends?"

Addie grabbed a pillow from a chair and tossed it at her mother, who laughed heartily.

"Goodnight, darling," Rachel said. "It's nice to have you here, a little like the old days, isn't it, even with the boyfriend on the couch." Rachel smiled.

"Yes, Mom, love you too."

TWENTY

Two murders, neither solved. July 4 loomed, the heartbeat of the summer tourist season. The island folk raced to get ready.

Rachel unpacked the boxes of merchandise she'd stored last fall to restock "The Lorelei" shop. Sean made sure his exercise machines were working properly, and the Be Fit operated longer hours. The medical center added summer staff, and appointments were booked solid. And Dita was given a list of article assignments. The task she let slip was the background checks on Bunny that she'd promised the Chief. He'd already called and asked if she'd gotten to it. That's why today she sat hunched over her laptop, looking through businesses in Bunny's hometown of Westport, reading the local newspaper, searching for Bunny's obituary, trying to find some clues as to her life. There were no relatives besides Bernard listed.

Then she searched Jessica's name. She found a listing for Jessica's financial management office. Nothing more. She was frustrated, but then she formed a plan. She'd speak to Bernard to get some names of people she should speak with. Then she'd go to the mainland. She couldn't leave Janie here, so she'd need to bring someone along to help. Sean was too busy. Everyone was, even her mother, who had landed a job as a part-time hostess for the BeachDune restaurant. She called Addie and begged her.

"You want me to leave the island when the medical center is busiest?" Addie asked.

"Aren't you getting medical residents?" Dita asked. "And a nursing student?"

Addie's response was immediate. "I have to supervise the nursing student and help orient the residents, too."

Dita was not to be deterred. "What about the weekend? There aren't any regular appointments, just emergencies and sniffles. It's still before the 4th; shouldn't be overrun. We can have some fun, too, you know. I'll call my old friend Janice, and we'll stay overnight with her in Milford."

"Why not leave Janie with Sean and Caroline? What are mothers for? Pump some milk for her and freeze it. My mom will help, too. Then we can go out and have some fun in the evening."

"I'll check with them and the weather report. I can't get stuck over there with Janie here if the boat doesn't run." Dita was reluctant to part from her little one even for a few hours, let alone overnight. She was just getting used to letting her mother babysit.

Addie pushed. "I'll get mine on board."

Dita called Bernard and drove to his house to interview him. He was all in; he said he wanted Bunny's murder solved. He gave her a list of names, a few of which were current. He went into the funeral guest book with her and showed her who'd posted or attended. She snapped a photo with her phone.

"I could come with you," he offered.

Dita almost agreed, but then she decided Bernard could still be a suspect and might influence her interviews. Though he'd been overseas, he could have recruited someone to carry out the murder. Besides, she didn't want to travel with him. He'd already hinted Jessica and he weren't exclusive. She had a feeling she'd be fighting him off.

Bernard brought coffee and settled into a chair with his. Dita pulled out her pad and a pen. He seemed eager to talk.

"Bunny and I were born in Westport, and I wouldn't be surprised if her old friends are still there," he started. "She came back to the area, bought a house in Wilton, a neighboring town, about ten years ago after her husband Jack died. We all had lived abroad, in Spain. I landed first, when I was posted there in the Navy. Bunny came to visit and decided to stay a while. That's where she met Jack." He paused, concentrating on drinking his coffee.

Dita made a note to check the neighbors in Wilton. She'd forgotten that Dahlia had told her Bunny was living in Wilton.

"Did they have any children?" Dita asked in her most neutral voice. She had wondered if there were other heirs being pushed out of the picture.

Bernard was forthcoming. "She did have a child, a boy, but sadly, he died in infancy. After that, she didn't feel up to trying again."

Then she slipped in an important question she'd been wanting to ask since she met him. "Were you ever married?"

"No. I spent a lot of time at sea, even when I retired from the Navy. I was an officer on a cruise line. We don't make good husbands. I have had girlfriends though."

"Interesting that a life at sea condemns men to bachelorhood," Dita said, and she considered that. Her own father-in-law had been in the Navy, and he was married. But then, he'd been married four times.

"Not everyone thinks that way," he said, "but I thought it best. Now that I'm on land, who knows, I'm trying out marriage. And given how I love the water, living here part-time might suit me. I'll buy myself a sailboat and get out on the water again. I probably would have visited Bunny and might have made the same decision if she were alive. I'm going to miss her."

Bernard sipped more coffee, then looked across the room at Dita. "She was the life of a party, you know," he added.

Dita tilted her head. "No, I didn't. In fact, no one here knew anything about her, even Dahlia, who sold her the house. Josh Martel might have spoken with her more than anyone else."

Bernard leaned back and reminisced about Bunny. "She sang with a band for a while," he said. "Had a wonderful voice. When Jessica had her gathering a few weeks ago, if Bunny was around, she and some friends would have played and sung some jazz. She was considering buying a club somewhere around Westport and bringing in bands from New York. Last time I spoke with her, she mentioned having a comedy night as well."

Dita had begun to form a picture of Bunny's life. "Was Jessica in on this? I know you said they were friends."

Bernard shook his head. "Jessica's interest is not in real estate or running businesses. She's strictly into stocks and bonds, what I call passive investments."

Dita pried a bit more. "Was Jessica disappointed that Bunny planned to put her money into a club?"

Bernard laughed. "My sister had enough for both. Her husband, Jack, was a banker, had a lot of money, and he left Bunny well off. But she made her own money, too. Her singing brought her in contact with other artists, and she represented quite a few of them. She was an agent and did quite well. I never realized how well until, well, until I inherited her estate."

He threw up his hands and raised his voice. "What I can't figure out is how she ended up dead on Block Island. She'd just signed the papers that spring, hadn't even spent time here yet. She didn't know anyone except the realtor and that guy she hired to do work on the house. I hadn't yet retired from the cruise line, so I was sailing around the Mediterranean Sea when all this happened."

No one had yet figured out how Bunny ended up dead on Block Island, Dita thought, and she commiserated with him before she asked her next question, "How close were you to Bunny?"

"Not super close," he answered, "but we enjoyed each other's company. We got along. We talked even when I was aboard the liner. Last time I spoke with her, she told me about Jessica, how she hired her to invest, and they became friends. I was planning to come for a visit. Thought I might invest with Jessica myself."

"Were you surprised that she named Jessica executor of her estate?"

Bernard hesitated a moment before responding.

"At first, I was. But then I realized with my cruising schedule, Bunny might have thought I wouldn't be able to carry out the tasks. So I'm good with Jessica doing the paperwork."

Dita felt that he was truthful. She didn't think he would have killed Bunny.

"Bernard, is there anyone you can think of who had a grudge against Bunny, someone who might have been angry enough to kill her?"

"I can't. Most people liked Bunny, and we weren't so close that we knew each other's enemies. There were things about ourselves we didn't share. We led fairly separate lives, got together on holidays and for occasional dinners. Once every few years, she took a cruise on one of my ships. I didn't follow her day to day, even then. That said, losing her put a large hole in my life. She was my only relative."

"Jessica seems to be trying to fill that hole," Dita blurted out, and immediately wished she hadn't. But the implication seemed to go over Bernard's head, or he didn't mind it, because he didn't get angry or defensive.

"Yes and no," he replied. "We are enjoying each other, I'll give you that, but we're not tied emotionally like Bunny and I were. Even if we didn't see each other frequently, there was a family bond that Jessica and I have yet to form. Jess and I are financial, and might I say 'fun,' friends, married friends. But right now, our relationship is open." He stared across the room at Dita and tapped his fingers on the coffee mug. "I think you understand what I mean."

Dita had known they weren't exclusive, but his statement was a total denial of emotional involvement. At Jessica's investment party, Dita could have sworn they were more of a couple, particularly from watching Jessica, who seemed quite invested in him. She wondered what Jessica would think about what he just said, and what she would say about the relationship when Dita got to interview her.

She finished her coffee and got up to leave.

"You will let me know what you learn from any of those people, won't you?" Bernard demanded.

"Of course, if anything new or important comes up," she said, and she was out the door.

TWENTY-ONE

Connecticut's Fairfield County is one of the wealthiest areas of the United States. The suburban maze of tony towns is so wealthy, it is known in other parts of Connecticut as the Gold Coast. And though Dita had technically grown up in Fairfield County in Milford, CT, that town was almost in New Haven County and was miles away from the fashionable towns. It was the affordable place where workers who commuted to the richer areas lived. She'd been to these aristocratic enclaves to visit her father at the school where he was a principal, or to whiz through on the train to New York City, but she still needed a map to find her way around when she went there. Today she had Addie read her the directions from the GPS once she left the highway. Like Dita, Addie had only zoomed through the county when she took the Amtrak train to New York, and there was not much to see beyond the tiny train stations and, when the train tracked along the Long Island Sound coast, estuaries and boatyards.

Their first stop was to be an interview with a friend of Bunny's from the music industry. Dita and Addie followed the directions along narrow, winding roads, up and down gentle slopes. It almost looked like they were in a wild forest, given the tall trees that lined the New England stone walls along the lanes, but the trees were hedges to hide the huge homes lurking behind them and, like ancient city walls, to keep strangers out. Eons ago, these were the woods and farms New Yorkers fled to in order to escape city life. Now so many New Yorkers had arrived, the farms were gone, and only these remnants of the hardwood thickets remained.

The driveways were narrow and disguised by thicker vegetation, often green fir trees grown to full height. Dita almost missed the opening that led to the house they were trying to find. Just a small mailbox with the numbers 2052 painted on it marked the entrance. The driveway was even narrower than the street and, like its neighbors, occluded. Addie spotted it almost too late. "Turn!" she shouted, and Dita hit the brakes, jolting the car.

"I said to turn, not kill us," Addie chided. "Good thing we're belted in."

She had never been to Fairfield County, having been brought up in Rhode Island, and as the car chugged uphill toward the house, she wondered if they were in the right place. "Are you sure there's a house back there?" she asked. "We've been driving forever."

"Only a couple of minutes," Dita replied, laughing. "A lot of these homes have long entrances."

"Long? This is without end. Who plows this in the winter?" Addie asked.

At last, a home loomed ahead, an enormous white, double-winged colonial with a long front porch.

"Holy moly. I think this is a hotel. We must've made a wrong turn," Addie exclaimed. "Talk about big. Humongous! I'd hate to pay their heating bill in winter."

They pulled up to the door in the circular end of the driveway and parked.

"We're here," Dita almost whispered.

"You go first," Addie said. "How much you bet they have a maid answer the door?"

They rang the bell, and a woman in ripped jeans and a cut-off top with a mane of black hair and long, loopy earrings opened the door.

Not a maid, Addie thought.

"You found the house," Melinda Barnett said, a sassy smile on her perfect face.

"Almost thought we were at a hotel," Addie answered. Dita gave Addie a look, but the woman just laughed.

"Yes, this is rather a large house," she said without further explanation. "I'm Melinda Barnett. You must be Dita and Addie, from Block Island." She held out her hand and shook theirs, as they each introduced themselves.

"Come in. I know you want to talk about Bunny. She was a good friend, more like a Granny to me," Barnett said as she ushered them down the hall and into a snug sitting room with a desk in the corner and large windows overlooking a flower garden filled with irises in purple bloom. The seating area had but one floral print easy chair and a red couch with a footstool as a coffee table. "I'll get a tray for us. I'll just be a moment."

She swept out of the room, leaving Dita and Addie on their own.

"Comfy," Dita said. "And beautiful."

Addie agreed. "I could stay here the rest of the afternoon." She put her feet up on the footstool and closed her eyes. Moments later, Melinda returned with coffee and lemon squares.

"So, my husband and I, we were devastated when we heard about Bunny. She was just back from Spain a few months and had purchased the house on Block Island. She was looking forward to spending summers there, Bernard visiting, and hosting us, too. I had hoped."

"How did you meet her?" Dita asked.

"She was friends with my mother, so I knew her all my life. She was a little older than my mom, and I always looked to her like a grandma. Then when I grew up and started a career in the music business, I contacted her in Spain, and she helped me, advised me, talked to people for me. I owe my success to her help."

Addie tried to place her name. Her face was familiar, but she couldn't think of anyone in music with that name. Addie must have appeared puzzled.

Barnett laughed, a small, bell-like tinkle of a laugh, and explained. "I perform under the name Melilly."

Now both Addie and Dita recognized her and in unison sang the first words of her most famous song, "Under the roses...."

"That's it," Melinda said, and she finished the first line. "Call me Melilly. Everyone does. It's fine."

They were both awestruck, neither of them having ever met a real celebrity before. Without the façade of the nursing uniform and cap that contained her at the medical clinic, Addie totally lost control of her emotions. "We, I, didn't realize we'd be interviewing someone like you. I mean, I just thought you were a friend," Addie got that sentence out in a jumble of uh's and ums.

"I was a friend. And I loved Bunny. If you were going to ask who I could think of that would murder her so savagely, or even just murder her, I can't. I wish I could. She helped so many people in the business. I mean, she didn't represent me because she spent most of her time in Europe, but she found someone for me."

"Do you know if she had any disgruntled clients, people in the industry who resented her?" Dita asked.

"The music business can be vicious, but I wasn't aware of anyone angry at Bunny. Her business was mostly in Europe, so I didn't follow her life that closely. Once in a while, she'd come to New York, and when my mother passed, she came for the funeral. I never would have expected... well, this," she said, waving her hand.

"Did you know Bernard, also?" Dita asked.

"Of course. They were our family's friends."

Dita tried to be gentle with her next question. "Do you think he could have had anything to do with...this?"

Melilly shook her head as she spoke. "Oh, no, no, no. I could not imagine Bernard hurting Bunny. He was so supportive after Jack, her husband, died. For all Bernard knew, she might have left her money to the charities she supported very publicly. She was known as a philanthropist. I don't think Bernard expected her money. I do wish I could help with the murder investigation. I have tried to come up with someone; Bernard did ask me, but I haven't been able to."

Dita finished her lemon square. Addie expected Dita would give her the signal they were leaving, but Addie did not want to leave yet. She wanted to continue talking with Melilly, maybe see the rest of the house. She was happy when Dita shifted in her chair, put her pen tip onto her pad, and asked yet another question.

"I do have another area to clear up," she said. "Do you know Jessica Crandall? She was Bunny's financial advisor and is now involved with Bernard, Bunny's brother."

"The one with the investment club? Of course. We all use Jessica. In fact, I recommended her to Bunny. I didn't know she'd taken up with Bernard. I thought she was involved with some other guy; I've forgotten his name. If you want to talk with her, I think she's in town this weekend. She was at her office yesterday."

"So, Jessica and Bunny are not old friends from school or the music business?" Dita asked.

"No, definitely not. Jessica just moved here a few years ago from, hmm, was it New York? Come to think of it, I don't know if I ever knew. I think I just walked into her office one day after seeing an ad online. I did check out her investment past, but not where she'd lived."

"And you trusted her?" It was Addie who asked this question. Trust was a huge issue for her right now.

"I did," Melilly said, "and I do. I only invested a small amount at first. She's made me a fortune on top of what I earn from concerts and recordings. She and Bunny really hit it off, used to see them around town shopping together, eating at restaurants. If anyone would know who Bunny considered an enemy, it would be Jessica. You should talk to her."

"We will," Dita said, and she continued with her interview. "We were told Bunny planned to open a night club in town with a partner, Armand Gillette. Were you aware of that? And did you know Mr. Gillette?

"Bunny told me about the club. I offered to help her get it going by performing a few sets there whenever I'm in town. I didn't know Mr.

Gillette, but expected to meet him eventually since he would be running the place. I think it would have been a success. The town has restaurants but no entertainment, and people don't always want to go into New York on the weekends when they're there for work all week. You know, most people who live here have jobs in the city."

Dita closed her notebook and stood up.

"Before you go," Melilly said, "I want to say what a loss Bunny's death has been for me. I may not have seen her for a few years at a time, but I did speak with her occasionally, and knowing she was always there was a support. I could call her for advice when I needed it. I miss her."

Dita acknowledged her loss and thanked Melilly for her time. She turned to leave, but Addie was not yet ready.

Turning as red as her hair, she asked, "Melilly, would you sign an autograph for me? I mean, for my son. He's a big fan," and she grabbed Dita's pad and pen before her friend could slip them into her large black pocketbook.

"Of course," Melilly said. "What's his name?"

"Danny."

Melilly filled out the page, and Addie followed Dita out to the car. Once inside, they both screamed. Meeting the singer, who was a real celeb, was quite an unexpected surprise.

"Danny's the big fan?" Dita chided. "Not you?"

Addie turned bright red again and said, "Made this trip worthwhile. No wonder the house is so big. It belongs to a real-life star."

Dita looked back and saw Melilly still at the door waving to them. "I don't think she killed Bunny, do you, Addie?" she asked.

"Of course not," Addie responded. "Why would she?"

"Well, if a deal went sour...but Bunny didn't represent her," Dita said, her voice trailing off.

"You do know we have to interview the man Bunny was going to start the nightclub with next, before we see Jessica," Addie suggested. "Maybe that deal went sour and he got angry."

"I'll call him while you drive," Dita said. "I'll ask if he can meet us in the village for lunch instead of us driving all over Fairfield County to find him."

TWENTY-TWO

Nana's deli was located in Westport among the row of shops that fronted the main, quaint lane of the village. Dita pulled the car into the lot located behind the shops.

"These aren't like the stores we have in Rhode Island," Addie said. "Maybe we could take a few minutes to shop when we're done. And look, Jessica's agency is here, too."

All the shops, including Jessica's, had back doors with signs so customers would not have to walk to the end of the street to go around to the front.

"Only here on the Gold Coast," Dita remarked, thinking of all the times she'd hiked from parking lots to stores. "Where's Nana's?"

"Down there," Addie responded, pointing five shops to the left. "What's that guy's name, and what does he look like?"

Dita checked her notes. "Armand Gillette. Will be wearing a maroon tee shirt."

"Is that an unusual color for a tee shirt? I mean, there won't be ten men in maroon?" Addie asked, already worrying about the meeting. At least, she thought, it would be in public.

Dita shrugged. They were already striding toward the deli. Once inside, they searched the busy booths. The restaurant was bustling, and a buzz of voices rose around them. A stocky, balding man half stood and waved to them from his seat in a four-seat booth. He was wearing a maroon sweatshirt. They headed his way.

Dita wondered whether everyone filling the booths in the deli lived in the village. How else would he have known they were the ones looking for him?

Addie wasn't thinking of him at all now. She was busy sniffing the deli's air as though she'd been out of breath for a thousand years. Scents of pastrami and corned beef, chicken soup, pickles and slaw, the miasma of her childhood, wafted all around her. Her mouth watered, and her stomach called out. This was what she missed and couldn't have on Block Island. She slid into the booth behind Dita and opened one of the menus already strewn on the table, but she already knew what she would order: hot corned beef on rye, and she hoped it would be stacked high.

Addie would let Dita do the talking while she did the eating.

"Mr. Gillette?" Dita asked.

"That would be me," he said, a friendly smile on his round face.

He had a thick neck, Dita noticed, and large shoulders and biceps. He looked like a weight lifter. If he had killed Bunny, he'd have had no problem lifting her body and shifting her to a vehicle, then dumping her by the estuary.

She said instead, "Nice to meet you. I'm Dita Redmond, and this is my friend, Addie Berliner. As I said on the phone, I'm writing an article about Bunny Butler for the *Block Island Gale*, and I'm hoping you can help. I think you probably know Bunny was murdered, and the police are still looking into it. I understand from Melilly that you and Bunny were planning to operate a nightclub together."

"We were. In fact, we looked at several properties together and were about to make an offer on one. Then she just disappeared."

The waitress came and took their orders.

Armand continued his story. "She ran an agency for musicians, mostly in Europe, but she knew a lot of people in the business, and we planned to use her contacts to bring in performers. She was a friend of Melilly's, who agreed to drop in to sing when she was in town. That would have guaranteed us customers."

Dita made a mental note that his story corroborated Melilly's about that. Armand was still talking, so Dita tuned back in. "Bunny was most of the money, and my part was to set the place up and run it. Bunny had no experience in that, and I do, so I was going to be the general manager as well as part owner."

This also fit with what Dita had already heard. She wondered how Armand and Bunny knew each other and got involved in this business venture.

"Were you long-time friends?" she asked.

"No, we were not, and we weren't involved, either. I mean, we weren't a couple," Armand said. "I met her brother on a Mediterranean cruise, and we struck up a friendship around the fact that we were both from around here. Bernard knew I was in the restaurant/bar business, so when Bunny moved back to the area, he called and told me she was toying with starting a music club. He was concerned that she knew nothing about the business except the music part and suggested I talk to her to help her out. We got on well, and I was between projects, having just left a job at a club in the city. One thing led to another. I fully expected to be operating a club by now."

Dita found it interesting that Bernard had sent him to Bunny. Maybe this was the connection between Bunny's murder and Bernard. She didn't have to prod him. He continued to explain.

"I have to tell you I was worried when Bunny disappeared. We had just found a property we both liked, and then she ghosted me. Sometime in October, maybe? I called, I went to her house, nothing. I even called Melilly. She thought maybe Bunny went to Block Island to her new place, but she'd have taken her cell with her, I thought. When she didn't answer and her voicemail box was full, and she didn't come back, I figured she'd gone back to Europe, and I gave up on the whole endeavor."

"You never checked with Bernard?" Dita asked.

"We were casual acquaintances, and he was out at sea much of the time. When he originally called to say she was around and maybe I could help her, that was a one-off. We didn't keep up."

Dita was surprised he sounded so nonchalant about ghosting the deal, so she pushed. "Were you angry that she disappeared like that?"

Just then, their food arrived. Addie was ecstatic. She could care less about Bunny now that her plate of cholesterol-laden delights was in front of her. She grabbed her corned beef sandwich and took a huge bite even before she slathered on mustard.

"Mmmm," she said, a huge smile lighting up her face. "Delish!"

Sometimes Dita wondered if Mel had left Addie because she was more excited about food than him.

Armand took a large bite of his hot pastrami special and agreed with Addie. "The best."

Dita was working on her coleslaw, but she hadn't forgotten that her question was not answered. She asked again. Armand waited until he swallowed a few more bites to reply. She wondered if he was really this hungry or using the food as a delaying tactic. Dita was beginning to suspect him. Wouldn't it be normal to be upset that the other party in a deal just dissolved into thin air? Would you really have to think to give a simple yes answer, unless, of course, you knew where she was?

"I wouldn't say I was angry. I was more disappointed, deeply disappointed," he said slowly. "But you have to understand that this kind of thing happens all the time. People back out of deals because money falls through or other opportunities open up, and everything sours. So no, I wasn't angry so much as disappointed and frustrated. No money had changed hands as yet. I hadn't given her the small amount of money I was investing in it, so time was my only loss."

*Does that really happen a lot?*Dita wondered. She'd never experienced that. If Teddy had disappeared after offering Sean a chance to start the fitness center, wouldn't they have tried to find him? Wouldn't they have been concerned if he didn't answer their calls or email back? They'd have turned the world upside down looking for him.

"It seems odd to me that no one reported her missing," she said, thinking out loud. "No one on the island even knew who she was until Dahlia, her realtor, saw her picture and recognized her."

This time Armand responded without hesitation. "As far as I knew, there was no one who would have been upset or surprised that she'd gone—well, besides me, that is. She had just bought the house on Block Island. People here might have thought she'd gone over there. Melilly went on tour; Bernard was not here. I don't know if she had other close friends."

Even more reason to suspect Armand and Bernard to be in cahoots in this, Dita thought, and she poked Addie under the table. After her first few bites, Addie had listened with one ear while she enjoyed her lunch. Now that she'd finished and gotten her cue from Dita, she had a question. She cleared her throat, pushed a few curls off her face, and asked, "Armand, when did you hear her body had been found and she'd been murdered?"

"When Bernard returned here and called me. Then the next day it was in the newspaper. I went to the funeral. After that, I didn't hear from Bernard again. I took a job at another club and went on with my life."

"Do you know Jessica Crandall?" Addie asked.

"Jessica, hmmm, Jessica, I'm not sure," he said, thinking aloud. "Wait, I might have met her at the funeral. Is she the investment counselor? She must have known Bunny, but other than the funeral, no, I don't know her. What does she have to do with all of this?"

"A close friend of Bunny's," Dita said, surprised that Armand didn't know her.

"She never mentioned her to me," Armand said. "Like I told you, Bunny and I were business partners, not close friends."

Dita couldn't think of anything else to ask Armand, and Addie appeared to be done also, so she signaled the waitress for the check and thanked Armand. As they left the deli together, Armand turned to them and said, "I hope you find whoever did this. Bunny did not deserve this brutal death."

"No one does," Dita said. "And I'm sorry your plans together evaporated."

He shrugged and then turned toward his car on the other side of the parking lot.

Dita kept quiet until he was out of earshot and she was inside the car. Then she turned to Addie and frowned, declaring, "He's high on my suspect list. On the face of it, he was better off with her alive than dead. But why didn't her sudden disappearance and prolonged absence trigger questions for him? I don't buy his explanation that deals fall through all the time. Why didn't he search for her? Maybe what happened was she backed out of the deal at the last minute, told him she changed her mind, and he got angry and lost his temper. He's a strong guy. Did you notice?"

Addie had. She nodded.

Dita continued to think out loud. "He could have overcome her, and I wouldn't be surprised if he carried a gun. Locking up a bar at night with cash receipts, a gun would make sense." Then she turned to her friend. "Addie, what do you think?"

Addie agreed with Dita. "I think if I was a bartender or club manager and someone offered to put up money for me to be a part owner of a music club in the Gold Coast, I'd really be psyched. And then if that person suddenly disappeared when we were on the verge of buying the building, I'd want to know where she was and why she vanished. Look how mad I am at Mel, and I know where he is. Sometimes I feel like I could tear him to pieces. I think Armand is lying," she declared.

"Yes, only there's a hole in this explanation," Dita said. "A big one. How did Bunny's body end up on Block Island? Did Armand come with her to see her house? How would he know to dump her by the estuary where no one would be walking until spring?"

"He would have needed an accomplice, someone who knew the island, like Josh Martel, or even Blaze, who claims he accidently discovered her when he was clamming," Addie suggested. "We didn't ask Armand if he had ever been to Block Island. Lots of people from New York and Connecticut visit the island as tourists. Or Bunny might have brought him with her when she came out after she bought the house and hired Martel. He might have met Martel with her."

Dita was annoyed at herself for not asking that question. "Some reporter I am. You just hit on the most important question, the one neither of us asked him."

Addie heard the frustration in Dita's voice. "Do you want to call him and ask?"

"No, now he'd know we suspect him. It's too late. There's another thing that bothers me," Dita said. "It's really hard to believe no one missed Bunny in the months between her purchase of the house and her body being found. She bought the house in September, disappeared a month or so later according to Josh Martel and the nightclub guy. Then she wasn't found until early spring. Okay, Melilly was on tour, Bernard on a long cruise, and Armand claims he's accustomed to deals falling through, but someone in her life must have noticed she was gone."

Addie shifted in her seat and raised her voice in response. "I get Armand as a suspect, but what about Jessica? She was Bunny's investment counselor and friend. In fact, she was a close friend, so close that Bunny trusted her enough to make her co-executor of her estate. Wouldn't Jessica have noticed that Bunny disappeared? Wouldn't she have called her, and then called Bernard if she couldn't find her?" Addie was so worked up she lapsed into her Rhode Island dialect, rounding her syllables. "I'd draw a suspect chart with arrows between them on your reporter's pad, but, Dita, there'd be so many we probably couldn't decipher it. The months she lay in the bog with no one searching for her doesn't make sense."

"No, it doesn't," Dita quickly said. "Hold on, I'll call the chief to find out if there were calls to Bunny's phone."

"I thought they couldn't find the phone."

"You're right, but they know the number and the phone company keeps records of calls."

Addie thought for a moment. "That long after? It was months before her body was found."

"I don't know. We'll ask Chief Gomez," Dita said, getting her phone out of her bag. "Then Jessica is our next interviewee. I think we should come up with our questions for her first, now that we think she's a suspect, not just an informant."

The chief didn't answer her call, so Dita left a message. Then she pulled out her pad, looked down, and began writing.

"Dita!" Addie exclaimed, grabbing her friend's writing arm. "Look! Look quick, right now."

Dita looked up. She drew in a deep breath, and her hand flew over her mouth.

"Do you see?" Addie demanded.

Dita slumped as low as she could in the driver's seat, even moved it back so she could get lower, but she put up her hands and snapped blind photos while she did. As she moved down, she whispered, "Addie, duck before they spot you."

"That's the guy that's been dating your mother," Addie said.

"With Jessica," Dita said, as Jessica gave Artie a hug before stepping back into her office. Artie walked through the parking lot right past their car, whistling. The two women waited until he was gone.

"What was he doing here?" Addie wondered. "What kind of hug was that? Was that a polite 'nice to do a deal with you' hug or a 'I can't wait to have sex with you again' clutch?"

Again, Addie's new mistrust of men led her. "That whistling gives him away. What else could have made him whistle? Not joining an investment club, for sure."

"Could have been. Maybe he already made a lot of money," Dita said. "It was almost a body to body but not quite. Maybe overstepped the business clutch a tad, like guys do. I don't know."

Addie dismissed this. "Not," she said.

"He did tell my mother he invested some money with Jessica," Dita reminded her. "And he was at that party they threw. Remember?"

Addie did. "He was stalking your mother there. I remember that."

Dita thought some more. "But he didn't say he and Jessica were friends. I need to ask Mom if he ever told her where he lives when he's not on the island. Is this his hometown? Did he know Jessica before?"

"Either way," Addie said, always food-oriented. "Something's not kosher about them, just like that deli. Did you notice they had ham on the menu as well as chopped liver?"

"No, but I noticed the food was really good," Dita said. "Since when are you kosher?"

Addie smiled. "I was just noticing. Enough about the food," she said, patting her stomach.

"Really? That is so not you," Dita was laughing.

"I want to solve this case for Bunny," Addie lamented. "Call Chief Gomez again. Find out about Jessica's phone records before we see her."

"Okay. I'll fill him in on our interviews with Melilly and Armand too, if he answers."

"While you're on the phone, I'll be in that shop right there," Addie pointed. "Looking at clothes will remind me how much more fun it is to be this slim."

When Dita finished speaking with the chief, she caught up to Addie in the upscale clothing store. She told her the chief had found a few calls to Bunny's cell from Armand and from Jessica, but he'd also said that a killer would want to leave evidence that they were concerned about her to cover their crime. He was grateful for their information and cautioned them to be careful when they met with Jessica.

As they picked through piles of sweaters and cotton tees that were way above their In their price range, they discussed questions for their interview. Then they tore themselves away from the clothes they could admire but not buy and headed to Jessica's investment office.

TWENTY-THREE

Addie had spent much of her adult life working in health care facilities, in hospitals, and, for several years, the island's outpatient clinic, where the waiting room furnishings were designed to be pleasant but not lavish, the expenditures on décor chosen with thrift in mind. The seating would be comfortable enough not to offend a tush during a twenty-minute wait, but not as welcoming as home theater chairs where people spend hours sitting. When she walked through Jessica's door into the financial office and looked around, she turned to Dita, who was right behind her, and mouthed, "Wow!"

None of the usual office accoutrements were visible in the furnishings, no metal file cabinets, no faux-wood-topped desks with computer screens. This space was as comfortable as Melilly's sitting room, even more lavish. The couches—there were two—were a chocolate leather as luscious as bonbons. There was a modern glass coffee table in the shape of a large teardrop with a supersized vase filled with white roses and red carnations, and two cream-colored sink-into easy chairs, all set into a thick, plush white carpet that Addie was afraid to step on. Two leafy philodendron plants stood behind the couch, where light from a large window filtered in through a sheer white curtain. Silk wallpaper embossed with lilies covered the walls, except for two doorways, each of which led into a modest, normal office with two less-cushioned and less-easy chairs facing glass desks with a computer monitor, behind which a financial advisor could sit.

A third door, wallpapered like the walls so as to disappear, opened, and Jessica appeared, holding a large watering canister. Her eyebrows went up, and her mouth formed an 'oh' before she motioned them to take a seat on one of the chocolate couches.

"Hello, welcome," she crooned. "I didn't hear you come in. I was filling a beaker to water the plants."

Dita and Addie had been hovering near the back door. Jessica, so preppy on Block Island, blended into her décor with a cream-colored pencil skirt-suit and coffee voile blouse. Had she not been wrapped in Artie's hug, they might have noticed her clothes when they saw her earlier. And, of course, she wore color-matched spiked high heels with a signature sole that signaled they were hand-crafted by a famous shoemaker. Dita felt naked in her island best jeans and sweater, as did Addie in her mom top and skirt. They gave each other furtive glances.

"Nice to see you," Jessica said. She was already trickling water onto one of the plants.

"What brings you off the island and here today? Are you interested in joining the island club? Artie was just here with some questions. Perhaps you bumped into him outside?" She cocked her well-coifed head sideways as she asked, her lips drawn into a practiced smile. "I wonder who else might wander in from the island."

Dita shook her head and responded, "Oh, he was here? I'm sorry I missed him."

But as Addie also shook her head, her color responded with a slight pink tint climbing up her neck to her cheeks.

Dita noticed Jessica taking this in and wished upon wish that Addie could stop that automatic blushing. What was it Addie had told her? It was the sympathetic nervous system that caused blood vessels to open in response to the heat anxiety roused? Did she have it right? It didn't really matter, did it? That blush had caused the vigilant Jessica to catch their lie. Suddenly Dita had an insight about Addie. She couldn't do her job at the clinic if she blushed her way through the day with patients.

The nursing cap was a lid, a real lid, that reminded her to hang on to her emotions. Oh that she'd had it with them today.

Jessica nattered on about Artie. Dita thought she must be concerned that she'd been seen in his hug, which would mean Addie was right that it was romantic, not chummy.

"So happy to see you," Jessica cooed, reaching her hand out to take either one of theirs. She asked again, "Have you decided to join my island investment club?"

"We're actually here to ask you some questions about Bunny's disappearance," Dita said, explaining that she was writing an article and Addie was interested in helping find the killer.

Addie spoke for herself. "My brother was murdered two years ago. When Bunny's body was discovered, I felt obligated to help with the investigation," she said.

"And what about poor darling Cathy," Jessica added. "Haven't the police identified someone? I thought that scarecrow who was working at the house had confessed."

Though Addie thought Josh was as skinny and ragged as a scarecrow, she never would have identified him that way. She disliked Jessica a bit more than she did before. "Josh Martel?" she asked. "No, he denies it."

Jessica finished hydrating the plants and took the watering can back to the open wallpapered door, stashed it inside the bathroom and returned to the couch.

"Are there other suspects?" she asked, crossing her knees and dropping her hands to her lap.

Dita responded to her this time. "We don't know if the chief has anyone else in mind. Since I planned to write an article anyway, he asked me to speak with you, Melilly and Armand. Do you know them?"

"Not well. Bunny introduced me to Melilly and she told me about Armand, but I hadn't met him until Bernard introduced me at the funeral. Bunny was a wonderful person. She became a close friend so quickly. If I can help with the investigation, I am more than happy to do so."

They settled back into the plush furniture, and Dita fired away with her questions. Jessica claimed she'd called Bunny several times, trying to contact her on the island and in the village, all to no avail.

"I thought she'd probably made an unscheduled trip back to Spain, that a client had needed her. She'd told me that happened now and then, and she would just book the next flight out. She warned me she could just leave for a while without prior notice."

Addie squirmed in her seat. "But Jessica, it was months before her body was found. Didn't you wonder why she was gone so long? I thought you'd become close."

Jessica unfolded her hands and gestured. "We had, but darlings, there is close and then there is close. Jessica invested with me, we shopped together and had dinners with each other, but she never shared the details of her business. She was setting up some sort of club with Armand. I knew that, but we didn't discuss the ins and outs. I didn't tell her about my other clients or investments. I knew nothing until Bernard contacted me."

"Had you met him before?" Dita asked.

"Never. He told me he lived in Spain and that he shipped out frequently. In fact, Bunny never mentioned she had a brother. Ours was a fairly new friendship, and we were both women of a certain age. There was a lot of back-story that we hadn't yet shared. I know little about her before I became her investment counselor."

When Dita felt they'd gleaned what they could from Jessica, she stood up and dropped the most important question. "You said Artie stopped in. You do know he's taken my mother out a few times. Does he live here when he's not visiting the island?"

Dita thought Jessica looked wary. Her brows contracted, creating a wrinkle between them.

"I have his address since he invested with me, but I can't share it except to say he is from this area, yes."

"I worry about my mom. Do you know anything about him?" Dita asked.

Addie knew her role was to watch Jessica carefully as she answered Dita. She thought the woman's shoulders tensed up considerably, but her face remained stolid.

"I met him shortly before Bunny bought the Block Island house. He did some electrical work for me at my house. He told me he spends much of the summer on his boat at the island, and I told him about Bunny looking for a house there." She paused.

Dita waited, reluctant to jump in and alter Jessica's train of thought while the woman seemed to be thinking.

Then Jessica patted her skirt over her knees and explained. "Artie has been divorced for a year or two. His wife moved to Florida before the divorce was final. My friends recommended him when I needed to rewire my kitchen. I found him personable and reliable. Then, when I started my investment club on the island, I invited him. That's where you met him, right?"

Dita couldn't recall whether she'd met him at the Be Fit before that party, so she just nodded in agreement.

"Did he know Bunny?" Addie asked.

Jessica thought for a long moment. She stood up and looked out the window. "I don't know," she said slowly. "I don't think so. I might have mentioned him to Bunny as a person to call if she needed an electrician when she found a building for her club. Otherwise, I don't think I ever ran into him when I was with her, and she probably wouldn't have met him somewhere else. You don't think Artie had anything to do with her death, do you?"

Addie answered. "We're just trying to eliminate people who might be suspects."

"So then, am I one of your suspects?" Jessica asked, looking back at them, her hand locked around her chin.

Dita shot Addie a look to tell her to keep quiet, then answered. "Jessica, Addie and I are trying to collect information about Bunny's life and find other acquaintances she might have had. Since you and she were friends, we figured you might know who else we should talk to. We thought you would want to help learn how she ended up lying in that swamp. I'm sorry if we've upset you, and as far as Artie goes, I just want to prevent my mother from being hurt."

"My dear," Jessica said, "as far as I know, Artie has not settled on a girlfriend. I've seen him around town escorting several divorcées, and he's made advances toward me. I am only interested in his business, so I turned him down. Even if I didn't turn him down, it would have only been for a fling. I'm surprised he hasn't approached you, Addie, being a new divorcée."

Jessica went into her office and retrieved papers from her desk, so Addie's blush was only seen by Dita.

"Here," Jessica said, returning and handing pamphlets to them. "This is more information about my investment clubs. There's one for people your age who want to start saving for retirement. You need to think ahead, even though you're young."

"Thank you," Dita said. "Sean and I will consider it, although with his new business, we have no extra money right now. Maybe in a few years."

Jessica addressed Addie. "I have a college fund also. Let me get you the info on that."

She disappeared into her office again, and the sound of a file drawer opening and closing broke the silence of the waiting room. When she returned, she gave them each a small hug, smaller Dita thought than the one she'd given Artie, and told them she had to get back to her work.

"But," she said, "if I think of anyone else who might have been a friend of Bunny's, I'll let you know."

They were ready to leave anyway. Jessica was not going to tell them anything of importance.

"We didn't put Artie on our list," Addie said. "Should we?" She asked Jessica, who shrugged and folded her arms over her chest.

"You could," she said in a nonchalant voice. She moved quickly to the door and waited for Addie and Dita to go out.

They took the hint and left. The door shut behind them, with Jessica on the other side. The conversation had left Dita feeling uncomfortable.

Caroline, though not deeply involved as yet, was seeing Artie. And it looked to Dita like he might be seeing Jessica as well, who was also involved with Bernard. Was Armand the only one not having a triste with one of that triad? Dita felt like her mother would accuse her of interfering if she questioned Artie. Dita didn't want to get involved in that.

"Who really are these people, Dita? We know so little about any of them. Bunny lived in Spain, and besides being a music agent and knowing Melilly, why was she living over there? Who were her friends there? How did her husband die? And Jessica, who seems to have just materialized in Westport from who knows where?

"None of these people had a real Block Island connection. Even Artie, who stopped in on his boat summers. What's his back story? If you think we need to interview him, Addie," she said, "you do it the next time he's on the island. Let's just wrap this trip up and go home. I need to see Janie. The texts from Sean are getting more frantic."

Addie sighed. "I don't really want to, because he's already hit on me."

"He does pick up jobs on the island. He did the wiring for Teddy at the Double Ender," Dita said. "Someone might know more about him."

"Let's leave him for the Chief if you don't think you're up to it. That's his job," Addie said. "You go back today, but I want to spend one more night on the mainland. Danny's with his friends, so he doesn't need me. I think I'd like to stay at the Shady Beech Inn and get into their hot tub. I brought my suit, just in case. Can I use your car?"

"Sure. Drop me at the boat, and it's all yours. Maybe pick up some apples for me if you go to the grocery. You fell into them instead of buying them for me last time you went, remember?" Dita laughed.

"Ugh, don't remind me," Addie griped, not laughing at all. "But, Dita, we need to talk about Artie even if we don't interview him ourselves. Suppose he is involved. Your mother could be in danger."

"Do you mean if he's involved with Jessica or in Bunny's death?"

"Either, or both," Addie said. "That hug, I'm leaning toward intimacy, not acquaintance."

"Me too. However, he never told my mother he was only seeing her.

You heard Jessica, she said he gets around. I don't want to ruin it for Mom. I think she's feeling attractive again, like you with Harry."

Addie bristled. "That's different. We've been friends for years. I know who he is."

"And that he runs around with a lot of young women, like Artie," Dita said.

"I think we should stick to the case. Who killed Bunny, and why?"

"And who killed Cathy? If, say, Artie did it, what was his motive?"

As they drove further along the highway, each lapsed into their own thoughts. When they exited and were on the straightaway to the ferry turn, Dita tapped her fingers on the steering wheel and blurted out, "Artie and Jessica are the killers. I don't know why they killed Cathy, but I'm pretty sure Jessica wanted Bunny's assets and enlisted Artie's help. She did say she's known him for a few years, and Artie's been coming to Block Island even though he doesn't have a house. He comes sporadically in the winter and most summer weekends. He'd know where and when to dump a body without being seen."

Addie wasn't totally convinced. "But Bernard got everything," she said, "except for the executor's fee."

"Maybe Jessica didn't know about him, and maybe he's next," Dita argued. "I will make sure my mother doesn't end up on his list. I'm going to warn her off."

"I think you're right. He probably shot Bunny inside the house," Addie said. "Or maybe he took her to a romantic cove and killed her outside where he didn't have a mess to clean. Would've had to be after Columbus Day when the island empties out, maybe down Coastguard Beach where no one would hear. Still, why Cathy?"

"Gives me the creeps. I think we need to keep an eye on him, but I'm not sure an interview is safe."

They reached the ferry landing, and Dita got out; Addie switched to the driver's seat.

"See you tomorrow. Have some fun," Dita said as she strode to the gangplank. Once aboard, she found a seat with some neighbors and texted her mother to pick her up. That would give her an opportunity to talk with her about Artie, and also, Sean wouldn't have to interrupt whatever he might be doing at the time, probably working at the Be Fit, with Janie sleeping behind the counter. Dita knew she had a lot of admirers at the gym who didn't mind amusing her if Sean got busy.

The gossip aboard the boat was usually intense on the trip over to the mainland. On the way home, most folk were tired from racing around the mainland doing errands and were more likely to share tidbits about the shops or doctors' offices they'd been to than trade information about island doings. That was true today, but Dita noticed a dark pall hung over her tablemates, like a morning fog shrouded around them, damping down the usual laughter and camaraderie. Dita knew the murders, though unmentioned, were on everyone's minds.

Carolyn texted her that she was waiting when they made the turn close to the island, and the ferry sailed parallel to the beaches before reaching the harbor. On beautiful days, and this was one of them, Dita loved spotting the dunes behind her house and then the peak of her roof. She broke away from her friends and stepped outside to the railing, where she could breathe the sea air and feel the wind as she watched the beaches and cottages go by. She still couldn't believe she lived in this wondrously beautiful place, and today it seemed egregious to her that someone had stained her Eden with murders, far worse sins than the original one, she thought, than Eve taking a bite out of an apple. Poor Eve, forever censored for one juicy bite of joy, such a small transgression. Dita was roused from her reverie by the sounding of the boat horn. They were about to enter the harbor.

Carolyn was waiting in the car. Dita hopped in, leaned over to give her a hug, and decided to tell her about Artie when they hit the straightaway on Corn Neck Road.

"Mom, pull over a minute so we can talk. I need to tell you something," she said.

Carolyn's face tightened. "Did you find the killer?" she asked.

"Maybe. We eliminated some suspects, but aren't sure about others."

Dita told her about Melilly and Armond, and then she got to the meat of the story, to Jessica and Artie.

Carolyn listened quietly, and when Dita finished, she put her hand on Dita's arm and told her she never really was interested in Artie anyway. The more she saw him around the island, the less she liked him. "Don't worry, honey, I'm not heartbroken, and I lost nothing by seeing him a couple of times. But I am interested from the standpoint that he urged me to invest with Jessica. I bet he's profiting from her business somehow."

"I'm so glad you're not upset, Mom. I was worried about telling you."

Carolyn laughed. "He was never really a contender. Ready to go home now? Sean just pulled up in back of us with Janie."

Dita turned around and waved, and they proceeded home.

TWENTY-FOUR

When Addie parked Dita's car in the ferry lot on her way home the next morning, she felt renewed. She'd run into a friend from the library book club at the hotel, and they shared a meal as well as some recent gossip at a nearby Italian restaurant. Then she had spent an hour alone in the hotel whirlpool before retiring to her room. This morning, she did her shopping, and now she carried two bags of groceries, including Dita's apples, across the parking lot as she walked to the dock, stopping several times to reposition her bundles. She dragged her small overnight case behind her as well. She was about to cross the street when an arm reached out and grabbed the larger bag.

"Here, let me help you with these," a male voice resounded close to her ear.

Addie startled and stared. It was Artie, also on his way to the ferry, wearing the same red windbreaker he'd had on yesterday when she'd seen him hugging Jessica. She wanted to refuse, as she could see only a murderer as she looked at him, but he was still talking and was hurrying off with her bundle. "I need a ticket. Do you?"

She didn't. She had her roundtrip. She shook her head. She ran to catch up and retrieve her bags.

"I'll just be a second," he said, peeling off toward the ticket window.

There was no line. He would be quick. Still, Addie was terrified. She decided not to wait so she wouldn't have to chat with him. She continued on her way and boarded the boat, placing her sack of groceries and suitcase in the bin on the forward wall of the car deck. Artie wasn't far behind, so she motioned to show him where to put the bag he carried, and she proceeded up the staircase by herself to the cabin at a much quicker pace than normal for her. Artie was clearly a man who took charge of things, she thought, sizing him up. Maybe she should interview him during the voyage. But that was way too scary. Maybe she would go up to the top deck behind the wheelhouse and smokestack to avoid him. Which would it be? She needn't have worried about which. He caught up to her while she deliberated and apologized for not being able to sit with her. He had a meeting with a client who needed an electrician. Addie felt a wave of relief wash over her. She barely heard him invite her to his boat.

"Come out on my boat. It's supposed to be nice this week," he said.

She didn't want to go boating with him. She didn't want to be alone with him period, especially not on his boat, especially not after her brother had been murdered by drug-dealing sailors on a fishing trip. She might never set foot on a boat other than the ferry again. She felt the heat of a blush as she pondered what to say.

Artie tried to put her at ease. "This won't be just us, Addie. I'm not asking you for a date. I'll invite Caroline and Jessica or Bernard if either of them are here, or even your mother. I'll call you at the clinic when I set it up."

Right, she thought, *more people to murder me.*

They'd reached the second deck. He stepped ahead of her and opened the door. When they were through it, he rushed ahead to find his contractor.

Addie almost blurted out that neither she nor her mother would get aboard a private boat, but he stepped away before she could speak. She took a seat at one of the empty picnic-bench tables bolted to the floor along the windows and gazed out the salt-sprayed glass as the ferry pulled away from its berth. Rushing over today's half-hearted waves, no turtles floated by, nor did any whales surface, just seagulls flocking to catch any scraps—potato chips, crackers, or popcorn—thrown to them by the children on board. Halfway across the expanse to Block Island, she felt restless. The trip always seemed to take forever when she was alone. She didn't see any neighbors or islanders to chat with today, so she went upstairs to the top deck and stood outside, letting the wind flow around her. For the second time that day, she felt a hand grip her arm. This time, however, it wasn't Artie's friendly clasp. It was Mike, and once again, he looked as angry as the heft of his grip. Addie steeled herself.

"You followin' me again?" he asked, shouting over the sound of the wind and the engines.

She knew why he thought that, and she rushed to explain. "No, I didn't even know you were on the boat," she shouted back.

He pulled her toward the railing.

"Mike, stop, I'm not following you," she protested, trying to free herself, thinking this could not be happening, but the pain of his hand wrapped around her arm told her it was. She pleaded with him again, telling him that she had totally written him off as a suspect.

"I only came upstairs for some air. Mike, I had no idea you were aboard."

Her excuses did not deter him. He whined in her ear, "I was the one who came up here to be alone and get some air. The police asked me the same questions you did, about did I call 911. I thought about it, and no, I didn't call 911, but I did call the firehouse, and the police verified that. Still, everyone looks at me like I'm a killer, and you, you seem to be everywhere accusing me of murder. I warned you to leave me be."

Addie realized he was deranged. "I'll go back downstairs if you want. Please let me go," she said as nicely as she could, smiling.

Instead, he pushed her and pinned her against the railing. He was a burly guy, and she was no match for him. She panicked.

"Mike!"

He laughed and held her there. She turned her head and looked over the edge. The water was at least 20 feet below them. She would never survive in that water. It hadn't warmed to the summer yet. He shook her shoulders, and she almost lost her footing. In her panic, she asked herself,

'*Is this how Joel died?*' She began to hyperventilate; she couldn't catch her breath. She tried to plead with him, but her words emerged as gasps.

Mike scrunched up his face and bared his teeth. In the moment, looking at him, she saw an attack dog, not a human. Then he growled. "Scared?"

His face was right in hers and reformed as human. She noticed the wide bridge of his nose, the rage shooting from his eyes, the receding cowlick of his hair. Why had she never noticed how homely, how fearful he looked? She had an insight; that was how her taller friend Dita always saw men's faces, straight across and full featured. She, on the other hand, was much the shorter and was always looking up, seeing their square or flattened chins, their lower lips and cheek bones, and the size and shape of their nostrils. What a thing to have in your head when you're about to die, she thought.

He was talking at her again. She wheezed deeper, and when she took air in, it was his sour breath. She instinctively leaned back over the railing. She must not lean back more. She must not fall.

"I can tell by your face it scares you," he taunted. "Likely no one will see if you go overboard. I could just say you jumped, or I could head downstairs before anyone sees you drop, if they ever do. It's a pretty empty boat, and not many people looking out the windows. No one else is up here."

She hadn't believed Mike could have killed Cathy before, but now she did. Had he abused Cathy before he ran her over and killed her? Maybe Cathy was trying to break up with him. What to do, what to do? She perseverated in her head, trying to figure a way out.

"Please, Mike. There are crew up here, they'll see you," she blurted out between her deep heaves.

He looked around. "They can't see us from the wheelhouse. Nope, I got you and I can do whatever I want."

Addie knew she needed to keep stalling him until someone else might come upstairs. "Is that what happened to Cathy? You got her?" She said it with as much aggression in her voice as she could muster.

He whined, the man who was threatening to kill her actually whined. "That's what I mean. I never did nothing to Cathy, but all you busybodies want to pin it on me. Why would I run my girlfriend over with my truck?"

Addie did not want to die. She especially did not want to leave her Danny, and she really did not want to leave him to Mel and a stepmother who would become his new full-time mother. She steeled herself to resist whatever Mike was getting ready to do to her, when she heard the rustle, and again a rustle, like someone with a wide skirt was coming up the steps. She couldn't place it, and suddenly there were full-blown howls, like a pack of coyotes calling in the wilderness. The sound pierced the air above the chugging of the engines, and it pierced the human heart. Mike lost his footing. He let go of Addie and stumbled sideways, then he plunged against her, a hard, unchoreographed shove that sent her stumbling across the deck. She fell, her entire weight onto one knee that slammed against the wooden planks. She cringed with pain, but she knew she had to stand back up and disappear down the stairs before Mike came at her again. She tried to catch her breath so she could move.

"Run," a high, thready voice called.

Addie looked up. Celia was striding toward her, her ubiquitous full skirt rustling, and she reached out a withered hand to help Addie up.

"Not good," Celia said.

Celia's howl had reverberated down the staircase, and deckhands were rapidly ascending. Addie couldn't run. She embraced Celia, and the two huddled while they watched Mike, who had climbed the deck railing and was perched on it, his back toward the water.

He looked at Addie, straight into her eyes, and slowly enunciated the words in his growl, "It wasn't me." Then he backflipped over the edge and dropped down, flailing until he hit the water below. The crew shouted "man overboard," and one ran to the wheelhouse, the other down the stairs. The P.A. system came on with the man-overboard broadcast. The boat stopped moving forward.

Addie reeled and clutched Celia closer. She knew the drill; she'd seen the crew practicing it from the beach by Dita's house. In midsummer, tourists crowded on the sand, the ferry would leave port and hover in the water, leaving all the people on the beach wondering what they were doing. Well-practiced, they could perform the drill without hesitation. Today, fast as they were, Mike had drifted too far from the boat for the rope with the ring to be thrown. They dispatched lifeboats and headed toward the disappearing speck that was Mike.

Addie remembered a golden retriever puppy had once jumped overboard, and long ago a jilted lover. Both had been rescued. Would Mike?

Celia was still standing right next to her. "Not your fault," she whispered. "Bad man."

Addie had not been feeling guilty, just relieved it wasn't she who was overboard and shocked that Mike was. But now that Celia brought up guilt, she did start to feel responsible for having started this chain of events in the first place. And she realized that in what seemed to be his dying declaration, he had denied killing Cathy. But was it a dying declaration, or was it a last punch at Addie? She wondered how Cathy could have fallen for Mike in the first place. She and Celia hugged and waited for the rescue boats to return. Finally, Addie spotted the motorboats returning, one with an extra man. Cheers arose from the ferry where all the passengers were lined up along the windows and the railings, watching. The boats were hauled aboard, the engines revved up, and the ferry moved forward toward port again. The passengers moved away from the railings and windows and resumed sipping their cocktails and chatting.

Celia unclasped herself from Addie and reached out to take her hand again. Then she led her to the staircase. Addie hobbled down step by step, her knee stinging. She needed to get off the boat as soon as she could when it docked and go to her mother's or Dita's, not home, where she'd be alone until Danny got out of school. She wondered whether the guys, Sean, Karl, and Harry, had paid Mike a visit and gotten him worked up. She should have listened to Dita and not followed him that day. Who knew he'd carry that this far? One thing she knew for sure, this kind of detective work didn't suit her one bit. Maybe Dita didn't mind when people followed her and threatened her, but she, Addie, sure did.

When she reached the cabin, she thanked Celia, who smiled and said, "You were gone too long, so I came to find you. Bad men on board."

Addie's eyes teared up. This ancient woman who almost never spoke had watched out for her. She drew Celia into an embrace once more. Then the woman rustled off to her seat, closed her eyes, and nodded off.

Addie tried to calm down. She couldn't watch the water. It had lost its calming effect. Now it made her think of drowning. She looked at her phone instead, about to text Dita to see if she'd gotten home, but then she saw Mike, wrapped in an old blue woolen blanket, being carried into the cabin by two crew members, who laid him on a bench on the other side of the ferry. Was he alive or dead? She needed to pace, so she went to the concession stand to order a glass of wine, then changed her mind. She sat back down at her table but switched seats to the other bench so her back was to Mike. She needed to block him from her mind. She wasn't on the work roster today, so she wouldn't get called to the medical center for Mike if he was still breathing. It didn't occur to her that the police would be waiting at the dock and would want to question her about Mike, suspicious that she might have shoved him overboard. Dita would have realized that, but not Addie, who'd never hurt anyone except when she gave them a shot or cleaned their wounds.

She was focused on how tough being single could be. She didn't want to go home. There was no one there to comfort her. Well, later there'd be the 11-year-old, but she couldn't complain to him. She liked to think of herself as liberated, but when a man pushed you around, what recourse did you have? If she complained to the police, next time Mike had her alone, he might really hurt her, that is, if he was alive, or kill her, as he had threatened. When Mel was her husband, he'd have sat down with Mike and convinced him to back off, unlike Sean or Harry, who would threaten him to get him to stop. Mel would have smoothed everything over. That was one of the things she'd liked about him. He'd probably been smoothing things over with her, too, for a long time, and she hadn't realized that's what he was doing. Was she just stupid that it took her so long to get it?

By the time the ferry was close to docking, she was so rattled she hobbled downstairs before anyone else could line up and unhooked the rope that cordoned off the staircase from the car deck. Passengers weren't supposed to be on the car deck during the voyage, and the crew let the cars leave first when they docked. That kept foot passengers out of the way. She ignored the rules, walked over to her packages and bag, and looked into the parked cars. One of the other island mothers, Martha, was sitting in her vehicle, something Addie often did when she had a car on board, even though that, too, was against the ferry company rules. Addie went over to her and knocked on the window. Sometimes, especially in summer, the crew squeezed the cars in so close that passengers couldn't get out. To exit, they either had to leave before the car backed in, or climb over the center console, not an easy feat. Martha was in a spot where her doors could open, and she unlocked them for Addie. The camaraderie among parents was one of the nicer aspects of the island. Addie never worried about Danny when she needed to be off island or at the clinic. He was always able to bunk in at a friend's house, and she opened her home to his friends as well. Parents pitched in for each other without hesitation.

"Martha, can I ride off the ferry with you? I'll get out at the Pub since you don't go my way and hitch a ride home from there." She'd said that automatically. She just as easily could have said, "Drop me at Dita's," if she didn't want to go home to an empty house, or her mother's shop. But no, her heart pointed her to Harry. Was she so dependent she needed to run to a man?

"Hop in," Martha told her. "I'll take you all the way home if you want."

"No, I don't want to hold you up," Addie said. She felt like she was still shaking, like her body hadn't caught up to the fact that she was safe now.

"You hoping Harry's around?" Martha's eyes sparkled, and she broke into a smile.

Addie felt the heat around her neck starting. She determined to hold it there and not blush. "Maybe," she said, for the first time acknowledging to anyone besides Dita that she might be interested in seeing Harry. But then she tempered that. "Or Karl or Sean might be around. Either of them could give me a lift in a while."

She needed to learn to play it cool. The whole island would be jibber-jabbering about her and Harry. That was the downside of a close community.

"Sure," Martha said, playing along. "Wherever you want is fine."

"Actually, if you could drop me at the post office, that would be good."

"How will you get your bundles home? I'll get my mail too, and then drop you at Harry's bar."

"On second thought, drop me at The Lorelei Shop afterward. My mother should be there. I'd really appreciate it." Addie realized stopping to see Harry would lead to spending the rest of the day with him. Rachel would be training her new helper, Doreen, today. Business was brisk on weekends, and next week, the 4th of July, summer season would begin in earnest every day.

Seeing her mother would ground her. She could calm down beside her. Maybe her mother would drive her home and stay with her a while, have lunch. She wouldn't tell her about Mike. No need to worry her. She'd call the Chief later and tell him. Maybe he would send a patrol past her house tonight, even come through the driveway to make sure she was all right. She wanted to be able to forget about Mike later and prepare a nice supper for Danny.

"Yes, I'll go to The Lorelei to see Mom. That's closer for you."

"No problem," Martha said. "Did you see Mike go overboard? I got texts from three people. Wish I'd seen it. What a jerk! I guess he's alive. Good thing the crew drills on that."

Martha seemed unfazed. All part of living on the island, Addie thought, trying to stop the shaking that had not yet abated.

TWENTY-FIVE

The bell on The Lorelei's front door tinkled when Addie opened it. She took a few paces sideways to glance down its three narrow aisles, looking for Rachel. She didn't see her.

"Mom?" she called.

"Right here," Rachel replied, straightening up. She'd been bent over, filling the shelves below the counter with jewelry too expensive to be left out in the open on top.

"Oh, okay. I didn't see you. Where's Doreen?" Addie asked.

Doreen was the summer worker Rachel had hired. Now that she and Teddy were about to marry, she could spare the money to have help at the shop. "I sent her to the post office with some orders to mail. Doesn't the shop look lovely?" she asked, sweeping her hand in a flourish.

Addie looked around. It did indeed look lovely, and she said as much. Tourists flocked to The Lorelei. Her mother had always stocked the most interesting curios on Block Island: indigenous dolls from South America, gold rings crafted in India with semi-precious stones, colorful embroidered dresses and blouses from Guatemala, stone Buddha fountains from Nepal. This year she had large feathered bird statuettes. Addie didn't know where she'd found those, but the real difference in the shop was the gleam of the floor and the ceiling, the upgrades Teddy had helped her with over the winter. Addie felt safe here among her mother's treasures.

"Sit," Rachel said, patting the seat next to her. "What happened to your leg? You're limping."

Addie had hoped her mother wouldn't notice how flustered she felt. She'd forgotten about her knee. "I fell. If you give me a ride home, I'll tell you all about it. Have lunch with me."

She put her bundles down on the floor. Their conversation was interrupted by the chiming of the doorbell. Doreen was back. She announced she'd overheard a group of tourists talking about The Lorelei as they grouped together for lunch outside the Island Inn. She hoped they'd wander over after their lunches.

"Then I'll be back after lunch," Rachel told her. "I'm going home with Addie for a while. Call me when they get here, and I'll drive back. Come, Addie, let's go."

"I need to either stop at Dita's with the groceries I bought her, or invite her over," Addie said as they left through the small stock room and out the rear door.

"Invite her over. I haven't seen Janie and Tuffy for a while," Rachel replied.

At the house, Addie limped upstairs to change and to call the chief, leaving Rachel downstairs to make their salads and wait for Dita and Janie. She shut her door and punched in the chief on speed dial. When he answered, she thought he sounded alarmed. He'd sent Karl to meet her at the dock, and when she wasn't there, they worried that Mike had hurt her. They knew he hadn't pushed her, but maybe she'd fallen when she was leaving. They searched the whole vessel unsuccessfully. Addie realized he was angry at her for disappearing, but she'd been so scared. He told her to stay home, and he'd be there in an hour or so when they'd processed Mike, after the Coast Guard helicopter arrived to transfer him to a hospital with a psychiatric emergency room on the mainland. Addie thought she would feel relieved that Mike was alive, but she wasn't. She was scared he'd come for her again when he recovered. She clicked off and heard her mother downstairs chirping at Janie. Dita had arrived with her troop. It was time to tell them her story.

Rachel clucked her tongue throughout the entire recitation. Dita relived her own near-death experiences as she listened and expressed sympathy for Addie's. Both women reached out to comfort Addie, who was finally able to let the tears she'd been holding back leak out. They let her cry until she had no more tears left. She dabbed her eyes and sniffled.

And then Dita speculated about Mike. "Mike used to be known as mild-mannered, but did any of us really know him? People come here and they play the part of new worker, new resident, and they try to control themselves so they don't get pigeon-holed as just another crackpot washashore. They're on their best behavior, but after a while, they can't help themselves. Their true natures emerge."

Rachel agreed. "For that matter, what do we really know about Cathy? We all mourned her loss because she was the nicest person, but she'd only been here less than a year. We know little to nothing more before that except what her parents included in her obituary. And look at Mel."

Addie glared at her. "Let's not bring him up, Mom."

"Or Harry," Rachel quickly said, correcting herself. She reached over and picked up a pile of envelopes from the table. "I almost forgot. Here's your mail, Addie. I took it out of the bag when I was putting away your groceries. You might note that there's an official-looking envelope."

Addie took them and dropped all but the letter from the state court into the empty shopping bags. She ripped the letter from the court open. Her face brightened as she read it.

"Mom, Dita, look! My divorce—it's official." She waved the letter toward Rachel, who grabbed it from her and skimmed through it. Then she reached out and hugged her daughter.

"My dear Addie, it's over. Now you can go on with your life," she murmured.

"I don't know whether to crow or cry," Addie admitted. "I feel relieved it's over, yet part of me wishes it never happened."

"I know. You can move into my cottage if you want and sell the house.

It's all yours. I told you that already. You'd make a good bundle of money. Ask Dahlia what it's worth."

The idea made sense, financially at least, but Addie thought it was too soon. Mel might realize in his haste to dissolve his marriage he'd made a mistake signing the house over to her and take her back to court. She didn't know if that was a legal possibility, but what if? She didn't want to start haggling with him all over again, so she told her mother no, for now.

"Mom, you should rent the cottage out this summer. It's not too late to find some tourists. Dahlia has a waiting list. I think I should stay in my house for a while. Danny's had so much change with Mel leaving and a stepmother over on the mainland. I want to keep him in his home a little longer."

"My house isn't new to him. He's comfortable there," Rachel said, "and you could use the money."

"I've been thinking of taking in a roommate to help pay the mortgage," Addie said.

"I don't like that idea," Rachel said, "not after what happened with mine."

Addie and Dita both knew she was talking about their former friend Loretta, aka crime family member, drug dealer, murderer—the epitome of the washashore who assumed a role to hide who she really was.

Addie decided not to argue the point. Her mother was right. She could get by a bit longer without the extra money.

But Rachel wanted to make sure of something else. "And don't invite Harry to move in, not that we don't know the real him: womanizer, barfly, guy's guy."

Addie started to turn red with anger. "First of all, we're not serious. Second of all, he's a bar owner, not a barfly. And third, why would I do that with Danny needing to get over Mel? You really don't know me, Mom, your own daughter."

Dita was shocked. She'd never known these two to have an argument like this. Rachel and Addie always were so la-di-dah close they made her feel like a terrible daughter. She suspected there was more to this than what she was hearing. How did Rachel know about Harry? Had she caught them together? She couldn't resist egging them on.

"Don't worry, Rachel," Dita said. "Harry's got his own place to take Addie to."

The two women clammed up, and Dita knew it was time to go.

"Ciao, my friends. I need to bring Janie home for her lunch."

"And I need to get back to The Lorelei," Rachel said, following her out. She knew she'd overstayed her welcome also.

Addie didn't try to convince them to stay. "The Chief's coming over to interview me, or maybe interrogate me, about Mike. You don't think he believes I pushed Mike overboard, do you?"

Dita laughed. "Mike's only three times bigger than you! Don't be ridiculous."

Addie wondered if she should feel insulted. Once he was on the railing, if he wasn't holding on tight, she thought she could have pushed him over.

"I do think you should tell him we're suspicious of Jessica and Artie."

It wasn't long before the chief showed up. He looked official in his gold-buttoned uniform. Addie had not noticed before that he was a handsome man with a physique that spoke to his daily exercise routine. Sean had mentioned that the chief was not only a member of the fitness center, he showed up every day. In summer, he donned his wetsuit and went spearfishing. Unlike other police chiefs who'd come to the island for a few years after retirement from more dangerous postings on the mainland and who never really become islanders, he had totally adapted to island life.

"This won't take long," he said.

"I hope not, George. I'd like not to have to tell Danny."

He laughed. "Addie, don't you think the kids are all talking about it already? This is the age of instant messaging."

He was probably right. How was she going to explain herself to her boy? First things first. She offered the chief the last cup of coffee that was still in the pot, and he accepted, so she reheated it and then answered his questions. But as she relived the scene, she grew scared yet again. Her hand shook as she poured the coffee into his cup. He reached out to steady it, acknowledging how frightening this must have been for her. And he urged her, and Dita as well, to leave the sleuthing to him from here on.

"I guess it was a mistake for me to ask Dita to do some interviews. I never expected you two would sleuth around Mike. He has a record, you know, and he did some jail time before he came here," he said.

The chief believed her version of the story, though Mike had told him Addie'd gone to the upper deck to bother him.

"If you make a complaint," he said, "I could charge him with assault. I have only your word, and Celia's. She didn't see it start."

Addie demurred. "I don't want any more trouble with him. I'm not charging him."

"Hopefully he'll move on to another place where he can slip into anonymity for a while," the chief said. "I still suspect Josh Martel for Bunny's murder, but I've got no evidence on him other than the fact that he worked for her and sneaked into her house to sleep."

"George, I think Dita's right. He's just a poor, homeless guy," she said. She launched into the suspicions she and Dita had about Artie and Jessica.

The chief heard her out, and then he buttoned his jacket, put his hat back on, and went to the door. "I'll have the guys watch your house tonight. Call if there's any problem."

And while Addie met with the chief, Dita and Janie stopped in to see Caroline again. Though Dita had told her mother about Artie, she felt she needed to convey how dangerous Artie and Jessica might be. She rehearsed several ways of delivering the message on the way over, but none felt comfortable. Caroline was surprised to see her. Usually Dita texted before she came. Still, she was pleasantly surprised. She reached over and took Janie from Dita and was rewarded with a smile from her granddaughter.

"Look, Dita, she smiled at me."

Dita teased her mother. "It's just gas, as you know."

"Hah! These doctors and their tales," Caroline said.

Dita sat on her mother's couch. "Remember what I said about Artie? There's more." She launched into the suspicions she and Addie harbored about him and Jessica and finished with the hug between Jessica and Artie. "I wasn't going to tell you because I didn't want to interfere with your life, but I am worried."

Caroline was seated in the small-sized recliner, Janie on her lap. "I'm glad you did. Nothing about him would surprise me, but murder? That's extreme. How sure are you?"

"Not sure, but we're working on it—enough that I'm sorry you live right next door to Jessica."

Caroline ran her hand through her hair and said, "I wondered why he'd be interested in me. Men like him usually are attracted to younger women. I thought he was just wanting to try me out, and I suspected something between him and Jessica. Basically, the more I was around him, the less I liked him. So, nothing lost, my dear, except a couple evenings I would have spent alone here."

Dita was relieved, but she was also sad for her mother.

"Now tell me how to handle Jessica. She is my neighbor, and you suspect her of murder, too. Of course, I'll have to remember to keep my doors locked. I don't think I can avoid her, or she'll suspect I know something. I'm just going to tell her I decided it was too soon for me to date, and I'm not seeing Artie anymore. She's quite something, isn't she? If she is a killer, she wormed her way into Bunny's finances, now she's hooking up with Bernie, trying to wrangle money from all the old island folk and sneaking around with Artie. She's so busy, I hope she forgets about me."

TWENTY-SIX

Race Week on Block Island—the largest event of the year. Sailers from all over the country, and maybe even the world, converged on the island for an entire week of races in the Block Island Sound. The crews brought a special vibe to the island, high energy in comparison to the usual tourists who just wanted to lie back and vacation. Their graceful sailers bobbed at the docks between races, and the crews partied at the bars at night. The waters surrounding the island were flecked with color when they raced, the reds, blues, whites, and yellows of their sails billowing in the winds, drooping in a calm. Locals lined the beaches and cliffs to watch, especially the round-the-island race.

Addie was on her way to the marina where Artie's stinkpot boat was docked. He had invited Addie, Caroline, Dr. Bennett, Jessica, and Bernard to have lunch on the upper deck of the marina's bar and then to motor out to watch the afternoon races from the sea. There was no way she'd go out on Artie's boat, though. She even feared the ferry now. Addie would go home when the rest of them boarded his boat. She wondered if Caroline would even show up for lunch now that Dita had had her talk with her.

But first, Addie had a stop to make. She wanted to see Harry. She strolled into the pub, using the front door, sure of herself, not caring if anyone was watching. Sticking out of her pocket was the envelope with the official divorce papers.

She knew Harry would be getting the bar ready to open. She was excited. She couldn't wait to see him, but she had planned it so there wouldn't be time for him to wrangle her to his house. He'd be too busy.

"Harry! Harry, are you here?" she shouted, looking around. She went behind the bar and into the kitchen. She needn't have yelled. He was right nearby, leaning over the stove while stirring the contents of a large pot. He looked up and smiled. She watched the bulges in his biceps as he mixed the chili for tonight's special.

"Look, look what came," she said, waving the envelope over her head.

He stopped stirring. She couldn't hide her excitement as he reached for the dishtowel tucked into his waistband and dried his hands. He hustled closer to her, and she realized she couldn't even watch him walk without feeling aroused. She'd never been like this with Mel. She wondered, would she ever get over Harry and go back to normal?

She cleared her throat. "Harry, guess what this is!" She waved the envelope around again.

At last, he got it. "Our freedom?" he asked, and he grabbed the envelope. He scanned the letter and handed it back, his face brightening.

She felt his breath on her forehead. She felt her blood pressure rise. She felt alive. His face in hers, she noticed the arch of his brows, the line of his nose, his full lips. How totally handsome! He whispered in her ear, rousing her even more. "Good thing you came early. Gives us an hour before I need to be back here. Let me get tonight's chili off the stove, and we'll get out of here and celebrate." He pulled away and moved quickly, a new spring in his step, to get the chili into the walk-in.

She hadn't expected him to be more excited than she was, but then, he was a guy after all. Testosterone might just be stronger medicine than estrogen.

"I'm supposed to meet some people at Artie's boat. We're going to watch the race from the marina. I just stopped in to tell you this news," she objected.

He looked at her, his brows raised, and he rolled his eyes as if saying 'really?' and she knew she wasn't going to that boat, not today, maybe not ever. Collecting more information on Jessica, Bernie, and Artie would have to wait.

"I don't know if I can wait a minute more," he said. "In fact, I can't."

"*Wow*," she thought. "*Mel was never like this. No urgency there.*"

And she realized that she and Mel had never had that kind of chemistry. She and Harry had had a spark between them for years. Maybe everyone, including Mel, was right. She had not had an actual affair with Harry during her marriage, but her hormones had. And she had a sudden realization about the hug that Artie and Jessica had shared. It really was more than friendship. She could almost visualize the spark that had passed between them. How could she and Dita both have doubted that truth?

Then Harry was back; he held her close, and they unpeeled each other's pants. He mamboed her into the pantry, and she climbed his hips as they thumped against the spice shelf. The scent of the pantry spices—thyme, rosemary, and hot chili from the kitchen—swirled in the air around them as they clasped each other, lending an exotic aura.

Afterward she said, "Okay, my house." She could barely get the words out. Artie could hold his party on his boat without her. She didn't like him anyway, not one bit.

In his truck, Harry pulled her close. "No need to hide anymore, is there?" he asked, landing a sweet kiss on her curls. "Doesn't matter if Mel sees, or Dita sees, or your mother."

"Mine already saw, remember?"

"How could I forget?"At Addie's house, they started all over again, this time beginning on the stairs to her bedroom and moving in sync to her bed, unpeeling all the clothes in a more leisurely fashion. She'd never felt this intense need with Mel. This man was like the most powerful drug she could imagine. Does Dita feel this way about Sean? Was this always lacking between me and Mel? Am I doing the right thing? And then she stopped wondering because a flow of ecstasy eclipsed everything else, including her ability to breathe. Sweat poured from both of them.

"Addie, Addie, what you do to me, I don't know if my heart can endure you."

They lay next to each other, her head on his tats, his arm hot surrounding her, both of them used up like the fragments of firecrackers strewn on the ground in the aftermath of the big show. She kissed him, kissed the tats, his chest, his abs, his core, his thighs, his everything. He groaned aloud, "Addie, don't stop."

And then he was kissing every inch of her until she thought she would ignite, and that would be fine. All the darkness for the moment forgotten, and then they were done, and they both drifted into a light nap. When they woke, he looked at his watch.

"I've got to go open the bar. I'm late already. Come for supper tonight. Bring Danny." He was pulling on his tee shirt, buckling his pants, and she wanted him back next to her. Instead, he pulled her to her feet, into a deep kiss.

"Later," he said. "Summer crowd coming."

She'd be on call later, also. They would be up to their waists in work as the tourists flooded the island. This might have been a rare, stolen moment with summer coming on. Her whole body tingled. "Harry," she murmured.

"Don't worry. We're together now. This isn't like Mel. You own me."

"Harry." This feeling was so new. She didn't know what to do with herself.

He held her once more, squeezed her hand, and disappeared down the stairs. She freshened up and headed to the marina in case Artie and his invitees were still there. She had promised Dita she'd keep watch.

PART THREE

THE SUMMER SEASON

TWENTY-SEVEN

July 4th weekend was two days away, and still no one had been arrested for Bunny's murder, nor for Cathy's. Dita fretted about this as she took Janie's red, white, and blue summer onesie out of the fresh laundry basket. She knew who it was; why didn't George? Did she and Addie have to sleuth out everything? They were trying to come up with a trap, but so far, nothing they came up with seemed like it would work.

It was a hot, sticky day. The sun pierced through the bubbling humidity, and no one moved without effort this morning, not even the birds. A cardinal couple perched motionless inside the bushes in the front yard; the usually busy and chirpy sparrows nested in silence beneath the brambles. All the wood in the house was swollen. Dita couldn't pull any drawers open to find a hair ribbon for Janie; even the front door had to be yanked to open. Addie had stopped off to leave some muffins and thought the door was locked. It was not. In most of New England, these were called the dog days of summer. Out here on this island in the fetid ocean, they were the stuck drawer days, the days when the humidity was so thick you could almost cut it with a knife.

Dita and Addie chatted about the state of the murder cases over their coffee.

"Stuck, we're just stuck like the door," Dita groused. "The chief still thinks poor Josh killed Bunny, but you and I know it wasn't him; we just have no proof."

Addie agreed, and she commented on the spark they'd noticed

between Artie and Jessica. Maybe they could use that, set something up that revealed their liaison. If people had noticed her and Harry, might they not catch on to Artie and Jessica? At the least, they wouldn't seem trustworthy, and their financial scheme might sputter, because, Addie said, she was sure it was a scheme.

"Hmm, you recognize that electricity between people now that you and Harry are... you know," Dita said, looking at her friend and laughing.

Addie blushed. "Stop," she said. "We're talking about Artie and Jessica, not me."

"The chief is accepting Mike's denial to you as he went overboard as a dying declaration and took him off the suspect list," Dita said.

"But he was convinced that I didn't push Mike off the railing..."

Dita interrupted her. "Did you? I never asked you because you were so upset about the whole thing, but did you push him over?"

Addie turned purple. "Dita, stop fooling around. You know I did not. Now be serious, or I'll leave."

"Okay, okay, I haven't ruled out Mike completely even though the chief has, but I'm leaning toward Jessica. Maybe she thought she'd be Bunny's beneficiary. Then when it turned out to be Bernard and he came to collect, she decided to get close to him."

"Yes, interesting that she married him, right? He's next in line to die, isn't he?"

"I think it would be too soon," Dita said. "I think they're in cahoots with him."

Addie reached over to pat Tuffy, who'd curled up at her feet waiting for a muffin crumb to fall. "Poor doggie, you've been cast aside for a human pet," Addie said. "Maybe you should come live with me and Danny."

"Hmmf, cast aside, not. He gets more than his share," Dita protested.

"To get back to that hug, or whatever it was, between Artie and Jessica, there's something going on there. I mean, first Bernard tells us he and Jessica are just friends, meaning friends with benefits, and they see other people. Then suddenly they're married. Jessica tells us she and Artie are just friends, but that hug, that spark," Addie said.

Dita raised her eyebrows.

"Don't start," Addie said.

Dita smiled. "To continue, I don't trust that Artie at all, and I don't like my mother seeing him. I'm worried he'll wine and dine her, take a few turns in the hay with her, and dump her."

"Because he's really involved with Jessica?"

"I don't know, maybe," Dita said. "Is posh Jessica the killer?"

"I can see her killing Bunny, but why Cathy?" Addie asked.

"Maybe Cathy was on to her. Maybe she was in cahoots with Mike," Dita said.

"How would Jessica have known Mike? She never came here before Bunny bought the house, as far as we know."

Dita sighed. "We're missing something. Maybe we need to look a little deeper into Cathy's life before she came here. There must be a connection somewhere. For that matter, like your mother said, who among the washashores do we really know anything about before they came here? Even your Harry."

"He's not my Harry, and he's not a washashore. He was a summer kid. His parents owned a cottage out on the West Side. He even went to the Block Island School every year in the fall."

"Okay, we know about him then, didn't come here after being a hit man for the syndicate," Dita yielded, and then she added, "like Loretta."

They sat in silence over their coffees until Addie had a question for Dita. "Do you think Jessica suspected that we saw her and Artie in the parking lot that day. If she did kill Bunny and Cathy, or have them killed, we could be in danger."

"Don't let what Mike did make you scared of everything, Addie. Jessica didn't know we were out in the parking lot watching. She didn't know we delayed going in."

Addie wasn't convinced. "What if she talked to the shopkeeper in the dress store and found out I was in there for a while? She'd know we came earlier and might have seen her. We need to grill Dahlia more. She's the one who knew them first."

"I agree with grilling Dahlia, but I think your idea is farfetched," Dita said. "Calm down. Mike's off the island for good. No need to be fearful."

Addie got up and put her dishes in the sink. "Okay. Well, my friend, I think it's time to get on with my day. Is Sean closing up for the parade on the Fourth?"

"I'll meet him in town at the Gothic. Want to join us? We're watching from their stone wall."

"Not this year," Addie said. "Danny and I are going to join Harry on the front porch of his bar. Sure you don't want to come there with us?"

"I'll walk up after. We already told Karen and Bert that we'd come there. You can have fun with Harry."

"Stop smirking," Addie said. "He has to go back to work afterward, so I'll find you if I don't get called into the Medical Center. I think Danny's going to catch up with some friends."

"When Sean goes to the Be Fit, I will find Jessica and Artie to keep an eye on them. Maybe we should trade off watching them," Dita said, but then she remembered Addie trying to spy on Mike. "Or maybe it should just be me."

Plans made, Addie left.

Later, Dita had an idea. She'd do a follow-up article on Cathy, not to go in the paper during the week of the Fourth, but the week after, which wasn't as heavy a tourist week. There'd be room for a short piece, and she'd downplay the murder, focusing more on where Cathy had surfed and done before coming to the island. The obituary had not gone into details. She found the parents' phone numbers and email address with the information she'd received for the obituary. They still lived in the same town. She decided to call.

Cathy's mother answered and was forthcoming about Cathy's life before Block Island. Dita took notes while she listened. When Dita finished, Cathy's mother, Elizabeth, surprised her with a bit of extra information she never would have expected.

"When we came to the island for Cathy's paddle-out service, we stopped at a small cafe near the ferry..."

"The Books and Bakes?" Dita asked.

"Yes, I think so. While we were drinking our coffees, a man came in and picked up an order. I could swear he was from our village in Ohio. He used to run an ad in the back of the newspaper with his picture, maybe ten years ago, fifteen years ago. He was an electrician, Carter something or other. He wasn't someone we knew, we just remembered his ads because at one time we needed an electrician, so we didn't say hello."

"Did Cathy ever mention him?" Dita asked.

"Not by name, but she did say she thought she recognized someone from here. It wasn't important, so we never spoke about it again."

Was this the link Dita needed? "Elizabeth," she said. "What's the name of your newspaper? Does it still publish? I'm going to give them a call tomorrow to follow this up, and then I'll let Chief Gomez know. I think he'll be in touch with you, also."

Dita jotted down the name of the newspaper and the number Elizabeth gave her as well.

"Again," she said. "I'm so sorry for your loss. She was a lovely young woman. The whole island feels her loss."

"Everyone except the killers, but thank you. I'm grateful you're helping with the investigation."

As soon as the call ended, Dita found the newspaper online. Instead of waiting for the next day, she popped them an email asking whether they had back issues digitized. In the morning she phoned them, and after a brief conversation, she had the link to their archives, all their editions photographed and uploaded online. They even helped by trolling through their advertising history, finding the years that Carter, aka Artie, had paid for business card sized ads. Dita found the newspaper interesting and spent several hours zipping through it. When she found one of Artie's ads, she pinched it larger, and there was Carter "Artie" Crane, younger, of course, but unmistakable unless he had a twin. She screenshot several of his ads as she scrolled through the pages of the editions, and then a picture in a wedding announcement caught her eye. A local woman named Amy Parker married a man named James Carrigan. At first glance, she looked a lot like Jessica Glen. At second glance, after Dita increased the size, Dita thought she had to be a younger Jessica Glen. Dita took a screen-shot and then read the article. Jessica was a bank teller, her husband a carpenter. One of the ushers was Carter Crane.

"Sean," Dita screamed. "Sean, come look at this!" She ran from her desk into the hall and yelled down the stairs to him. "Come, come quick."

"Okay, don't wake the baby. I'm surprised she's not screaming already." He lumbered up the steps, and she sat down at the desk again and pressed print.

"This is the *Gazette* from that small Ohio town where Cathy's family lives. I asked them if I could go through their digital archives. Look at this, look."

He took the two pages from the printer trolley. "Holy guacamole, Dita."

"Right," she declared. "It's them, isn't it?"

"Where's the husband, then?" he asked.

"James Carrington?"

"He's not here on Block Island."

"Maybe I can put in a search query," Dita suggested. She scrolled, exited to the beginning of the archive, and typed his name into the search box. There were five entries, and the first four, including the wedding announcement, were not useful, but the fifth was his obituary.

Sean stood in back of her, reading over her shoulder again. "Sudden death from anaphylaxis," he mumbled in a reading voice, "allergic to shellfish. His wife thinks it was the fish soup she bought at the local fish market. Assumed it was just fish."

"She killed him, didn't she?" Dita was astonished. She pressed print again.

"On purpose, you think?" Sean wondered.

"Maybe. But why?"

Sean collected the printout and reread the death notice. "I think you need to call Cathy's mother back."

"I think you're right."

"You did warn your mother to stay away from Artie, right?"

"I did, and now I'll warn her about Jessica, too. First, though, we need to find a motive."

She already was ringing Elizabeth, Cathy's mother. After apologizing for bothering her again, she told her what she'd found.

"Amy is on Block Island? Maybe that's what Cathy wanted to tell me. I wonder if she saw her and said hello. Amy worked at the bank, and I used to take Cathy with me when I went there. She always got a candy from Amy, so she liked her, and I think she would have remembered her." She hesitated a moment. "You don't think Amy killed her, do you? People thought she was pretty stupid to feed her husband that soup, but murder?"

"She could have killed him on purpose. What do you remember of that period of time? Why would Amy change her name and move? Did people blame her, even if they didn't suspect murder?"

Dita was excited. She felt she was close to answers, and she wished Addie was with her. She grabbed a pen and a sticky note and wrote, *Call Addie to tell her,*and handed it to Sean. He nodded and stepped into the hallway to make the call.

Cathy's mother said that there was talk for a while, but there was an embezzlement at the bank soon afterward that became the number one topic in local circles. Her memory was spotty, but she recalled they never figured out who took the money, and the bank, a city savings and loan, closed soon after, with the officers under suspicion. Dita had a sudden inspiration.

"Tell me, was Amy wealthy? Did she and her husband have money?"

"I don't know, but she would have lost her job when the bank closed, and she no longer had income from her husband. I don't think her parents were wealthy. Maybe her husband had life insurance."

Yet, Amy came to Westport with a bundle of money and opened an investment counseling firm. How much life insurance would a carpenter's helper have had? And why would she kill him? Was she already having an affair with Artie? Was that enough motive instead of divorce? She was missing something. She'd let the chief know what she found, and she'd warn her mother again to remember to lock her doors.

"I'll get back to you when I know more, Elizabeth," she said.

She heard Sean at the door letting Addie in. She'd run right over when Sean called.

"Dita, I can't believe you found a house for your mother right next door to a murderer!" she called as she ran upstairs. "You need to get her out of there until they're arrested. Have her stay with you."

"Not a bad idea. I'm not sure I'll be able to convince her, though."

They called to tell Caroline, and she laughed at them. She thought Artie and Jessica were both slippery, but murderers? She said she felt like she was in a television show and they should come back to reality, but she was already locking her doors. With Josh roaming the island and them next door, locking up did seem necessary.

After warning Caroline, Dita called the chief on his cell phone. She could barely hear him through all the background noise. This was the busiest time of year for the local police, and even Chief George Gomez was out in the crowds keeping order. Dita felt relieved that he seemed to believe her, finally, and though he was up to the brim of his police hat over the 4th, he'd talk to the state troopers that had come to help about bringing Jessica and Artie in for a talk as soon as things quieted down a bit. That, Dita knew, would be a couple days. Maybe she could find out more before then. At the least, she and Addie needed to keep an eye on them. They might kill again.

TWENTY-EIGHT

On the night before the Fourth, Caroline didn't have company, and she didn't plan to go out. She was testing her newfound ability to be comfortable alone. It had taken her many months to accustom herself to singlehood after her husband's death, but she was there at last. Tonight she was having a moment, enjoying a glass of full-bodied Merlot at dusk in the tights and tank top that she slept in. She dimmed the kitchen light, thinking she'd mosey into the living room, spread out on the couch, and read her latest book club novel. She belonged to three book clubs, two of them on Zoom. It was difficult to keep up, but she couldn't decide which one to quit.

Suddenly, the lights next door flicked on. Jessica, wearing a pink print sleeveless shift, popular with the doctor/lawyer cocktail crowd, she traipsed into her living room. When she reached the center, she twirled around and, to Caroline's surprise, Artie, not Bernard, swooped in and caught Jessica in his arms, dipping her as though dancing to music. But maybe they were; Caroline could only see, not hear them.

"Hmmmf," she said, expecting Bernard to trounce in next.

But he did not. Instead, Artie lifted Jessica up from the dip, pulled her body to his, and planted a squishy kiss on her mouth. Jessica placed her hands over Artie's ears, holding him close. Caroline's mouth flew open.

"Hmmmf," she repeated, a bit louder. She was totally caught up watching, standing in place, her wine glass tipping in her hand.

Now Artie was running his hands all over Jessica, unzipping her as he went. She was unbuttoning the waistband on his boater shorts. Once that was open, they shed clothes like they were peeling banana skins. Caroline was transfixed. She couldn't pull herself away. When the two were totally naked and Jessica climbed onto Artie, she let out a "holy hmmmf" and spilled all the wine out of her glass, almost dropping it.

She held her breath when they fell onto the couch. Their living room faced her kitchen, and the couch faced her. *Ohhh*, they were really working out on that soft, immaculate, new couch. She leaned over sideways to figure out just what they were doing. *Huh*, she said. Then, *ew*! *Really?* She raised her free hand to cover her mouth.

But where was Bernard? Was he going to arrive any minute and jump onto the couch with them? He had said they weren't exclusive, but then he hadn't said they did threesomes. He and Jessica were married now. Would he get a gun and shoot them if he walked in?

She was so glad she'd been smart enough to keep Artie at arm's length, that her couch hadn't become yet another to bear his bare bum. She'd seen enough, actually more than enough. Jessica and Artie were still locked together like two stray dogs. Caroline decided to turn her back to them and walk away, but then they looked straight at her and waved. *Oh, no*. She'd been so engrossed she'd forgotten her kitchen light was dimmed, but not off. She realized they could see her silhouetted in her kitchen, standing and watching them. Should she wave back, and then tactfully retreat? But, double *oh, no*, Artie was gesturing, beckoning her to come join them. She grimaced and turned as red as Addie often did, almost tripping over her own feet to race out of the room. She did not stop to pull the shades first. She left them open and would not return to the room until morning. She checked the lock on the front door on her way and ran upstairs to her den overlooking the high hedge on the other side of the house.

What had just happened? Caroline could never face Jessica again, or Artie. The first man she'd dated since.... She turned on the small TV and tried to watch something, anything, but her mind was whirling. Was this really her life now? And her daughter thought the couple were murderers. Could she stop the sale of her house on the mainland and go back to her old life where people were normal, even in their sex lives? What had she done?

TWENTY-NINE

July 4th could be called the pinnacle of the island's summer season, that is, if the weather is good. This year it was stellar. Optimists saw the Fourth as the official opening of summer season when money would come pouring in; pessimists dreaded being overrun with slap-happy visitors for eight more weeks. And this year, the Fourth actually fell on the weekend, on a Saturday, so more people were able to come. Dita looked forward to seeing the parade with her mother, showing her how the island could celebrate. She was sad that thus far her mother's experience as an islander had been negative, what with the murders, and Jessica and Artie. She hoped Chief Gomez would arrest the two quickly and the island would once again be their Eden.

When she went to bed on Friday night, the harbor pond was dotted with the tiny mast lights of sailboats and the occasional lanterns of motorboats, mooring together or anchoring in for the holiday. On Saturday morning, Dita looked out her front window and thought she could probably walk across the harbor with small leaps, going boat to boat. The water between vessels was barely visible, and in the distance, where the Coast Guard cut entered the pond, boats were still streaming in from the sea.

There were yachts and cabin cruisers, speedboats, cigarette boats, dayboats, and schooners, large sailers and even a commercial sailing cruise ship from a port in Connecticut. There were boats tethered together, flotillas of three to six, party groups. People were moving about on the decks, the water taxi was hauling boaters to and from shore. How Bobby the baker found room for his skiff to motor through the pond selling his breakfast pastries she didn't know, but he was out there in his little motorboat, calling to customers to buy rolls and doughnuts and muffins, all made fresh in his bakery that morning.

"Get your fresh bread!"

"Sean, come see!" Dita shouted.

He stepped beside her and whistled. "The Double Ender is full also, not a room left. I heard Carrie at the Chamber say everything's rented all across the island. That was yesterday."

"Where are they sending people?" Dita asked. She knew it was the Chamber of Commerce that kept a listing of lodgings that could take people who missed the last boat off the island.

"I haven't a clue. Maybe back home? Is Janie ready?"

Janie was on the deck in her carriage, dressed in red, white, and blue with streamers on her carriage. Sean and Dita wore some red, white, and blue also, but not quite as much as the family that always vacationed on the island and came to their beach with the dad and two boys in patriotic bathing trunks, hats, and shirts. That guy was always wheedling his way onto their deck to get a beer and a chat from Sean.

"If that patriot guy comes by to bum a beer this afternoon, let's sign him up for the gym," Dita said.

Sean chuckled. "Let's go."

They drove to town, snuggled the truck into the small parking lot behind the hotel buildings, and joined their friends, the owners, along the street.

Was the parade a big deal? As parades go, it was minor. But as the island went, it was great; no, it was the greatest. At the head of the marchers, three islanders, steeped in the lore of the island, marched in Continental Army uniforms, a fife-and-drum trio, the same three every year. Uncle Sam, tall and even taller with his top hat, wove in and out, the same man every year. Marching bands from the mainland, fire department fife and drum corps, high schoolers from along the Connecticut shoreline, all came to march. And then there were the antique cars, the floats from the island's businesses, the shops, restaurants, and hotels. On their floats, some of the bars carried the rock bands playing their venues that weekend. Even The Lorelei sent a car float with an island teenager dressed as a mermaid. The local volunteer fire department ran some of their trucks and threw candies out to the children. Almost the whole island participated in the parade. There was even, one year, a float from the peaceniks, people protesting the Iraq War. Bringing up the rear, always, were the horses from the rental stable.

There was a theme each year. This year it was businesses people loved that were now gone from the island. Dita, cynical as usual, thought the theme this year should have been island murders, will they ever be solved? As she obsessed about this, she wondered whether the murderers were at the parade. Addie had already been attacked by Mike; would her suspects Artie and Jessica be stalking them?

"Dita, the baby's howling!" Sean brought her back to the now.

"You're her father. Pick her up!" she retorted, surprising even herself. The newness of motherhood, the excitement, was beginning to wear off. The short trip to the mainland with Addie had restored her personhood apart from her motherhood.

Sean hustled to pick up Janie, and Dita plopped down in a chair her friends offered her. Josh Martel stumbled by, apparently already drunk or just disabled, not with any marchers but going with the current through town. Dita wondered why the chief still suspected him. The man seemed almost ready for check-in at a hospital.

Not far behind him came Artie with a folding backpack chair and an open beer in hand. He spotted them and let out a cheery hello, then beelined toward them.

"Uh oh," Dita mumbled to Sean. "All yours." She wondered, were they being stalked?

"Good customer," Sean whispered back. "Remember? He signed up for the summer."

Artie gave them a hearty hello, even feigned interest in Janie, reaching out to give her an awkward pat on her arm, not a movement anyone who loved babies would do. Dita restrained herself from pushing him away, but one pat was all Artie could muster up. He and Sean exchanged how-are-yous and so on, and then Artie got to the point.

"I was looking for Jessica and Carolyn. I thought they might be with you," he said.

"Were we meeting them?" Sean asked Dita.

"I don't know why we would. Why would they be with us? Maybe they're with Bernard," she suggested.

"Not Bernard. He left," Artie replied.

"He did?" Sean asked. "He was at the Be Fit a couple days ago, and we had a long chat. He didn't say anything about taking off. In fact, we went through summer membership pricing. He was considering adding weekly training with me."

"I think the cruise line called and asked if he would do one more, a turnaround from Miami to Barcelona. They were short officers for the trip and offered him a bonus. He could have taken Jessica, but she wanted to stay here."

"I'm surprised Jessica didn't want to go," Dita said, but she was thinking that fit in with Artie and Jessica being the real couple. Despite her recent marriage, Jessica didn't seem emotionally connected to Bernard, maybe to his money.

Artie answered her with confidence. "I'm not in on all the details, but I think her business is booming right now. She mentioned that she had a lot of new clients. She was quite excited about her clubs," he said. "When she does well, I do well."

"Oh?" Sean asked.

"I invested quite a bit in that club she formed for us here. I think your mother did too, Dita, didn't she?"

Dita was not aware that Caroline had placed a large amount of money with Jessica. In fact, Caroline had said just the opposite. She'd told Dita she had put in a very small amount to test it. At least he didn't know her financials."I guess your mom isn't coming," Artie said, and he put on what

Dita thought was a very exaggerated disappointed face. "By the way," he continued, "we, I mean me and Caroline, had quite a nice time at lunch last week. She wouldn't come out on my boat, though. I took Rachel and Teddy, and Jessica and Bernard, and Dahlia." He looked at Dita. "Your friend Addie was supposed to go with us also, but she never showed up. I heard she's frightened of boats, but is your mother frightened also?"

Dita had told Caroline not to go, and she knew where Addie had been that day, but she wasn't about to tell him. She shrugged. The corners of her mouth turned up ever so slightly, but those corners came down pretty swiftly. She couldn't stop thinking about the day on the mainland when she and Addie had seen Artie fondling Jessica, because by now, that's how Dita thought of it. That hug in the village parking lot may or may not have been innocent, but in her mind, it had grown into outright fondling. As the days passed, it had mushroomed like an H-bomb, and she felt angry at him for pursuing her mother while she perceived he was involved with Jessica. She wondered whether his goal was to notch another sexual victory, or was there more? Fleece her savings and commit another murder?

"I'll just wait," he said, unpacking his chair and opening it, giving a nod to the owners before he sat. Dita had had enough of him. Whereas previously she just found him distasteful, now she downright detested him. She needed to get away and to find her mother and warn her Artie was with Sean and Janie.

"Maybe I'll go find Addie," she said, "that is, if you can mind Janie, Sean."

Janie was sound asleep. Sean looked over at her and nodded to Dita to go. She threaded her way through the crowds along the sidewalk. A midnight blue vintage Pontiac convertible was passing by with Celia in the back seat. A banner on its door declared she was the parade's Grand Marshal, a title reserved for the oldest person on the island. Dita waved to her, and Celia waved back, half rising out of her seat to throw a kiss to her. After she had passed, Dita crossed the street, sprinting between the cadres of marching bands to squeeze through the throngs to make her way to the Washashore Pub.

It took her five minutes, though it was normally a twenty-second stroll. The outside tables were filled, and the outdoor bar was overflowing, three people thick. To Dita's surprise, Addie was helping take orders, but she looked up and spotted her friend.

"Want a beer? It's all I have time to bring you," Addie said.

"No, I just came to chat, but you're way too busy."

"Not. I stepped in to help because I had nothing else to do. Harry's the one who's way too busy. He can't hang with me, but he has enough servers to bring drinks out." She was untying her apron as she spoke. "Just let me tell him I'm taking off." She disappeared inside and returned a few minutes later. "Where to?"

"I should relieve Sean. He's watching Janie, and then he needs to open the fitness center, so let's go sit with them. Also, I'm trying to find Caroline."

They retraced Dita's steps back to Sean, who was still hanging with Artie.

"Yuk, you didn't tell me Artie was here," Addie complained. "Let's go over to the library to see the end of the parade."

Artie stood to say hello to Addie, but she turned her back to him and marched away with Dita following.

"Sean, I'll meet you at the steak fry afterward," Dita shouted back, and to Addie, she said, "If I were him, I'd be wondering what I did to you. I mean, I have a grudge because he's wining and dining and sailing my mother when I think he has another lady, but we don't want him to think we're on to him. And remember, I want us to keep an eye on him and Jessica."

"He did come on to me once or twice," Addie said. "Remember that?"

Dita focused on finding her way forward between people. Finally, they reached the library lawn. It was shoulder to shoulder, and they still hadn't spotted Caroline.

"Let's cut through the back to The Lorelei. We can talk there," Addie said.

"Maybe that's where our mothers are. Odd she hasn't called or texted either."

The Lorelei was open for business when they reached it, and Rachel was behind the counter. She hadn't seen Caroline.

"She's probably with Artie," Rachel said. "He's been on her trail a lot lately."

"Trail or tail?" Addie quipped, laughing, bobbing her red curls.

But Dita was not in the mood for that sort of joke about her mother, and she knew her mother was not with Artie. She tried calling her again, but still no answer.

"This isn't funny. I haven't seen Mom in a few days," she said, "I lose track of everyone else when I'm with Janie. When was the last time you saw my mother, Rachel?"

"Um, when we went to lunch and the rest of us went out on Artie's boat. Teddy and I have been making wedding plans, plus I have the shop, so I haven't been in touch with Caroline."

"Should I be worried?" Dita asked, because she was getting worried. She called Sean and asked if he'd seen her. She hadn't shown up. He suggested Caroline might meet them at the steak fry after the parade.

THIRTY

Caroline slept through her alarm on July 4, and that's why she was late. She panicked when she realized she might miss the parade. She'd promised Dita she'd meet them all to watch it.

Late or not, she needed coffee to start her day. As it perked (she still had one of those old-fashioned electric pots), she checked her phone. She had a message. It was from Jessica. *Ugh*, she thought. Last night's next-door antics came rushing back. Without thinking, she went to the windows and pulled the shades. Daylight or not, those would stay down, shut, forever. She really didn't want to see or speak with Jessica.

She played the message as she drank her first cuppa and ate a muffin with cream cheese. Jessica wanted her to come over. She shuddered. She would never lower herself onto that woman's couch again. Besides which, Dita seemed convinced the woman was a murderer. Jessica sounded all chirpy. *Hmmf*, Caroline grunted. *After her night, she should be exhausted.*

Jessica was not to be ignored. "Caroline," the message chirped. "I want to apologize for last night. Let's talk. Please come over before you leave for the parade."

Caroline didn't think she ever wanted to go next door again. They were neighbors, and maybe someday they needed to talk this out or she would forever feel awkward around Jessica. It didn't seem like Jessica would feel awkward around her, though. The phone rang again and it was Jessica yet again. The woman was certainly persistent. She let it go to message and played it right away.

"Caroline, I'm leaving for a few days so please come and let's talk now. I don't want any feelings from last night to become permanent blocks to our relationship. Please."

Her voice sounded less upbeat this time. In fact, it was a bit terse. Once again, Caroline ignored her pleas. She showered and dressed, pulling on a t-shirt and lightweight gym tights to go to the parade. She turned the ringer off and stuffed the phone into her bag so she wouldn't be bothered all morning. She was hoping Jessica'd already left. She marched downstairs, grabbed an apple to bring with her and was almost at the front door when she heard knocking, and her name. She recognized the voice: Jessica. There was no avoiding the woman. She opened the door and Jessica pushed into the hall.

"Darling," she crooned. "I am truly sorry you saw that last night."

*Darling?*Caroline thought to herself. Since when had Jessica acquired this affectation?

"I know what you must be thinking," Jessica said.

*Really?*Caroline thought. How ever would Jessica know what she was thinking?

Jessica continued, "Artie and I were just having a bit of fun. We're not really lovers. How do the kids say this...we're friends with occasional benefits, just fooling around. I'm not interfering with you and Artie. You have a relationship."

Carolyn's eyebrows shot up. *Really?* She wanted to say, we don't have anything, but instead she emphasized that she and Artie had dated once or twice and that was all.

"I hope I haven't gotten in the way, darling," Jessica drawled.

There was that darling again. Caroline just replied, "Everything is fine, Jessica. Not to worry. Now, I was on my way out." She put her hand on Jessica's back and guided her out the door and followed, shutting it after herself and turning the key in the lock.

"Are you on your way to the parade?" Jessica asked. "It already started and you're late anyway, so how about taking a ride with me? I'd like to show you something."

Caroline couldn't imagine what Jessica would want to show her. "I'm late to meet the kids," she explained.

"Caroline, the reason Artie and I got together yesterday wasn't for what you saw; it was for business. We're buying a commercial property together. Come see it with me, and I'll drop you near town afterward so you can watch the parade where you want."

What a way to seal a deal, Caroline thought. She was not getting into a car with Jessica knowing that Dita suspected her of murder. "Is it so far we can't walk? It's such a beautiful day. Otherwise, I can see it another time."

"I suppose we can walk."

They started down the hill, cut through town, and Jessica led Carolyn down Corn Neck Rd, turning at Beach Avenue. They heard the bands playing. The parade was in full swing.

"Can you guess which property we want?" Jessica asked.

"No, unless you're buying the firehouse or police station," Carolyn replied, as both were on that block.

"You really have a wonderful sense of humor, darling," Jessica said. "Of course not."

Carolyn's hackles were up. That was the third darling. She couldn't imagine that Jessica would want to kill her for catching her with Artie, but then, maybe. Maybe she should be careful.

They crossed the bridge over the stream that flowed out of the Salt Pond, a place Carolyn usually stopped to watch the water eddy over rocks, and at night, small-celled creatures light up as they were swept along in the current.

"Are we almost there? I'm even missing the end of the parade," Carolyn said. She was getting suspicious of Jessica's intentions.

Halfway down the block, Jessica stopped, waved her arm, and said triumphantly, "Here we are!"

Caroline was confused. They were standing on the sidewalk in front of a hulking but decrepit and deteriorating ghost of a building, once the annex to the Hygeia Hotel across the street that had been torn down decades ago. The paint was peeling, indeed in many spots had totally disappeared, the porch sagged, and almost everyone who saw it for the first time when passing by wondered what had happened that it had fallen into such disrepair.

"I love the Mansard roof, and the fact that it's 2 1/2 stories, so typical of the island. And, the covered porch. Artie and I want to restore it," Jessica said.

Caroline liked this. "So you'll move?" she asked.

"Oh, no, we'll turn it into a hotel. It's a business venture," Jessica said. "Artie's friend Blaze is a contractor here and will do the work for a good price. I'm not sure we'll be able to get it, but we have a good chance. The owner is holding a contest for people who are interested, and I hear a relative of the original family who lived there is applying also. We're just going to offer a bundle of cash," Jessica laughed. "Cash usually works."

Caroline recognized Blaze's name and almost asked if he was the guy who found Bunny's body, but she stopped herself before it popped out. She didn't want to say anything connected to the murders, not to Jessica.

"Come around the back and look at the view of the pond from the yard. I bet it's even better from inside."

"I'm running out of time," Caroline said, thinking her daughter was correct about Artie and Jessica being the real couple, not Bernard and Jessica. She wasn't convinced they were murderers yet, but she was not convinced they were innocent either. "I've seen the view before from the hotel next door. I need to get to the parade to catch the kids." She listened for a moment. "No more music. It sounds like I may have missed the entire parade. See you later."

"Wait. Please don't tell anyone you saw us last night, not even Dita. You know this is a small island. It will destroy our businesses. Can I trust you to keep my mishap to yourself?"

Caroline noticed there was no *darling* at the end of that sentence. She looked Jessica in the eye and touched her finger to her mouth. "Of course, but Jessica, please pull your shades from now on." As she spoke, she spotted a stocky, well-muscled man in a black tee shirt and jeans come around the corner of the house and beckon to Jessica. Suddenly the two of them were on either side of her, whipping her around and pulling her toward the backyard. They turned the corner of the house, and Jessica ran ahead and opened a door.

"I'm so sorry, darling, but we really can't trust you not to tell anyone," Jessica said.

"Beware of those who say darling," jumped into Caroline's head as her feet dragged across the grass and dirt of the building's neglected back yard.

The man dragged her into a dark, dank cavern. A vile, noxious stink hit her. "Hold her a minute," Blaze ordered Jessica, and he moved to the center of the room where he pulled a barely visible string. A lightbulb came on. Now Caroline could see what appeared to be a thousand cob-webs and scurrying mice. In the back corner of the mostly empty cellar, she saw a blanket thrown across an old mattress. Along the concrete front wall was a long green plastic box with a handle, not unlike the container Addie sometimes used for transporting packages to and from the island, the one Danny named, "the coffin."

Blaze returned with a rope and secured Caroline's wrists. Then with one arm, he covered his nose. "He's getting rancid," Blaze said, pointing to the coffin.

Jessica turned toward it. "Blaze, we really have to do something about him. The smell is overwhelming. It's going to seep outside. And that vagrant, Josh, seems to have been sleeping in here."

"Artie is bringing the boat, and we'll load them both," Blaze said.

"Where are you taking me?" Carolyn asked. She felt goose bumps erupting all over her body, though it was not cold in that cellar. "You're scaring me."

"Darling, you should be terrified," Jessica intoned.

Carolyn screamed. She screamed as loud as she could and struggled against Blaze's grip. "Let me go!" she yelled.

"Get her phone," Blaze ordered.

Jessica yanked Caroline's bag off her shoulder and searched inside it. When she found the phone, she turned off the ringer.

"Put it on airplane mode. Turn it off," Blaze said.

"Please, I didn't see anything but a bit of hanky-panky. Why are you doing this? Please let me go," Carolyn pleaded.

"Hand me the rope near Bernard," Blaze said. "We need to tie her legs when we get aboard Artie's boat."

Carolyn's heart wobbled. She didn't see Bernard, but she did see Jessica walk over to the green container and reach down for a coiled rope.

"*Oh, no,no, no, Bernard. He's in there, they killed him. The smell. That really is a coffin now,*"she thought.

THIRTY-ONE

Addie picked up her car, and she and Dita drove to Caroline's house to find out whether she had just overslept or forgotten about the parade. There was time to search before the fire department steak fry began. They hoped Caroline hadn't had a mishap. Dita told Addie that her mother had high blood pressure, a fact Addie already knew because she had taken Caroline's vital signs several times.

The front door was locked, but Dita had the key. She searched for it in her bag, opened the door, and shouted.

"Mom, Mom! Caroline!" She waited a moment. "No answer," she said, perplexed.

She headed into the living room and went through to the kitchen. No Caroline. The room was as Dita would have expected; her mother's half-empty coffee cup unwashed and abandoned on the table, and crumbs on the yet unwiped counter."It looks like she's had breakfast," Dita said, a frown creeping over her face. "But her car is still here."

"Maybe she's sleeping in?" Addie suggested. "Upstairs?"

"It's almost noon," Dita said. "She's an early riser."

She swept up the stairs and peeked into the bedroom Caroline had furnished as her master. The bed was empty, but unmade, the sheet on the bed rumpled, not done tight as Addie had taught them all to do. The other two rooms were empty. Now Dita was seriously concerned. That her car was parked in the driveway made it even stranger.

"Maybe she went back to Connecticut to visit friends," Addie said, trying to calm her down.

"Without her car? How would she have gotten there? And wouldn't she have told us? She doesn't answer her phone." Dita couldn't imagine where Caroline could have gone. "She's not with Artie. At least we know that."

Addie went into nurse mode, trying to find reasons for Caroline being AWOL. "She must have walked to town. She's probably wandering around shopping or having lunch with some new friends, maybe even Dahlia. She's made some social connections since she moved here."

"Why doesn't she answer the phone or text, then?" Dita asked.

"I could barely hear you when we were in town watching the parade, let alone a phone alert. It's noisy down there with all the crowds. Wait until later. Then you'll find her. It's kind of a switch, you worrying about her."

Yes, but Dita knew her mother, and disappearing was not one of her habits.

"Okay, I'll leave her a note," she said. "If I don't hear from her later, I'll get hold of Dahlia. Dahlia usually knows everything that goes on here."

"Good idea," Addie said. "Chances are she's with her or Jessica. Wasn't Jessica AWOL also? Remember, Artie was searching for her."

Dita was not reassured. The knot in the pit of her stomach told her to worry no matter how many times Addie told her everything was okay. The memory of the Washashore gang and her own near-death experience forewarned her that something indeed was very wrong.

"Let's stop at Jessica's. Maybe they're both there," Dita said.

They rang the bell, they knocked, but no one answered the door. Addie looked in the backyard in case they were sitting outside, but no one was lounging in the chairs. Dita tried the front door. It opened. She stepped in.

"What do we say if Jessica comes back while we're here?" Addie whispered as she followed her friend.

"We don't need to whisper," Dita said. "We want her to hear us, right?" And she began to call Jessica's name.

"Doesn't sound like she's here. Let's go upstairs first," Addie said. "But Dita, remember, we think she's a murderess. Let's go through the rooms and back out again, fast."

Jessica's house was much like Caroline's upstairs, except with lower ceilings: three bedrooms, one of which had been made into an office. Addie couldn't resist looking into Jessica's closet.

"These clothes, so preppy," she said. "Like the ones the women used to wear on their husbands' sailboats. You know, back when all the WASPs used to spend the summer in cottages—ahem, what we call mansions—and they sailed and drank Manhattans. But there aren't many. Just a few. I would have thought Jessica would have more to wear here. There are hardly any shoes."

"We're not here to look at her clothes," Dita reprimanded. "It was you who said we should get in and out fast. Just see if there's anything of my mother's lying around anywhere that would tell us she'd been here."

"Where do you suppose Bernard keeps his things?" Addie asked, undeterred by Dita's urgency. "There's nothing of his in here."

They searched the other rooms. There were no men's items in either closet, nor, Addie noticed, were any drawers in the bureaus being used.

"This is odd," Addie said. "Her desk is empty too. Does she keep everything in Fairfield County? You'd think she would have some records of the new investment clubs here."

"Maybe it's all digital now. Hmm, there's no computer either," Dita noted. "But we're looking for my mother, not inventorying Jessica's clothing and papers. I'm going to search the kitchen and basement."

"The basement? What would she be doing down there?" Addie asked.

"I don't know. I just think we need to be thorough," Dita said.

The kitchen was spotless. Addie opened the fridge. "It's empty. It's as though no one lives here," she remarked.

"Let's go," Dita said.

Addie checked her watch. "I think it's time for the steak fry. I'm sure we'll find Caroline there."

"I hope so. I don't want to go home first to leave your car off, but it's going to be mobbed near the firehouse. Where do you think you can sneak in to park?" Dita asked.

"How about the Hygeia driveway? No one's been to that place in years to check," Addie said.

As they passed the firehouse, Dita spotted Sean in the crowd. It looked to her like he'd grabbed a table for all of them.

"Danny's there with Sean," Dita said.

She texted Sean to tell him where they were parking and asked if he'd seen Caroline. He replied with "No."

They pulled in alongside the old hotel and parked on the grass in the back.

"Isn't that Artie's boat tied up at the dock?" Addie asked.

Dita knew it was. Maybe her mother was on it, with Jessica. She was half out of the car before it rolled to a stop. She was about to run toward it when the basement door opened, and Jessica popped out. Right behind her, Blaze was holding Carolyn, her wrists tied behind her back, a scarf trailed out of her mouth.

Dita froze in place. "Stop!" she called. "Mom!"

Blaze's head snapped around. He pushed Caroline to Jessica and reached for the gun holstered on his hip. Artie jumped from the boat to help Jessica drag Caroline.

Addie was still in the car texting Sean to come pronto and to bring the cops.

"The police are on their way," Addie screeched out her window. "It will only be worse for you if you hurt one of us."

Sean was already rounding the corner with Sgt. Karl Schultz on his heels.

"Drop her," Artie told his accomplices. "Get to the boat."

The three ran across the backyard, less than a football field, more than a suburban patch, to make it to the boat. Dita rushed to her mother.

Chief Gomez, who had been at the station catching up on the morning's calls before the afternoon's festivities began, arrived with two more police officers.

Artie and Jessica were boarding the boat, and Blaze was backing toward it, his gun pointed at Sean and Karl as they closed in.

Chief Gomez shouted in his most powerful voice, the one police use to frighten people into obedience, "Drop the gun and put your hands up. You're surrounded."

Artie started up the motor and pushed off the grassy bank with a pole. He'd only gotten a foot or so when the two state troopers assigned to the island for the Fourth came around the other side of the building and sprinted toward the boat. Sgt. Schultz and Sean were on their heels, and they all hopped aboard before the boat could back out and motor off. They wrestled Artie and Jessica to the deck. Blaze, still on shore, was surrounded by Chief Gomez and his two officers. He threw his gun down and fell to his knees, his hands raised.

Dita embraced her mother and was huddled with her on the grass where Jessica had dropped her. With the sound of handcuffs jingling and clicking closed, Dita felt safe enough to call for someone to come and cut the ropes binding Carolyn's wrists.

"Thank goodness you're here," Carolyn cried. "How did you know?"

"We didn't. If we knew, we'd have come earlier. We just decided to park here. Are you okay, Mom?" Dita asked.

"Yes, yes, I'm fine except for my wrists," Carolyn replied. Then she startled and collapsed.

"Mom, Mom!" Dita cried. "Help! Mom fainted."

Addie called for an ambulance and rushed over to help. She took Carolyn's pulse. "Dita, she may have had a stroke."

The ambulance rolled in almost immediately from across the street, and the volunteer EMTs lifted Carolyn onto a stretcher and inserted a line in her arm before wheeling her into the vehicle.

"I'll go with her to monitor her, Dita, you take my car and meet us at the medical center," Addie said.

Sean ran across the street to the steak fry to fetch Janie, and Dita stopped to pick them up as she drove by.

THIRTY-TWO

Though the Medical Center was only a short quarter-mile away, the streets were clogged with tourists in cars, on bikes, and walking. They all moved at the pace of a snail, and Dita felt panic rising in her throat. She wanted to jump out and shout to them all to get out of their way. The siren was sounding ahead of them from the ambulance, but it had no effect.

She turned to Sean, "What's wrong with people? Don't they know they're supposed to get out of the way when an ambulance is trying to get through?"

Sean shrugged. "This happens to us all summer. The tourists, they're on vacation, and so are their brains," he said.

At the Medical Center, Dita watched as the volunteers wheeled Caroline inside and slid her onto an examining table. She heard them report the medical details to Dr. Bennett's summer medical resident, Dr. Ashutesh Pandey, who had arrived on the island that morning.

Addie remained in the examining room to monitor Caroline's vitals. Caroline seemed semi-conscious. Dr. Bennett was tending to another patient in the adjoining examining room, but Dr. Pandey came right in.

"Caroline," Addie said. "Can you hear me?"

Caroline tried to respond, but her speech was garbled.

"Dr. Pandey, should we give her something for her blood pressure?" Addie asked.

Dr. Pandey stepped closer to Caroline and raised her left hand and arm. He asked her who that arm belonged to. Caroline, again in garbled speech, responded that it belonged to him.

"No, Addie, I think this is a stroke. Get Dr. Bennett."

Addie had the doctor at the doorway in a nanosecond.

"Dr. Bennett," Dr. Pandey asked, "we need to start a stroke protocol. Where is the CT scanner, and do you have TPa here?"

Dr. Bennett hesitated. "We need to identify the type of stroke before rushing to use it. We have no CT scanner, but yes, we do stock the medicine here because we were hoping to buy a scanner soon."

Addie went to the waiting room and explained the procedure to Dita. "TPa, tissue plasminogen activator, dissolves blood clots. It must be administered within 4 and a half hours of the onset of a stroke, preferably within three."

Dita interrupted, "Then do it. Do it now," she said.

Instead, Addie took Dita's arm and brought her to the flowered couch. When they both were sitting, she continued to explain. She hadn't had time to put her cap on, but she was all professional nurse now.

"In addition to strokes caused by blood clots, there are also brain bleeds, strokes caused by hemorrhaging inside the brain. It can be dangerous to administer Alteplase, a TPa clot buster, in the case of a hemorrhage, as it would increase the bleeding. Normally, a CT scan is done to ascertain the origin of the stroke." Addie paused before delivering the bad news. "CT scanners are expensive for a small medical center to purchase. We don't have one."

Dita already knew the medical center had decided recently not to purchase one.

Dr. Bennett came out to the waiting room and gestured for Addie to return to the examining room. "Addie, monitor the patient. I'm calling the Coast Guard and the CT hospital helicopter to get a timeline on how soon either of them could get a copter here and transport her to the helipad at Providence Hospital. I'd rather be on the safe side here time-wise as far as treating her with a drug that could make her worse. Keep checking her blood pressure."

Then he turned to the medical resident. "Check her carotids with the ultrasound. It's on the wall over there." He pointed. "And do a neuro check."

He swooped out of the room. The resident began to perform a neurological exam. Caroline's eyes flickered open, and he flashed a penlight into them. Addie heard him ask Caroline her name, to which she responded slowly. He nudged her to move her fingers and toes, one extremity at a time, and to lift her unhurt leg.

"Dr. Pandey," Addie said. "Here's the ultrasound."

He ran the carotid duplex ultrasound over the carotid arteries in her neck. Addie knew he was looking for narrowing, often a cause of clot formation. Then he moved the wand over her head, looking for hemorrhages or clots.

Dita, at the doorway while Dr. Pandey was working, spotted Dr. Bennett on the phone in his office across the hall. He signaled to her to sit. When he finished his call, he informed her he'd just spoken with the Connecticut Hospital Helicopter Service who, given the good weather and lack of fog, said they could be on the island in 30 minutes and back on the mainland in less or the same amount of time. Dr. Bennett reviewed all the options with Dita. She asked for his opinion. He thought they should send her to the mainland, but he warned Dita her insurance might not cover the cost, which could be considerable, up to $10,000. Dita knew her mother had a nest egg, but not a huge one, and she and Sean did not have an extra $10,000, or even $2,000, yet.

"I wonder if Mom is awake and talking?" Dita was hesitant to make the decision for her.

"Let's go in and see," Dr. Bennett said.

Dita rushed back into the treatment room. Addie moved over to make room, informing her Caroline's eyes were open and she had just been speaking. When Caroline saw her daughter, she attempted to speak again, but only guttural sounds emerged. Dita panicked. She looked at Addie.

"Don't worry. She said her name when asked a few minutes ago. She just woke up, and it probably will take a while to return to normal,"

Addie told her, putting her arm around her friend. "Try asking her simple questions she can nod or shake her head to. Let's see if she has that movement now. When you are ready, I'll have the resident return to conduct another neurological exam."

"Mom, do you know me?" Dita asked.

Caroline nodded.

"Do you want some water?"

She shook her head. Addie said she didn't recommend it anyway, as they didn't know whether she could swallow. She brought some ice chips.

When Dr. Bennett returned, he explained the options again and said they would have to make a decision quickly. Did they want Caroline helicoptered to the mainland where they could assess her for TPa medication, or have him administer it here, or just let her recover as she seemed to be doing, though there was the possibility of some loss of brain function or movement.

Dita thought of the joy her mother seemed to experience holding and rocking Janie, cooing and kissing her soft cheeks. She wanted Caroline to be able to continue interacting with her grandchild.

"Mom," she said. "Shake your head or nod. Do you want to be flown off the island? I would like you to go to have further assessment, as the TPa could damage instead of help if it's given before we know the type of stroke you had. The downside of that is the ride could cost up to $10,000. Do you understand what I said?"

Caroline nodded.

"Do you want to be transported off?" Dita asked.

Caroline nodded again. She uttered some guttural noises and then found her voice. "Take money from Jessica club," she enunciated slowly, hesitating between words.

Dita looked at Dr. Bennett. "Get the helicopter." Then she leaned in to her mother. "Right on it." She doubted Caroline would ever recover that money, but decided they would worry about paying for the transport when the bill arrived.

"Okay," Dr. Bennett said. "Keep the patient comfortable, Addie, monitor her, and get her ready for transport. I'll have Dr. Pandey in here to do another neuro check when they arrive."

With that, Dr. Bennett did his usual swift disappearance from the room, this time to make his call. It was still July 4th, and there were other patients waiting to be seen for accidental injuries or sudden illnesses, like a little boy with a bad sunburn, a teenager who'd drunk too much alcohol, a boater who'd dropped the anchor on his foot.

Dita waited right next to Caroline until the helicopter arrived. She couldn't ride with her, partly because of Janie and also because only the injured person was allowed on board. Caroline would have to travel alone with the flight nurse.

"Can Sean fly with Island Airlines and meet Caroline at the hospital?" Addie asked Dita. "I don't think you should bring Janie there."

"Do you think Rachel might go?" Dita asked.

"Maybe, but a family member should be there anyway in case decisions have to be made and Caroline is not able."

Dita gave Addie a panicked stare. "I thought you said she was better."

"Just in case," Addie said in her calmest voice.

Dita thought this through aloud. "The Be Fit opens tomorrow morning though. I'd have to get Janie dressed and fed early and go in for him. People can use their key cards, but I would need to check everything, and we might get weekenders coming in for a workout. The weather is supposed to turn nasty tomorrow, and everyone will want their exercise."

She really wanted to be the one who went with Caroline, but with a storm moving in, she could be marooned on the mainland for days. She couldn't leave Janie that long.

Addie waited. She tapped her foot in impatience.

"I guess I could cover the fitness center instead of going," Dita said, and she called Sean.

Addie called Rachel, who said she would fly over with Sean.

Soon they heard the sound of the helicopter in the distance. The rhythmic putt-putt of the engine grew louder as it came closer, and then they heard it hover over the front lawn of the Medical Center's neighbor, a benevolent man who allowed the copters to land there. The onboard flight nurse came through the door minutes later and met with the staff. Two island ambulance volunteers had returned to help move Caroline's stretcher to the copter, where they shifted her onto the aircraft's stretcher for transport. While the paperwork was exchanged, Dita kissed her mother good-bye. And as the helicopter lifted off, Dita covered her face with her hands and burst into tears.

Addie put her arm around her friend and assured her her mom would be all right. The CT scan would show any damage or clots, and the proper treatment would be applied. Addie spoke calmly to her friend, although she was perturbed that the Medical Center had decided against purchasing a portable CT scanner. Addie had fought to have a fundraiser to purchase one.

She decided she would start working on that again, perhaps as soon as they sewed up these island murders.

"Come on, Dita. Let me take you home. I'm assuming you don't want to come to the fireworks party tonight."

"Nope. Might not even stay awake until it starts."

"I get it. I have to go because Danny's all excited. Get some rest, my friend," she said as she let Dita off home.

THIRTY-THREE

The fireworks were the most awaited event of the weekend. They were set off on the town beach, down the road from Dita's house. Dita and Sean usually invited everyone they knew to come watch from their place because the works flashed on top of them and were super loud.

Most years Mel and Sean had a back and forth over whose house was a better place to watch. Mel and Addie could watch the rockets rise into the sky over the Great Salt Pond, then see them reflected in the water, a double bang for their buck. Sean and Dita heard a bigger bang, being right next to them. Truth be told, the island was so small that almost everyone could get a fine view from their own homes and lodgings.

In years when the weather was too wet for the show to go on, there was widespread disappointment. Many of the tourists had to leave before the rescheduled date, often the next day.

Though Addie was not in a party mood, she was happy to get to the party before all the food was gone. She was starved after her intense day of searching for Carolyn and meting out nursing care to sick and injured island visitors. She was reaching for a hot dog when she felt a tap on her shoulder. She turned and was pleased to see Dahlia next to her. Dahlia smiled back and began to speak.

"I'm so glad to see you here. I was going to call you, and then I got so busy that I never got around to it. Let's go over to that table at the edge of the yard to talk for a few minutes. Gather up your food, and I'll meet you there." She waddled across the yard in her wedgies, which she always wore. Addie grabbed her food, picked out some coleslaw, potato salad, and homemade baked beans. Then she strode over to join Dahlia. She hadn't yet found Danny, but then she spotted him playing ball with some of the other kids and smiled. He noticed her and waved.

She plunked her food down on the small table and sat down across from the realtor. Dahlia adjusted herself in her chair and leaned in. Addie thought she was being quite conspiratorial.

"What's up, Dahlia? You seem anxious," she said, hoping she wasn't about to hear more bad news.

Dahlia peered around, making sure no one was listening. "Before Cathy was so brutally run down and," she stopped a second to stifle a sob, "killed, she told me something important. I never mentioned it to the police afterward, because I was so scared."

Now Addie leaned forward to make sure she heard every word. The yard was crowded with islanders, all talking, laughing, shouting, and singing, filling the yard with loud noise.

"Go on, Dahlia."

"Cathy recognized Jessica from her home town."

"I know," Addie said.

"You do?" Dahlia was surprised.

"I called Cathy's mother, and she told me she thought she recognized Artie from her town. She said Cathy had wanted to tell her something but hadn't had the chance. I did some research and found they both were from there. In fact, Artie was best man at Jessica's wedding, only her name was not Jessica."

"No, it wasn't. Cathy told me it was Amy Carrigan. The bank where Amy worked closed, and Cathy forgot about her. But one day on Block Island, they came face to face on the street, and Cathy said, "Hello, Amy." She said Jessica looked startled, then pulled herself together and tried to look puzzled instead. She told Cathy her name was Jessica, not Amy. Cathy was quite sure she was not mistaken, but she apologized and walked on. When she spotted Jessica again, she looked carefully from across the street where Jessica couldn't see her, and once again was certain that she was the person she knew from Ohio. Cathy had been to that bank with her mother quite a few times and had often been in Jessica's line."

Addie was as tense as a drumskin. "Go on," she said, certain that Dahlia hadn't gotten to her point.

Dahlia put her finger on her lips. "Cathy still had friends in her former hometown. She called one of them to find out if Amy still lived there, thinking there was a small chance she could have been wrong. Cathy's friend said Amy's husband died and then she moved away."

Dahlia paused. She drew in her breath and looked around to make sure no one had come close to them. It must be hard for her, Addie thought, to keep her voice down. Dahlia moved in, her face almost nose to nose with Addie's.

"Knowing Amy was now well-heeled and collecting money under an assumed name here and in Fairfield County also, Cathy wondered if she had embezzled the bank in Ohio and gotten away with it. And she wondered if she was embezzling here. But before Cathy could tell anyone besides me, she was killed."

Addie's eyes widened. She placed her hand over her heart. "You said you hadn't told the police. Had you told anyone else?"

"I did. Jessica was paying me a commission for every person I sent to her club who joined, so I told her," Dahlia admitted. "I thought Cathy might have imagined it all or spread a fake rumor.

"You told Jessica!"

"I did," she said. "And now I feel like I killed my dear Cathy. Addie, I'm so shattered."

"Dahlia, why didn't you go to the police? How could you do that?" Addie asked. "What made you think she wouldn't kill to keep her secret? You're lucky they didn't kill you."

Tears bubbled from Dahlia's eyes and rolled down her cheeks. "I'm sorry, so sorry. Yes, I should have known but I was so sure the killer was Josh and I didn't think. To tell the truth, I was scared of Jessica. I didn't believe Cathy. I thought she had quite an imagination and had made a mistake. I told Jessica that."

"Jessica needed to keep Cathy from talking to anyone else. Call Chief Gomez and tell him. You'll probably have to testify in their trials. This is just awful. Poor Mike and Josh Martel, accused of murders they didn't commit, and Caroline frightened into a stroke because she caught Artie and Jessica being a couple."

Dahlia began to weep harder. "And Blaze? I never would have suspected him."

Dita had, right away, but with time, she'd forgotten to follow up on his background. Everyone who came to Block Island had a past life somewhere, unless they were among the few who had been born here.

"I invested some money," Dahlia complained. "A significant amount of money before Cathy told me her suspicions. The first month or two I got statements, but one was due at the end of last week, and I haven't received anything. Were she and Artie planning to run off with our money?"

"My guess is they're not going anywhere but prison, but as for the money, who knows where it is? I'm trying to figure out, are they serial killers or career thieves who kill their marks. What do you think, Dahlia?"

She was speaking to empty space. Dahlia had wobbled off on her wedgies. At least, Addie reasoned, the killers had been passed on to the authorities. She felt a tap on her shoulder. Danny stood next to her with Harry behind him.

"Come watch with us," Danny said.

Harry reached out for her hand. She felt her face flush and looked down at Danny, but he was oblivious. Harry and Danny had colluded to nestle up to her. She and Harry were no secret anymore, not even to Danny.

"Did you close up the pub?" she asked, knowing he would never close on the busiest night of the year.

"During the show, there's a lull. I have staff who can handle things until later," he said, placing his arm around her. "Danny showed me where you were."

As darkness fell and the sun's puddles of scarlet faded on the Great

Salt Pond, the first fireworks of the official show exploded.There with Harry and Danny, Addie felt comfortable with herself for the first time in a year. No recriminations, no questions, not about her life anyway. And as always, when Harry held her hand or put his arm around her, she felt fireworks lighting up within.

Dita watched the show from her upper deck. She hadn't fallen asleep after all. She was too worried about Caroline. Tuffy, who detested and feared the great booms and understood them not, lay indoors on the floor snoring, medicated with pills from the traveling veterinarian who came to the island monthly. The new black and white kitten, an island stray, curled up against his belly. Janie snuffled in her crib. It would have been the utmost scene of domestic bliss had Caroline not been lying in a hospital with Sean sitting watch. Dita was waiting for him to call with an update. She kept her phone on a small table in front of her so she would know when it lit up, as she never would hear it with the din going on in the sky. She looked out over the pond, lit up too, but by the lights of the hundreds of boats weekending there, or was it thousands even? Between the cracks and booms above, she could hear the tinkling of the wind in the sailboat masts, the low background hum of many people talking out there, the barking of an occasional boat dog, and the far-off mourning of the bagpipes, played by the same sailor each year.

She couldn't silence the voice inside her that kept crying, what if we hadn't found Mom in time? She knew that the hospital had administered the clotbuster after seeing the CT scan that they ran. Now she just had to wait to find out whether it had worked. She didn't want to call Sean again. She knew she should wait for him to report to her, so she kept herself from touching her phone, and finally it lit up.

"Sean," she said. "How is she?"

"Better. Recovering, Dita, the TPA is working."

Tears seeped from Dita's eyes as she broke down. "Sean, oh, that's so wonderful."

"Yes, and she's awake again and seems to have all parts moving. The doctors think she'll make a full recovery. She recognizes me," he said. "They're going to move her out of the ER to a room. It was a small stroke, thank goodness. She probably can come home the day after tomorrow, back to Dr. Bennett's care.

"I think I missed the last boat back and the last plane too. I might as well wait here and bring her back in the car. I spoke with Doc Bennett and he'll talk to the ferry office about putting me on in the stand-by space, that is, if the boat runs in the storm tomorrow."

"Where will you stay? The hotels are probably booked."

"I called Mel. He's got room for me."

Dita's stomach turned. "Don't be too nice to him, and don't be at all nice to that Addie replacement." She was still angry at Mel for Addie.

"Of course not," he replied. She couldn't see his grin. "I think you can handle the Be Fit for a day or two without me. Oh, and by the way, there is some bad news. Guess who else is in the E.R.? Celia. She was visiting her daughter and fell. Addie, she may not make it."

"Sweet Celia. I hope she pulls through," Dita said. "Give her a little kiss on the cheek for me, Sean."

"Will do. Love you. Don't forget to open the Be Fit."

"I won't. Love you, too. And thank you for doing this."

As she signed off, the grand finale began.

The fireworks were perfect on a far from perfect night.

THIRTY-FOUR

And before anyone could say, 'I'm sick of tourists,' the July 4th weekend was over. Those tourists left, and new ones replaced them. Every available room and cottage on the island was fully rented at summer rates. Only the house next to Caroline's stood empty of human life, an anomaly in the high season. From her short time in the Hygeia basement, however, Caroline knew that battalions of field mice would soon climb out of the cellar and take up residency.

She was no longer bedridden but remained physically weak. She worked with a physical therapist who came to the island twice a week.

Chief Gomez called Dita and asked her to put a notice in the *Island Gale* calling for a meeting of the members of the investment club. Dita suggested it be held at Caroline's house since she was not yet well enough to go to a meeting at town hall; he agreed to that.

While he had her on the phone, he let her know that it was Bernard's body in the basement of the Hygeia. He knew she suspected that, but now he affirmed it.

When the club members gathered in Caroline's living room, they commiserated about the disappearance of their money. Chief Gomez delivered an update on the case. Addie and Dita had both come, Dita to gather information for another article, Addie because she'd helped uncover it and also because she thought Rachel had invested in the club, although she hadn't.

Gomez told them things they already knew, and some information they had not been aware of. He started with what they already knew.

"The telephone in Jessica's office clicks into message immediately upon ringing," he said. Each one of them had tried to reach Jessica more than once. "What we haven't told you yet is that the mainland police got a warrant to search the office there. But I'm sorry to tell you, they didn't find any paperwork. The file drawers are empty, the desk is empty, no computer was found."

"Even the printer?" Addie asked, thinking they could pull some information from the memory in that machine.

"Even the printer," Gomez said. "But there were some documents hidden under the floorboards in her bedroom here."

A voice in the back of the room shouted out, "So, do you know where the money is?"

In the back of the room, Dahlia cleared her throat. "Excuse me," she honked. "What about the possibility she had the money in Ohio under her former identity? Has anyone followed up with that?"

"We have," Gomez said. "Jessica Glen was indeed Amy Carrigan, who worked in the bank that went under. The FBI has fingerprints from that location, and we have some from her refrigerator on the island. But we haven't found any account in Ohio."

There was a hush in the room. Then everyone started speaking at once. Chief Gomez shouted for order.

"We believe that she and Artie murdered Bunny and orchestrated the deaths of poor Cathy and Bernard as well. It was Blaze's truck that crushed Cathy. He also helped dispose of Bernard's body, but Jessica and Artie were alone in pulling off their investment scam. And that, folks, is what the club you joined was—a scam. From the transaction papers we found in the bedroom, we know that Jessica transferred the money to a crypto account in an underground wallet group. The FBI says it is going to be very hard to recover it unless we can get her to talk."

As Addie listened, she thought of Celia at that first investment club meeting, circling the room uttering, "Not good." She wondered whether

Celia had overheard or seen something, or maybe the ancient island woman had amassed a lot of wisdom during her long life and saw through Jessica in a way the rest of them hadn't. She felt sad that Celia was struggling for her life.

And Dita was thinking about how naïve they all had been. Jessica was new to the island, but Artie had been coming for summer vacations on his boat and was recognized by the locals, who trusted him. It gave her the chills to think he had wined and dined her mother.

Gomez was on a roll now. "When Cathy recognized Jessica as Amy Carrigan, they needed to silence her before she told us. We now know for certain that Jessica, when she was Amy Carrigan, stole money from the bank in Ohio. We think she already knew Artie then and enlisted him to kill her husband. She could only have amassed enough money to start an investment firm by embezzling it from the bank. She and her first husband had nothing but their house and a small account in the bank she worked for. This stolen money must have grown in Westport when locals there placed their money with her, and then you people. These are professionals, long-time criminals. They will spend the rest of their lives locked up."

He paused and waited for questions, but the group was silent; their eyes, focused upon him, spoke volumes.

"Folks, Cathy told Dahlia, but neither of them told us. If either of them had trusted us enough to let us know, probably Cathy would be alive. Dahlia did tell Jessica, though, because she didn't believe Cathy. Then Cathy had to be silenced. They were paying Dahlia to bring them customers for their scam, so they figured they had her disbelief and her silence for at least a while."

A murmur of low voices filled the room and everyone turned to look at Dahlia.

"I'm sorry, so sorry," Dahlia said, wiping tears. "You all know I loved Cathy."

The chief continued, "Jessica's first husband was cremated, so there's no way to determine whether he was murdered, unless she confesses. I doubt she will. We believe that Artie and Jessica murdered Bunny to get her money and the house next door. We think the two of them had no idea Bernard existed. He still lived overseas. Jessica had not seen the actual will. She only signed papers to act as executor. She thought Bunny's money and her house would fall into her hands as Bunny had no living children, but when the estate's lawyer read the will, and he contacted Bernard, who came back to the U.S."

Dahlia spoke up. "How conniving for her to marry Bernard, and then to kill him."

There was a low mumbling of whispers. Dita moved closer to her mother so their arms were touching. She could have been next, Dita thought. They leaned into each other. Addie looked over and smiled, thinking they were more like her and Rachel now.

Gomez continued with his narration. "Artie's white van was parked at the airport where it always was when he left for home in Fairfield County, and his boat was in the Salt Pond. A forensic team from the mainland went through both for traces of blood, DNA, fingerprints."

"How do we get our money back?" someone asked.

Gomez told them the house Jessica had murdered for would be sold, and the proceeds would be divided proportionately among the swindled investors.

Caroline said in a low voice to Dita, "Dahlia told me my house was haunted. I think she made a mistake. It's Jessica's. I feel sorry for the next owner."

Dita chuckled.

"Unfortunately," he cautioned, "you are not the only investors. There are more in Fairfield County."

"Was she bonded? Was there insurance?" Teddy, who had accompanied Rachel, asked.

Gomez squirmed. He looked down instead of at them when he said, "I'm afraid not.

Since she was using a fake identity, Jessica did not bond herself or carry insurance on the investments. She couldn't risk that level of inspection."

Everyone shouted at once. Some people had placed their entire retirement funds with Jessica, aka Amy Carrigan, Dita was glad her mother hadn't trusted them with the lion's share of her money, but Caroline was even happier that she didn't become one of their dead victims. A small amount of money was a small price to pay for trusting them.

Gomez read the list of known investors on the island with the amounts they were owed. When Addie heard Mel's name and the amount of money he'd put in, she let out a whoop. She quickly covered her mouth and turned red with shame, but to her surprise, a few other people cheered. Then she laughed, and Rachel moved to her and embraced her. If this was her only revenge, it might be enough.

THIRTY-FIVE

Rachel and Teddy set the date for their wedding for September 10, several days after Labor Day. They reserved the entire Double Ender for their guests. The night before, Rachel sat down with Addie and Danny.

"Teddy and I are looking for a house south of Boston in northern Rhode Island so that we can commute to the city and here easily."

"Cool," Danny said.

"I'm telling you this because we think we'll get something large enough for the two of you to move in with us in the winters. It's time for Danny to go to a more rigorous school, and it's lonely for you, Addie, in the winter."

"But, Mom, are you forgetting I have a job? And my agreement with Mel is for Danny to remain in Rhode Island."

"I said we would buy over the border in Rhode Island," Rachel reminded her.

Addie was stunned. Just as her life was pulling together here, her mother decided she needed to leave. She knew Rachel disapproved of her and Harry, but they weren't getting married, not yet anyway.

"I'm not lonely, and I think Danny's happy here right now," Addie told her. "Plus, the school is good."

"Running around with Harry is not the answer to getting over your divorce," Rachel said.

Addie knew it wasn't the answer, but she really enjoyed it. She'd been thinking of the future, too, and it was her job that wasn't satisfying her enough, not Harry.

"I have plans too," Addie said. "I need to learn more about how to treat medical problems, to practice my nursing at a more independent level. I've decided to become a nurse practitioner, and I'm applying to several nursing schools with graduate programs, not for this winter, but for next year.

"I don't see Harry as an answer to anything," she continued. "I do know he makes me happy right now. We have no long-term plans at this point. We're just seeing where our relationship goes. If I am accepted to a school, we'll either have a long-distance relationship, or our connection will fizzle."

Danny shook his head. He and Addie had already had their talk about all of this. If they moved, she'd explained, he could go to middle and high school somewhere with a wider curriculum and real sports teams—and more girls. Addie had noticed he was beginning to be interested in them.

Addie thought Rachel looked surprised. How, Addie wondered, had she been so off-base that she thought her own daughter would be so dumb as to fall into another serious relationship so quickly?

"Well, that's good news," Rachel agreed, swallowing her embarrassment.

"You're the one who fell head over heels into a relationship quickly," Addie reminded Rachel.

"But Teddy is not like Harry," Rachel said.

"You don't know Harry very well," Addie responded.

Eager to move to other territory, Rachel asked, "Have you looked at any Boston universities? You'll need babysitting, I'm sure."

Now it was Danny's turn to disagree that he still needed watchers.

Addie laughed. "Of course, I'm looking at the Boston area," she replied, "but for this year I think we'll just visit you and Teddy. I'll stay in this house. You can sell your cottage if you want."

Rachel stood up. "I guess, then, this talk is over. I have things to do to get ready for tomorrow."

"As do we," Addie said. "What time should I come help you dress?" Rachel replied and left.

Teddy had turned the entire hotel and its grounds into their wedding venue. The rooms were filled with relatives and friends, a Chuppah erected outdoors in the wedding tent, antipasto and appetizers to be served in the bar, the dinner in the dining room building. He'd hired his favorite Boston band. He even wore a tux, a big concession for him. Sean was best man, and Danny the usher, with Tuffy his helper. Addie was maid of honor. All the locals were invited, and everyone who could leave their businesses for a few hours came. For one day, the entire island celebrated and tried to forget the financial losses they'd suffered.

Jessica and Artie, and Blaze were gone, transferred to prisons on the mainland. Chief Gomez was attempting to set bond extremely high, given the flight risk they presented.

Addie and Dita toasted the bride and groom, and then they toasted each other. Their teamwork had resulted in the arrests, though they both felt guilty about accusing Mike and contributing to his desperate suicide attempt. They felt they owed him an apology, and the whole town owed Josh Martel one. It was all too easy to accuse vulnerable people of crimes they hadn't committed. Dita and Addie agreed they hoped there would never be another murder or heinous financial crime on Block Island again, but if that did happen, they would be more cautious about pointing fingers at someone. For now, they both hoped they could just sink into the cloak of winter, when the island would calm down and they would deal with boredom instead of calamities.

But first, Addie whispered to Dita, "Beach and margaritas."

Dita was game. They sneaked away from the gathering, and Addie drove them to Dita's, where they slid into bathing suits, mixed up margaritas, and grabbed towels and boogie boards. Then, unusually for her, Addie led the way, racing to the water. Dita could barely keep up. They rushed in and caught the first good wave, landed on the beach laughing, drank some more margaritas, and went back in the water again.

"Do you think anyone noticed we left?" Addie asked.

"Maybe Janie, but she's with Daddy and Grandma."

"To us, to friendship forever!" Addie proclaimed.

"And to more margaritas and no more murders," Dita replied.

"Amen!" Addie crooned.

ACKNOWLEDGMENTS

Thanks to Jean Tabor for taking the time and effort to edit this book. Her comments are always welcome and necessary.

I am grateful to my nephew, the actor Gary Rubenstein, who narrated the audio edition and did a second edit for me. I am delighted that we were able to work together on a project.

A special thanks to Jack Hayback, special Block Island family friend, for engineering the audio version when I am sure he had more important things to do.

Dr. Nishant Mishra, neurologist, contributed medical advice, and Jennifer Rubenstein of Rubidoux Mortuary contributed advice on death.

And, of course, heartfelt thanks to my Zoom writers' group, Rebecca Green, Thomas Smith, and Leon Wann. They read through the chapters as I wrote, threw in constructive suggestions, and they offered support when I wasn't sure I should go on. Without them, I would not have completed this novel.

Always a hug to my husband, Ron, and my book-loving friends who read prior to publication, Lynn Kibbe and Fraser and Betty Lang, Rosemary and George Liebowitz for cheering me on, and for my son, Kevin, who jumps in to help with computer glitches.

A special thanks to supporters on Block Island, The Spring Street Gallery and the Glass Onion who sold my previous mystery, and to the Island Free Library, especially Susana Gardner, who helped spread the word about my works.

Finally, thanks to all my readers. I hope you were pleasantly transported for a short while from the tasks and toil of your daily lives to what I consider the most beautiful island on earth, Block Island, Rhode Island.

ABOUT THE AUTHOR

Judy Tierney lived as a "washashore" on Block Island, Rhode Island for fourteen years. Prior to moving there year-round she was a long-time summer cottager, vacationing there with her family, her beloved dog Tuffy and a cantankerous cat. She worked as a correspondent for the *Block Island Times* and won three New England Press Awards for her work at that newspaper. Her book of essays and memoirs, *Passing Time in Winter, Block Island Style*, written in 2021, recalls her life there.

In her mainland years, she was a nurse clinical specialist in psychiatric-mental health and an environmental activist.

She has two prior books, *The Washashore Murders* and *Passing Time In Winter: Block Island Style.* Available from islandj@gmail.com.

www.ingramcontent.com/pod-product-compliance
Lightning Source LLC
LaVergne TN
LVHW020705110826
845149LV00012B/2119